THE

SEASIDE

AFFAIR

The Seaside Affair

By

Vicki Hopkins

The Venturous Hearts Series

Book One

PUBLISHED BY
RED BRICK MEDIA
HILLSBORO, OR

DEDICATION

To my fifth great grandmother, Elizabeth Edwards
Birth 1694 • Sawbridgeworth, Hertfordshire, England
Death 1770 • Essex, England

CHAPTER ONE

Mourning's End

Beth stood at the end of her bed, clad in her white petticoat, chilled from the crisp morning air that permeated her bedroom. Goose pimples rose on her arms. The evening's fire had extinguished from the night before. With a quick rub of her hands together, Beth shooed away the shivers. A rush of enthusiasm curled her lips as she gazed at the day dress lying on her neatly made bed. The sage-colored garment looked subdued but so much brighter than her former attire. No longer would she have to wear the black paramatta silk that she had donned for the past year. The time for mourning had ended, but memories remained fresh in her mind as if it were yesterday.

It was a brisk April morning in the church graveyard a year ago when she said goodbye to her mother. The gusty wind swirled around the tombstones like flying ghosts, causing her skirt to billow in the air. Her gloved left hand clung to her small leather-bound prayer book while the other held a clod of earth in her palm. Beth bit her lower lip, remembering how she had done so during the funeral to suppress her tears. Even though her heart ached, she endured and kept her emotions contained. Her father would have been proud since his voice echoed in her head not to show weakness in public. Even though he too had passed away, Beth endeavored to be steadfast and unmoved by life's unsettling events.

The vicar's voice replayed in her mind. "We commit Catherine Edwards's body to the ground, earth to earth, ashes to ashes, dust to dust, in the sure and certain hope of the resurrection to eternal life through our Lord Jesus Christ."

The time to mourn had ended. Although the subtle grief of losing one's parent lingered, Beth vowed to return to more pleasurable pursuits in life. Today a smile replaced the grief-stricken expression of loss. The social protocol had been satisfied, and at last Beth could sigh in relief.

Whoever had written the communal conventions of bereavement had morbidly bound throngs of individuals in a dark aura of endless sorrow. Even her mother believed that three months for the death of a parent seemed far more reasonable than one year. Poor widows who lost spouses had to wear black for two. Perhaps it had been a cruel etiquette set up by greedy dressmakers, profiting off grief to make a lucrative business for themselves.

Nevertheless, since Beth's aunt and uncle were staunch proponents of propriety, she had observed the long year in honor of her mother's passing.

"Beth, are you ready?" Francis's voice boomed up the stairs, sounding like their deceased authoritative father, expelling frustration. She swore that each year her brother grew more like him, taking on his characteristics, whether it be voice or mannerisms.

"Give me a few more minutes, Francis," she yelled, grabbing the garment and dressing in haste. Thankfully, it still fit as Beth's bodily stature had not altered during the long year. A minute later, an anxious knock came at her door.

"Beth, the carriage is waiting outdoors, and they have loaded our bags," Francis announced in an exasperated complaint.

Beth tied the ribbon of her bonnet, grabbed her reticule, and opened the door.

"An ounce of patience, Francis, goes a long way," she scolded, pushing past him and descending the stairs.

"My, you look so bright and cheerful." Francis eyed her.

"Yes, at last I can wear color. With my fair complexion, I looked like a stick of chalk in black."

Francis bolted the door behind them and strode with a wide gait to the carriage. They climbed inside, and after closing the door with a bang, Francis knit his brows together. When the horses began their trot, Beth gave him a piece of her mind.

"Honestly, Francis," she protested. "I could have made this trip by myself if it upsets you so much."

"Do you actually suppose that, as your older brother, I would allow you to do so?"

"I understand your concern for me." Beth attempted to remain civil. "Let us not quarrel. I often feel like we are two dogs constantly nipping at each other."

"As do I." He tempered his tone. "My only request is that you understand and accept my concern. Since Mother and Father have passed, the responsibility for your well-being rests upon me." He sighed as if his task were a significant burden.

Aware that Francis suffered from a controlling personality, Beth attempted to allay her irritation with a bit of humor.

"Just loosen the leash a bit." Beth put her fingers underneath her collar and tugged on it. "You know how I jerk when restrained," she said with a sly smile.

"How well I know, sister."

Francis shook his head, leaned back in the seat, and glanced at the passing scenery. They had spent their entire lives in Dunwich, a small village an hour southeast of London. Beth and Francis had rarely left on any occasion except to visit their aunts, uncles, and cousins who lived in another village, accessible by a thirty-minute coach ride. Their family was extensive, with their mother having one sibling and their father six. Each married, having their share of children, giving Beth and Francis multiple cousins.

Beth's father had been a gentleman, having purchased a small country estate from the profits of a successful watch-and-clock-making business. Francis had learned the trade as a junior apprentice and continued to run the establishment upon their father's death. As a perfectionist, Francis focused on his craft with the same serious intent as his father.

Beth silently observed Francis as the carriage bounced over the potholes of the road, left behind by the harsh winter, pondering their dissimilarities. Even though they were siblings, they were opposites in personality and appearance. Francis had taken on their father's characteristics of dark hair and brown eyes. In contrast, Beth had her mother's fair complexion and golden locks. While her skin burned in the heat of the sun, Francis bronzed easily. She envied him that he had only to hide under a hat while she had to take cover under a parasol or large-brimmed bonnet to avoid the bright sun rays.

As she contemplated their differences, he returned his attention to her, noting her intense stare with displeasure.

"I am still unclear why you insisted on writing the Wilsons about Mother's demise," he remarked with a tone of annoyance.

"Because our mother corresponded with the couple for over twenty years; that is why." They had discussed the matter repeatedly beforehand, and it exasperated Beth that Francis decided to resurrect the question once more. "I will admit that I do not understand Mother's relationship with the Wilsons," Beth said. "Only that they showed her kindness when she was young and lived in Aycliffe."

"What could they possibly correspond about for so long?"

"Mother read a few portions of the letters to me. They contained tidbits about Aycliffe, people she once knew, and the weather." Beth contemplated the oddity of the ongoing correspondence.

"Did Mother keep them? I would be curious to read them, frankly, to better understand this strange friendship."

"It was odd that I did not find them among her things after her passing, Francis. I can only assume that she discarded each letter after reading it." Beth did think it bizarre. If the Wilsons had been such dear friends, you would think her mother would have kept a few letters as keepsakes.

Francis cocked his head and looked at her in disbelief. "Peculiar indeed, which is why I am uncomfortable that we have accepted this invitation. Neither of us knows anything about the Wilsons."

"True, but Mother held a fondness in her heart for them. Their invitation shows respect to her memory, and I did not wish to refuse." Beth lifted her chin, showing her determination to proceed regardless of Francis's doubts.

"Yes, that is one of your faults. The inability to say no. You're too affable, even to strangers."

"It's my nature." Beth shifted in her seat, intent on

defending one of her good qualities.

"What I don't understand," her brother said, continuing to balk, "is why Mother never returned to Aycliffe if these people were so dear to her."

"She told me that Father would not allow it because he hated the dampness of the sea air. Though I will admit I always noticed a bit of animosity rise between them whenever Aycliffe came into the conversation."

"I too," Francis admitted. "Well, at least we will finally gaze at the ocean since Father had no desire to holiday at a seaside resort. Frankly, it's the only reason I agreed to accompany you. Who knows, I may try my hand at deep-sea fishing."

"Deep-sea fishing?" Beth gasped in surprise. "I daresay you should fish for a nice young lady instead."

"It's been on my mind to seek a wife," he mumbled. Francis averted Beth's gaze as if it embarrassed him to admit it.

Beth grinned, hearing Francis's surprising statement. He had barely spoken about female companionship, even though he had entered his prime as a young man. Unfortunately, Francis had taken on far too many responsibilities since their parents' death. Of course, the thought of matrimony entered Beth's mind also. Now one and twenty, she did not want to be a burden to her sibling any longer. It would be unfair to rely on his care indefinitely. Although Francis attempted to control her every move, now that she was of age she could make decisions about seeking a future husband.

"And what about me? May I search for a companion, or shall your watchful eye prevent me from obtaining an ounce of affection beyond the confines of Dunwich?" Beth coyly teased.

Francis pulled his mouth to one side and eyed Beth with amusement. "I will admit it is about time you found yourself a husband. If the opportunity presents itself, I shall gladly hand over the leash to another man that I approve."

Beth rolled her eyes. "Women are not meant to be kept on a leash, brother," she asserted with pursed lips.

"Well, I beg to differ with you but shan't make it a point of contention between us. Besides, I have little concern that you shall fall in love with anyone within a fortnight."

Francis resumed his interest in the scenery, and Beth settled into a comfortable position. Their travels by coach would be for at least three hours. The only history Beth knew of her mother's trips to Aycliffe came from occasional remarks. As a young woman, she had been a governess in the household of a prestigious family. Oddly, her mother spoke little of the experience, except to reminisce about her love of the ocean. Beth recalled her mother's eyes filled with a mixture of sweetness and sorrow whenever she spoke of the past. Perhaps their visit to the Wilsons would provide insight into her early life. As much as she loved her mother, there were times that Beth wished they had been closer.

"Do you think Mother loved Father?" Francis inquired, turning his attention to Beth. His brow furrowed, showing his seriousness. The prying question caught her off guard.

"Mother was fond of Father, of that I'm sure." Beth spoke in a harsh tone, not wishing a lengthy discussion about their affections.

"That's not what I asked." Francis leaned forward, pressing the matter further.

Uneasy that he insisted on continuing the conversation, Beth fiddled with her skirt as she thought about the past. She had never observed a cross word spoken between her parents. Father doted upon their mother, and Beth perceived that she admired him in return. Surely love had been displayed through their actions in how they treated one another. Although physical affection had not been readily observed between the two. Naturally, she attributed that due to her father's character and not as an indication that he did not love her dearly.

"Since I am not an expert on marital love or behavior, I find the question difficult to answer. Nonetheless, the kindness they displayed toward one another has never led me to assume otherwise. Surely Mama loved our father."

Francis listened to her explanation. He acted agitated, glancing momentarily out the window. With a sigh, he leaned back into his seat.

"Father didn't seem to feel that she loved him with the same ardor," he divulged.

Aghast at his remark, Beth objected. "What are you talking about? Did he express such opinions to you?"

"Not in so many words," Francis solemnly answered. "Perhaps I formed the wrong notion by some of his statements. Nevertheless, it caused me to question Mother's sincerity."

"How could you question her sincerity?" Beth demanded. "That is an awful assumption to make on your part."

Francis lowered his head and dropped his shoulders. Beth thought that he regretted his words, so she dismissed the distressing insinuation. "They are both gone now." The reminder of their loss resurrected a pang of grief. The black dress had been put away, but sadness over her mother's untimely death lingered. "No matter," she added. "They are together now in eternity. There is no value in speculating about their affections or lack thereof. Do you agree?"

Francis remained speculative, glancing out the window. A few moments later, he answered. "Perhaps you are right. Forgive me for bringing it up. Besides, what do I know of love?" He flashed a lopsided grin.

"Nothing. We are inexperienced in such matters, but perhaps that will change one day."

The carriage rocked as they traveled the country roads, lulling Beth into a sleepy state of mind. She closed her eyes and forgot the heartache, hoping to wake at the sight of the ocean.

CHAPTER TWO

Shrouded in Fog

Beth woke at the jolt of a carriage and opened her eyes. After hours of travel, the horses trotted on a trail along the cliff. To her disappointment, rather than seeing the ocean for the first time, the landscape lay shrouded in fog.

"Shame it obscures the view," her brother remarked. He reached over and pulled down the window, and a burst of moist, cool air filled the coach.

"Refreshing," she remarked, sniffing the welcoming aroma. After a chill entered, she blurted. "Although, a bit chilly. Close the window, Francis."

He obliged and sat back in the seat. "It's getting late, so I doubt we'll see much scenery. Let's hope it burns off in the morning, and we can visit the beach."

"Will you sea bathe?" Beth asked, curious to know if he would partake.

"In that cold water? I would rather not," he harshly remarked with a scowl. "If it were the middle of summer, I might consider it."

"I hear that cold is good for you. Perhaps they have those bathing machines for the ladies." Beth wondered aloud.

"If you insist on it, as long as you cover from head to toe, I do not care if you freeze." Francis smirked.

"Yes, God forbid I reveal an ankle or elbow for a man to see," she said with a snicker. "I'll be the talk of the town."

The carriage descended from the hilltop into the city that lined the shoreline. The fog remained thick as potage, obscuring the view. The horses slowed their gait as they trotted down the main town thoroughfare. Small quaint shops lined the roadway, from clothing and housewares to seaside trinkets. They passed the bank and hotel, and Beth noted few people on the streets.

"There don't seem to be many individuals outdoors," Francis remarked, noting the lack of persons.

"Well, it's off-season and late in the day. Perhaps more tourists come during the summer for a holiday. With this weather, I'm certain the climate draws no one of importance." Beth assumed the seaside resort held the popularity her mother noted in passing. Now it appeared abandoned and solitary.

The carriage turned to the right and traveled a quarter of a mile, halting at their destination. A flutter of apprehension tickled Beth's stomach. She had no idea what kind of people the Wilsons were but hoped they were pleasant based on her mother's unceasing intention to keep in touch.

When the coach door opened, Francis exited and offered his hand to Beth. The driver untied their suitcases and trunk from the back. Even though everything around them lay cloaked in a misty gray cloud, the house emerged in all its grandeur. It rose three stories with a distinctive tower off to the right and a dormer to the left. Arch windows accented the facade, covered in lace curtains. A stained glass window highlighted the front oak doors.

"How lovely." Beth sighed, turning toward Francis.

He stood silently, admiring the architectural delight, which made their aging residence in Dunwich dull in comparison.

"Remarkable design," he pronounced.

Suddenly, the front door flung open. Beth observed a woman approaching, with a man not far behind. No doubt the Wilsons were about to descend upon them in greeting.

It didn't take long to confirm Beth's initial impression. She surmised the couple to be in their late forties based on her mother's stories of meeting them when she was yet but twenty and close in age. A plump, red-faced lady approached Beth, gasping in delight as if the few steps had overtaxed her heart.

"Oh, my dear, dear Elizabeth. I'm astounded at how much you look like your mother!"

Beth thought her facial features resembled her mother. Nevertheless, she never considered it a close likeness except for their complexion and light hair.

"I think we have the same nose and lips, but other than that, I'm shorter than Mama." Beth made light of the comparison.

"Believe me when I say the similarities to Catherine at her young age are astounding," Mrs. Wilson repeated. Her eyes roved up and down her frame, smiling approvingly.

"Miss Edwards." Mr. Wilson greeted Beth with a quick bow of the head. "Welcome to Aycliffe."

"And this is your brother, I surmise," Mrs. Wilson said, moving in front of Francis. "My, my, a handsome gentleman. You must take after your father, although I do see Catherine's eyes."

"Pleasure to meet you, ma'am," Francis said. He removed his hat and held it by the brim.

"Welcome, young man." Mr. Wilson held out his

hand, and Francis gave it a hearty shake.

"Now come indoors out of this dreary fog," Mrs. Wilson excitedly encouraged. "I had hoped you would arrive on a sunny day, but the ocean appears to have other plans. It is very unpredictable, somewhat like life."

"It is just the warm air blowing over the chilly water that causes the fog," Mr. Wilson interjected, glancing sideways at his wife. He grinned sardonically. "You'll discover that Mrs. Wilson is prone to adding life lessons in every movement of nature."

Beth and Francis glimpsed at one another and followed the couple indoors. A male servant collected their luggage and set them in the foyer.

"Wilford, take those upstairs to the bedrooms we have assigned for our guests." Mrs. Wilson gave a stern order, wiggling her chubby finger at the servant.

"Yes, ma'am." He grabbed two suitcases and climbed the stairs.

Beth admired the interior, suppressing a giddy grin at its decor. Francis, on the other hand, had no qualms about stating the obvious.

"You have a very fine home, Mr. and Mrs. Wilson. You must be proud," he commented. Francis glanced around, observing the furnishings.

"It's drafty," Mr. Wilson remarked with a smirk.

"No, it's comfortable," his wife countered. "Come dears and sit by the fire and have a spot of tea while we get to know one another."

Curious, but somewhat exhausted from the trip, the idea of a hot cup of tea led Beth forward with eagerness. They entered a high-ceilinged parlor. The intricate lace curtains caught Beth's fancy as well as the velvet settee in a deep purple. The color scheme of muted green and plum permeated the room, giving it the atmosphere of an arboretum. A tall plant, the likes of which Beth had never seen, stood in the corner.

"My goodness," Beth exclaimed, walking over to it. "What is that?"

"That my dear is a cataractarum palm, which is native to Mexico. It makes handsome indoor foliage and is becoming popular in England. You only need to water it every five days or so, and it seems to love the front window as you can tell." Mrs. Wilson looked affectionately at the greenery.

"Yes, my wife loves it and has the most splendid garden in all of Aycliffe. She will show it to you when the sun returns." Mr. Wilson motioned to the chairs. "Please sit. You must be exhausted from your trip."

Beth found Mr. Wilson possessed a cheerful demeanor in his mannerisms and facial expressions. His salt-and-pepper-colored hair gave way to a large bald spot on the top of his head. His stature was thin and wiry, akin to a skeleton, and she briefly wondered if he were ill.

Francis chose the settee, and Beth sat next to him. For a few seconds, the room grew quietly awkward as their hosts grinned and scrutinized them. A maid entered the room with a pot of tea and cups on a large silver tray. She set it down on the table and then scurried away. Beth took the liberty of speaking first.

"My brother and I wish to thank you for your generous invitation. I must admit that it quite surprised me to receive your letter expressing that you wished to extend such a courtesy. After all, we are unacquainted, although you knew our mother."

Francis augmented Beth's sentiments. "I agree with Beth. It is a thoughtful gesture on your part to invite us into your home. After a year of mourning, the invitation has been most timely."

Mr. and Mrs. Wilson smiled at one another,

acknowledging their pleasure. By the sparkle in their eyes, they exchanged a knowing glance but remained silent in their thoughts.

"Tea?" Mrs. Wilson asked, picking up the flowered pattern china pot and pouring a cup. "Milk or sugar, Miss Edwards?"

"Call me Beth, please, and a bit of milk will do."

"And how about you, Mr. Edwards?"

"No milk or sugar," he replied.

Beth noted her brother wished to keep the formality of not offering his Christian name. Until he felt comfortable with the Wilsons, he would remain cautiously distant.

After serving a steaming cup, Mrs. Wilson spoke in a compassionate tone.

"Your dear mother, God rest her soul," she began, "left you far too soon in life. I was so terribly heart-broken to hear of her passing."

Mrs. Wilson's eyes watered, while her husband sat quietly by, displaying his disenchantment by a frown on his face.

"I very much agree. Our mother's death was a shock to us all," Beth admitted. Painfully, she recalled the day she fell ill with the sniffles. A high fever followed, which turned into pneumonia. Only a year earlier, their father had passed away from a heart ailment. The gnawing sense of loss pricked Beth's heart, feeling cheated for not having them longer in her life.

"It was kind of you to remember us and let us know of your mother's passing," Mr. Wilson said. "We would have wondered had her letters ceased unexpectedly whether a misfortune had befallen."

"We were aware, sir, that our mother corresponded with you for these twenty-plus years, so it was the least we could do," Francis acknowledged. "She must have held you both in high regard to maintain contact."

Beth gave Francis a sideways look with one arched brow since earlier in the day he had scolded her for having written to the Wilsons. He could change his mind on a whim to suit the situation, and Beth wanted to give him a sisterly jab with her elbow.

"We held her in high regard," Mr. Wilson confessed. "A fine young lady who made quite an impression upon Aycliffe during her stay here. There are others who remember her with great affection, and they were sad to hear of her passing."

"Others?" Beth tilted her head at the surprising announcement and words of great affection.

"Old acquaintances," Mrs. Wilson clarified. "By and by during your stay in Aycliffe, you will meet them."

"I daresay," Mr. Wilson chuckled softly, "that my wife and I feel as if we know the two of you rather well. Your mother often wrote about you as you were growing into adulthood, and it appears that you turned out to be fine individuals."

"Sounds like Mother," Francis confirmed with a nod. "She had a way of singing her praises about us whenever the opportunity arose," he remarked in a melancholy tone. "Mother had the distinct gift of embarrassing me to the point of blushing."

"No, it was I who blushed," Beth clarified. As she finished speaking, a young lady abruptly arrived and stood in the threshold. Surprised by the unexpected intrusion, Beth put her teacup down, and Francis jumped to his feet.

"Ah, at last," Mrs. Wilson exclaimed. "May I introduce you to Celia, our daughter? She lingers at home, having yet to find a husband."

"Lingering, Mother? Really?" she chided. "You make me sound like a dawdling spinster." Celia displayed no shy hesitation. Instead, she boldly approached the visitors. "You must be Beth. I've heard so much about you over the years I feel as if we are sisters already."

Beth gave an incredulous look at the young lady. Before she could say anything, Celia gave her a warm embrace that took her off guard.

"It's a pleasure to meet you," Beth sputtered after she released her from the suffocating hug.

A moment later, she moved in front of Francis, who looked befuddled and awestruck. Undoubtedly, the young lady's demeanor and attractive countenance had caught his attention like a lightning bolt. She brandished a petite, well-endowed frame. A voluminous blue dress accentuated her assets. Lace trimmed the collar and the cuffs, and a pretty broach decorated her bodice. Curly honey-golden locks bounced with the same enthusiasm that she displayed in personality.

"Now, you must be the older brother." Celia studied him for a moment, eying him curiously up and down. "I sense that you will be protective of your sister while she is in Aycliffe, but I assure you I shall take excellent care of her wherever we go."

"I keep her on a tight leash," Francis proclaimed in stern seriousness.

"Too tight." Beth made known her objection.

"Then, Mr. Edwards, I beg of you to hand it over so I may free the young girl to have a marvelous time in the weeks ahead," she ordered.

"I may be inclined," Francis cautiously replied, "all in good time."

"Sly and controlling, I see." Celia narrowed her eyes at him with an impish smile. "We shall be grand friends too. Welcome to Aycliffe."

Francis and Beth exchanged glances as Mr. and Mrs. Wilson silently observed the antics of their daughter. It was clear to all in the room that the center of attention had arrived in the parlor.

CHAPTER THREE

Interested Parties

Prudence Wilson descended the stairs and rejoined her husband in the parlor. She glanced at him and heaved a sigh of relief.

"Well, they are settling in for a rest before dinner." After plopping on a wingback chair, she touched her forehead. "My goodness, Benjamin, I had no idea how closely either of them would resemble their mother. It's brought a flood of memories back that I find most disturbing."

"Yes, for the most part, I am prone to the same emotions." He frowned at Prudence. "While you were upstairs, I received a summons from Mr. Davenport." Benjamin pulled out the note from his pocket.

"Well, he has wasted no time at all. You better respond and tell him they have arrived." Prudence shooed him on with her hand. "Go on, but be back before dinner so I will have no need to explain your absence."

"As you wish, my dear," Benjamin agreed with a twinkle in his eye.

He grabbed his hat, slipped on his frock coat, and entered the foggy outdoors, sensing the evening chill approach offshore. The weather had been dreadfully dreary for the past few days, and he hoped that the sun would finally arrive to push away his doldrums and greet their guests.

The two from Dunwich were welcome indeed, and Benjamin was pleased to see the resemblance to their mother, Catherine Ashby. The young lady who came to work for the Davenports over twenty years ago had been unmarried, naive, but well liked by everyone with whom she became acquainted. Catherine had a way about her that attracted both agreeable and disagreeable personalities. Her beauty, golden-colored hair, blue eyes, and a flawless complexion drew the attention of many. To add to her attractiveness, Catherine's lips were rounded and plump, and when she spoke, her voice tingled one's ears as if she were an angel from heaven.

The Davenports were quite taken with Catherine when they employed her as a governess. They allowed her far too many liberties. Unfortunately, her tenure was short-lived, and she eventually departed Aycliffe under less than ideal circumstances. Alexander, Lydia, and Edwin had all benefited from her care and over-sight. Richard, the youngest in the family, hadn't the pleasure, having been born after Catherine departed.

Prudence and Benjamin were young newlyweds at the time. Since Benjamin worked for Mr. Davenport overseeing the construction of the resort, it had only been natural that their paths should cross. Prudence had become close with Catherine and maintained their steadfast devotion to one another throughout the years. Their ties ran deep, and Benjamin pondered the history that bound them together as he approached his destination.

The Davenports lived on the outskirts of town in a monstrosity of a house. James Davenport built it after being elected mayor of the city years ago. Unopposed by anyone else, Benjamin had no doubt that James would remain the mayor for some time to come. Even the city council members had no stomach to oppose the man. Undoubtedly, he owned their property, souls, and debts, which guaranteed his continued reelection in the conservative party.

With a quick rap on the door, the Davenports' stoic butler, Benson, welcomed him indoors.

"Mr. Davenport is waiting for you in the parlor, sir," Benson declared. "Might I take your hat and coat?"

"Yes, yes, please do," Benjamin said, handing them over. Afterward, he turned to the left of the foyer and entered the sitting room. Davenport sat in an oversized chair in front of the roaring fireplace. He appeared like a king on his throne, albeit without a crown on his head. In some aspects, he was the king of Aycliffe, although he lacked an aristocratic title. Only the resident noble, Lord Howard, owned that privilege. Regardless, Davenport possessed half the town and ran a tight ship, leading the community with a firm hand of purpose that faced challenges.

"Ah, Benjamin," he said, rising to his feet. "Thank you for coming so quickly." He motioned to a single chair, and Benjamin sat, out of breath from his brisk walk in the chilly air of dusk.

"Drink? Brandy, perhaps?" Davenport asked.

"Yes, please. Sounds delightful."

Davenport poured a glass and handed it to him. A moment later, his eldest son entered the room.

"Alexander." Benjamin noted his arrival, nodding his head. "Good to see you."

"And you as well, Mr. Wilson. I'm assuming you won't mind me interposing myself into the conversation?" he inquired with a sly grin.

Benjamin noted Davenport's fashionable elder son, impeccable and well groomed as usual. Alexander, now six and twenty, unmarried, maintained a close relationship with his father and nurtured entrepreneurial and political interests. Ambition should have been his middle name instead of Reginald. The young man maintained a highly regarded reputation in the community compared to his siblings. He was also easy on the ladies' eyes but held a bit of an air about him that could be off-putting to woman with reduced confidence.

Lydia, his sister, had been coined the most conniving young lady to walk the shores of the south coast. In contrast, Edwin, his younger brother, had shamefully taken on the reputation as the resident rogue of the seaside resort. When summer arrived, he was the first to follow the skirts of incoming ladies. Richard, the youngest, was far too interested in his pursuits of books and knowledge to care either way. He was neither mean nor unscrupulous, waiting for the day his father would send him to university.

"Pour yourself a drink, son," Davenport said, inviting him. "Make it quick, as I'm eager to hear what Mr. Wilson has to tell us about his guests."

"As I am," Alexander agreed. With a glass in hand, he sat across from his father with a keen glint of interest in his eye.

"Now that we are all settled," Davenport said, "do tell of their arrival."

"I must make a quick report as Mrs. Wilson has threatened me with bodily harm should I return late for dinner." He sniggered. After wetting his lips with a drink, he spoke. "They arrived a few hours ago, none the worse for wear from their lengthy trip."

"Good. Glad they made it safely to our shores," Davenport remarked.

"Pity that the weather has not been more welcoming," Alexander noted.

"What do they look like?" Davenport gripped the glass, anticipating a report.

Benjamin spoke about Francis first. "Well, the young man has brown hair and eyes, square jaw, and assured countenance. Other than that, he must take after his father and stands tall as your son here, shoulder to shoulder." He paused for a moment, noting how Mr. Davenport hung upon his words. "Soft spoken, I would say, in voice and manner. Beyond that, I have obtained nothing more of his disposition. Obviously, it will take time."

"And the daughter?" Alexander inquired, leaning forward with interest.

"Ah, now there's a beauty, much like her mother. Miss Edwards's hair is the color of golden wheat, fair complexion, gray eyes, petite, and attractive for a young lady." He paused and knitted his brow together. "Her clothing, however, is most commonplace, and I fear she will lack in proper attire while here. I must encourage my wife to do some shopping on her behalf."

"Is she timid, or does she have any spunk about her?" Davenport pressed his inquiry.

"She's pleasant in demeanor, but I sense her upbringing being somewhat ordinary. She may not possess the social skills needed to navigate Aycliffe," Benjamin surmised with a slight scowl. "Time will tell if she can rise to the task."

"Hmm." Davenport pondered.

"She sounds delightful," Alexander noted. "It will please me to make her acquaintance."

"And that is all it shall be," his father sternly counseled. "An acquaintance. Do not think I shall allow your affections to run rampant toward a girl with no fortune."

"Father, it is far too early to conclude whether or not I shall find her pleasant since I have yet to meet the young lady." Alexander downed his drink, appearing agitated by his father's edict. "I do have a mind of my own, as I've repeatedly emphasized in our private conversations."

Noting the evident tension between father and son, Benjamin remained cautiously neutral. "Well, on the morrow, you will meet Miss Edwards. I assume the dinner invitation stands." He turned and looked at Mr. Davenport for confirmation.

"Yes, it stands," he replied.

"I have yet to convey your invitation but will do so as we dine in the next hour," Benjamin said. He lifted his eyes to the clock on the fireplace mantel and noted the time. "Forgive me, but I must be away. I don't wish to be late." After gulping the rest of his glass, he rose to his feet and bowed his head. "I bid you a good night."

"Seven o'clock sharp tomorrow evening," Davenport said, reminding him with a firm voice.

"Sharp, it will be, sir." Benjamin nodded toward Alexander. "Tomorrow, you shall meet our guests, and I hope they are to your liking."

Benjamin left the company of the two and scurried down the road home. He pondered the growing animosity that appeared to develop between father and son over the past few months and wondered what cause lay behind it. By the time Benjamin had sprinted back to his residence, he had puffed his way through the door and lumbered into the dining room as everyone sat at the table.

"There you are," Prudence said, scolding him harshly. "Honestly, Benjamin, must you take walks at the most inopportune time?"

"Fresh air, my dear. Fresh is good for the lungs."

Benjamin patted his chest with the palm of his hand. He sat down at the head of the table and glanced at Francis and Beth, who watched his antics. Celia smirked and picked up her napkin, setting it upon her lap.

"Well, I'm home now. Let's not dally about. What's for dinner?"

"Pork roast," Prudence announced. "We are blessed with a fine cook."

"Mother was a fine cook," Francis stated. "I'm afraid Beth does her best, but we are currently without a cook of our own."

"Francis," Beth said, narrowing her eyes. "You're embarrassing me."

"Nothing to be embarrassed about. While you're here, perhaps Miss Princeton can give you some tips," Prudence suggested.

"That would be nice, but I fully intend to find a cook when we return home," Beth said. "I know where my talents lie and where they do not."

"Do you now?" Francis smirked at her remark.

"Speaking of dinner," Benjamin began, taking advantage of the opening. "We have received an invitation to dine tomorrow evening with the mayor, Mr. Davenport, and his wife."

"Peachy," Celia remarked, rolling her eyes. She turned toward Francis and Beth. "I shall speak to you ahead of time to warn you of the siblings who will be at the table."

"Warn us? I was of the impression that the children were now adults," Beth commented.

"Yes, except for Richard, who turned sixteen on his last birthday," Celia said, clarifying.

"Now, don't go influencing their opinions ahead of time. Let them form their own," Mr. Wilson said, keeping calm lest he showed concern.

"If you insist, Father." Celia scowled in disagreement.

Prudence glanced at Beth. "I hope you have brought attire that will suffice."

"Yes, I brought a gown in case there would be such occasions as a formal dinner, but it's rather out of date, I am afraid."

"Do you have a ball gown?" Celia asked.

"Ball gown?" Beth's eyes widened.

"Well yes, my dear," Prudence said. "You will attend the Howard ball while you are here."

Francis and Beth exchanged alarming glances between each other.

"Oh dear. I can tell you do not. Do not worry, as we can go shopping," Prudence offered.

"I'm afraid, ma'am, that our funds for this trip do not allow for frivolities of fashion." Francis spoke in a low tone, visibly uncomfortable at the admission. "I have packed no formal attire either for such a function."

"Now, no concern about that, young man," Benjamin declared. "You are Catherine's dear children, and we can supply you with the funds for clothing as needed. Lord Howard extended the invitation, and he is looking forward to meeting you."

"I cannot accept your charity, sir," Francis sternly asserted.

"It is not charity; it is a gift. Even your mother accepted gifts from Prudence and me over the years. You should have no cause for embarrassment to accept one from us," Benjamin pressured.

"Indeed, no cause," Prudence agreed.

"You better accept," Celia added. "Otherwise, they will hound you relentlessly."

"I don't see any harm in it," Beth said, leaning in toward Francis.

Francis's worry appeared to decline at Beth's persuasion. "All right then. It is very kind of you to offer."

"Ooh, a shopping excursion," Celia excitedly declared. "You know, Father, I could use a new frock."

Benjamin shook his head at how easily Celia turned the gift to her advantage. Naturally, he could not deny her in front of guests. "Yes, of course. A young girl your age can never have enough dresses." Though his pocketbook moaned at the added expense.

As they ate dinner, Benjamin glanced at his wife. All progressed as planned, and hopefully, as the days unfolded in the weeks ahead, all things would come together for good.

CHAPTER FOUR

Friends or Foes

Difficulty falling asleep wasn't what Beth hoped for after a long day of travel. The mattress was comfortable and the pillow fluffy, but her mind spun like a whirlpool offshore. It took at least an hour for her body to still from incessant tossing. As she listened to the faint roar of the ocean in the distance, it eventually lulled her to sleep.

After awaking, she lay in bed, wondering if the fog had lifted. Being in unfamiliar surroundings and among strangers was much like walking through the mist outdoors. She wanted to see with clarity, but everything remained shrouded and indiscernible so early in their visit.

At the end of the dinner the evening before, Beth experienced physical and mental exhaustion. The onslaught of conversation and announcements of the social gatherings sounded daunting. They would meet the Davenports, and later in the week have tea at the Howard estate, which frightened the daylights out of her. In all her one and twenty years, she had never visited the home of an aristocrat and had no idea how one should behave. Afterward, attendance at a ball. Dancing at the local town assembly hall was one thing, but attendance at a formal affair quite another.

As far as her garments for all these affairs, Beth

arrived woefully unprepared. When she accepted the invitation from the Wilsons, she had visions of leisurely walks up and down the beach, taking in the fresh air and clearing her muddled mind from the year of grieving. Never had she considered strangers would throw her into the throngs of Aycliffe society that her mother had once known years ago. Their statements about her mother befuddled Beth. The Wilsons did as well, and she couldn't shake an uneasiness that gnawed at her as she contemplated the day ahead.

Eager to see outdoors, Beth threw back the covers. While sleeping, a maid had come in the early morning hours and lit a small fire, making the room warm and cozy. Beth placed her feet upon the rug laid over the shiny wood floor, wiggled her toes, stretched, and released a rather loud yawn. The sun had risen, and Beth glanced at the clock on the mantel, noting the hour at seven fifteen. They served breakfast at eight, so she had enough time to freshen and dress.

Curious as to the weather, she pulled back the heavy drapes and light flooded the darkened room. After parting the lace curtains, she was pleased to see that the fog had dissipated, although gray clouds appeared above.

"I'm wondering if the sun ever shines in Aycliffe," she mused aloud. A soft knock came at the door, startling her. "Who is it?"

"Francis. Might I come in?"

Eager to speak with her brother, Beth grabbed her dressing gown, wrapped it around her body, and tied the sash. She opened the door and grinned at her sibling. Apparently, he had awakened much earlier and dressed for the day's activities.

"Come in," she said, pulling him indoors before anyone could see he entered. "I've been dying to talk to you since last night."

"And I you," he replied, closing the door.

"To be honest, I'm overwhelmed at the expectations being placed upon us by Mr. and Mrs. Wilson. Do you feel the same?" Beth inquired.

Francis leaned against the closed door and crossed his arms in front of him. By his leisurely stance, he did not appear too ruffled in the least.

"Not really," he readily admitted. "I am looking forward to it, although I certainly did not expect the obligation of formal dinners, tea with an aristocrat, and a gala ball."

"It is disconcerting to me," Beth pouted.

"Your shyness makes you as such, but perhaps you will enjoy it, especially getting a new dress." Francis encouraged her with a smile.

"I could tell that it mortified you accepting their generosity regarding clothing."

"Yes, indeed. I promised myself that upon our return home, I would send them the funds to replace whatever expenditure comes of today. Father would not approve of me being beholden to anyone."

"I thought you would, so I shall be prudent in the choice of a new garment."

"No need, Beth. You deserve something of quality. Please find a gown that pleases you." Francis smiled warmly. "Besides, you may catch the eye of someone special."

"I'd rather catch the eye of the open waters. Will we ever see the ocean or walk on the beach?" Beth groaned. She sat down on the edge of the bed.

"Oh, I'm sure we will. Let us satisfy whatever need Aycliffe carries to honor Mother, and then we shall do as we please." Francis patted his stomach. "I hope breakfast is as hearty and well cooked as dinner." He grinned mischievously. "Do take time out of our busy social schedule to obtain cooking tips from Miss Princeton."

"I will do no such thing. We agreed to hire a new cook and housekeeper upon our return," Beth reminded him in a stern tone.

"Well, in the meantime, it would do you no harm to learn a few culinary lessons before you become someone's wife," he teased.

"Oh you!" Beth grabbed a pillow and flung it at her brother. Francis caught it with his right hand and tossed it back in her face. By the time Beth relaunched it, he had opened the door and disappeared. She grinned, reminiscing how they tussled when they were younger. By all accounts, Francis was a good sibling. However, they had their heated arguments and disagreements now and then like any other. Since the death of their parents, he acted more akin to a guardian, which soured their close relationship. No longer a child, she didn't care to be told what she could and could not do.

Beth spent the next half hour readying herself for the day, choosing to wear a day dress of modesty that matched the blue ribbons of her bonnet. With a growling stomach, she made her way downstairs to discover Francis in conversation with Mr. Wilson. Celia sat across from Francis and motioned her to join her at the table. Mrs. Wilson sat munching her toast and boiled eggs as if nothing else mattered except breakfast.

"Sit by me, Beth, and let us speak of the day ahead," Celia offered. "There is toast, butter, marmalade, boiled eggs, and ham. Help yourself as we are rather informal with the morning meal."

Beth glanced at Francis, whose plate mounded with a sizeable portion. Beth took a smaller amount, wrestling with the anxiety about the day's scheduled activities. The looming formal dinner for which she expected to be well dressed and socially acceptable had pricked her nerves.

"Did you sleep well?" Celia asked, taking a sip of tea.

Her voice, clearly more reserved than when they first met, sounded inviting. Beth didn't like personalities that displayed high-spirited behavior but preferred more reserved and contemplative individuals like herself. Perhaps Celia possessed more agreeable characteristics that would emerge as they got to know one another better.

"Yes, for the most part," Beth fibbed. She buttered her toast and noted Francis deep in conversation with Mr. Wilson about the architecture of their residence. Mrs. Wilson grabbed another slice of toast, still focused on her morning meal. Beth took advantage of their distraction.

"Do you mind telling me about the Davenports before we dine there this evening?" she asked, leaning in toward Celia. "What did you mean by warning us?" It was one of the points that caused Beth's mind to twirl the evening before.

"It is a well-known fact that Edwin, the second son, is a ladies' man. If he shows any interest in you whatsoever, you would be wise to keep your distance and not fall victim to his flattery." Celia glanced at her parents, apparently making sure they had not noted their conversation and whispered. "Do you understand my meaning?"

Naive Beth, unfamiliar with the terminology applied to Edwin, pondered Celia's warning until she deduced the essence behind her advice.

"Oh, I understand the caution. And the others?"

"Lydia will be kind to your face, but she may speak of you behind your back in the vilest fashion. She is a gossip and meddler of the worst sort. You would do well not to become friends or share your personal thoughts or secrets with her. If you do, they will end up being the next topic of gossip in Aycliffe, fanned by her wagging tongue."

"Celia?" Mr. Wilson drew attention from everyone at the table with his stern voice. "Are you speaking of the Davenports even though I asked you not to?"

Unashamed and lifting her chin, she answered. "I am simply telling Beth to be careful of Edwin. You know his reputation, Father. Would you have her fall victim to his wiles and be harmed?"

Mr. Wilson narrowed his eyes at his daughter, Francis looked alarmed, and Mrs. Wilson lifted her head, hearing the conversation.

"I am grateful for the counsel," Beth said in Celia's defense.

"Husband, I see no harm in Celia speaking of it," Mrs. Wilson interjected. "We all know it to be true, and are we not behooved to protect Catherine's daughter?"

Mr. Wilson thought for a moment and sighed. "Perhaps you are right, as far as it goes with Edwin. However, I will hear no ill will spoke of Alexander, Richard, or Lydia for that matter. Is that understood?"

"Yes, Father," Celia sheepishly replied.

"Should I worry about my sister's welfare as far as this Edwin is concerned?" Francis asked with an alarmed tone.

"No, Edwin merely trifles with the ladies in a flirtatious manner," Mr. Wilson responded. "I shall speak with Mr. Davenport ahead of time to make sure the man keeps his distance where your sister is concerned."

"And should there be other reservations about the family?" Francis asked.

"Absolutely not," Mr. Wilson assured. "Alexander is one of the finest men in all of Aycliffe and well respected. He went to university and excelled in his studies and returned to work for his father. Richard is too involved in his education to be of a bother, and Lydia—well, Lydia just needs to find a husband to keep herself busy."

"Busybody indeed," Celia muttered. Mr. Wilson cast a stern gaze at his daughter, and Celia muttered, "Sorry."

Everyone at the table fell silent for a moment, returning their attention to their meals. Beth whispered to Celia, "Thank you."

"You're more than welcome." Speaking in a louder tone, Celia directed the conversation elsewhere. "Mother, what color would Beth look good in?"

"Oh dear." She dabbed her lips with the napkin. "With her fair complexion and light hair, I daresay we need something rosy to bring out the hue in her cheeks."

"Rosy?" Beth responded. "It sounds delightful after wearing black for the past year."

Francis cast a wary gaze in her direction, as if he objected to such a bright color rather than a muted one coming out of mourning.

"Well, mauve perhaps would be better." To Beth's chagrin, she countered the suggestion to keep Francis from balking.

"Well, it limits our choices as we usually hire a seamstress and choose our fabrics ahead of time. There is no opportunity to make you a dress before this evening. Still, we will see what Mrs. Price has available in her shop."

"Beth and I are of the same size, I would imagine, so I could lend her one of my gowns for tonight," Celia offered.

"True, but a new dress always is more preferable than used," Mrs. Wilson countered.

"And you, young man, I shall take you to the tailor and have you fitted for a new ensemble for Howard's spring ball," Mr. Wilson pledged.

"If you insist," Francis relented half-heartedly. Beth knew he would probably never wear the item again since the small village of Dunwich catered to no such formalities. Seeing Francis in such a fashionable garment would be enjoyable.

CHAPTER FIVE

Measurements of the Past

After breakfast, everyone went their separate way. Celia, Beth, and Mrs. Wilson scurried into town to the dressmaker. At the same time, Mr. Wilson and Francis headed out the door to the tailor shop. As they stepped outside, Francis noted the clouds above part and spots of blue sky peek through.

"Beth shall be happy to see the weather clear," he said to Mr. Wilson has they walked side by side. "I hope that we might find some time to see the ocean before dinner tonight."

"Oh, that can be arranged. Is this your first time to the coast?" Mr. Wilson asked, looking curiously at him.

"As children, we went to Brighton for a brief time with Mother and Father. Unfortunately, I can't say that I remember anything whatsoever from the age of two or three years."

Mr. Wilson laughed. "Well, I can hardly remember conversations with my wife, for that matter, from this morning. Although I remember a pleasant childhood, growing up in Aycliffe."

"Then you have been resident here your entire life?"

"Why yes, of course. Back then, it was a small fishing village that scarcely supported its residents, I'm afraid. My father was a fishmonger if you can believe that," Mr. Wilson conveyed.

"No shame in trade," Francis replied, thinking nothing of it. As they walked toward the main street, Francis noted there were more individuals out and about than late afternoon when they arrived. Perhaps the weather drew people out of doors.

"I'm assuming that you've watched Aycliffe grow over the years," Francis mused aloud.

"Oh yes, yes. Mostly because of the Davenports, who took family money and infused it into the town so it could grow." They rounded the corner and were a few yards away from the hotel. It emerged from the shadowy fog in all its glory. "The Aycliffe Hotel, one of the grandest on the coast for miles around," Mr. Wilson announced.

Francis tipped his head and looked at the six-story building that took up an entire block on the main thoroughfare. It was impressive, but the facade looked weathered. No doubt buildings on the coast were challenging to maintain due to the rainy winters and powerful winds.

"The top floor contains the most expensive suites, as they afford an ocean view," Mr. Wilson noted.

"Very impressive," Francis stated. Anxious to see far more than buildings, he inquired, "How far are we from the beachfront?"

Mr. Wilson grinned. "I say you are eager. Follow me, and we shall turn the corner so you can see." With a brisk step, he led Francis past a line of shops that included everything from sweets to seashells. On the opposite side of the street, clothiers, millinery shops, the bank, and other buildings passed one by one. As they came to Broughton Avenue, they turned to their right, which gave Francis an instantaneous view of the sparkling waters off in the distance.

"We have a rather nice pier but plenty of sandy

beaches to the right and cliffs to the left." Mr. Wilson inhaled a deep breath of air. "Ah, nothing like the smell of the ocean to fill your lungs." He gave Francis a pat on the back. "Take a deep breath, my boy, and enjoy."

Francis couldn't help but fill his lungs as a gusty breeze, the town's structures had previously blocked, grazed his face. It was exhilarating to say the least, and it unexpectedly brought a pang of guilt that he enjoyed the sight without Beth by his side. Mr. Wilson described the locale perfectly. A rather large pier jutted out into the waters. As he gazed to his left, the landscape made a gentle incline toward the cliffs. Below was a small cove with a few fishing boats anchored offshore.

He turned and glanced to his right, and as far as the eye could see were sandy beaches. The clouds parted, allowing shards of sunshine to hit the water and sparkle like diamonds. Seagulls squawked overhead. A few individuals enjoyed a morning stroll on the pier. Though the town was named Aycliffe Cove, it wasn't much of a harbor at all, and the fishing industry appeared nonexistent.

"Is fishing not a commerce continued in Aycliffe?" Francis asked.

"Oh, we still have a spattering of fishing boats, but it's more of a resort. We cater to the summer visitors who come clamoring for the ocean and all its benefits," Mr. Wilson answered. "During the summer, bathing machines line the beach. As you can see, it is off-season, but the crowds will return in June as they always do."

"It must bring in a rush of income to all the businesses." Francis wondered if they had a watchmaker in town. The idea of relocating to live on the ocean shores tickled his fancy, or perhaps opening a second location for the summer months. He could leave the shop in Dunwich in the expert hands of another.

Silently observing the gentle rolling waves filled his head with ideas.

"We shouldn't tarry too long," Francis confessed. "I would prefer to save a stroll on the pier or beach with my sister lest she bite my head off for going without her."

"Understandable." Mr. Wilson pulled out his pocket watch from his vest, flipped open the lid, and noted the time. "Well, let us make our way to the tailor. It's three blocks away."

"Sounds reasonable," Francis concurred. They retreated in the opposite direction. As they walked down the street, a tall gentleman approached. Mr. Wilson halted and tipped his hat.

"Good morning, Mr. Davenport," he said.

"Good morning, Mr. Wilson," the man answered, glancing at Francis.

"Mr. Davenport, may I introduce you to Mr. Edwards, our guest who will dine at your home this evening with his sister, Miss Edwards?" He turned toward Francis. "This is Alexander Davenport, the elder son of the family."

"Pleasure to make your acquaintance," Alexander said. "I hope you are enjoying our fine town."

Francis tipped his hat. "My pleasure," he replied with a grin. "Yes, I'm quite impressed with Aycliffe and hope to see more of it in the days to come."

"Well, we have plenty to keep you busy," Alexander announced with a surety in his voice. "Do we not, Mr. Wilson?"

"Yes, indeed, Mr. Davenport. Plenty to do in Aycliffe, both socially as well as indulging in its natural delights."

"Well then, I'll leave you, gentlemen, as I am on my way to the bank on a rush errand for Father," Alexander said. "I look forward to dinner this evening and meeting your sister. Perhaps we can further our conversation tonight."

He nodded in deference and continued onward. Francis found it difficult not to glance over his shoulder and watch the man's departure. An assured and robust gait led him ahead, impressing Francis by his appearance and confidence. Dressed in fine clothes, he sounded articulate in speech, with piercing gray eyes, wavy brown hair, and a well-trimmed mustache.

"Alexander is the joy of his father. The man has a solid head on his shoulders and entrepreneurial sense like the elder Mr. Davenport. He will follow in his father's footsteps in every sense of the word, both in politics and business." Mr. Wilson praised him as he watched him retreat. "He would make a splendid catch for some young lady, and I daresay the women of this town are eager to snag him, but no one has caught his eye yet."

Francis glanced at Mr. Wilson, speculating if he imagined Beth to be that young lady. "Set me straight, Mr. Wilson. Is he not one of the children whom my mother was governess to?"

"Yes, that is correct. Alexander was six at the time, Edwin four, and Lydia two. They were under her care," he clarified. "Come now, we must be off to the tailor."

Francis's mind filled with questions, but the moment to have the conversation eroded as they entered the shop. A bell rang above the door, announcing their arrival.

"Mr. Huxley, we need your help," Mr. Wilson said, entering like a stampeding bull. "This gentleman, Mr. Edwards, needs a new set of formal clothes for the Howard ball."

"I see," he said, adjusting his spectacles and

approaching Francis. With a tape measure dangling around his neck, he walked around Francis and noted his stature. "Well, you may be in luck as I doubt that I could tailor a new garment on such brief notice. However, Mr. Peterson came in a few weeks ago for a fitting. He decided halfway through my tailoring to cancel his order. Of course, I was extremely unamused, but I have a nice formal suit partially underway."

"Well, that is delightful news, indeed," Mr. Wilson said.

"Let me take some measurements and see what we can do," Mr. Huxley announced. Before Francis could get a word in edgewise, the tailor pointed him to the backroom for removal of his current clothing and measuring for the new.

"While Mr. Huxley is taking care of you, Mr. Edwards, I will run a quick errand and be back in a half hour," Mr. Wilson announced.

"As you wish." Francis had no choice but to be left behind.

"Come with me, young man," Mr. Huxley ordered. "Are you new in town?"

"My sister and I are guests of Mr. Wilson. We come from Dunwich."

"Never heard of it. Far from here?"

"A few hours by coach," Francis said, sounding downhearted.

"I see. Have you known the Wilsons for very long?" Mr. Huxley continued, as Francis removed his frock coat.

"My sister and I met them yesterday. They were friends of my mother and extended an invitation."

"You can leave on your linen shirt," he instructed. He stood behind Francis and measured him shoulder to shoulder, jotting numbers down on a piece of paper.

"And who is your mother?"

"Her name before she married was Catherine Ashby. She passed away a year ago," Francis said.

"Good Lord." Mr. Huxley stepped back and looked at Francis with large open eyes. "You are Catherine's boy?"

Surprised by the look of astonishment on his face, Francis nodded. "Yes."

Mr. Huxley's mouth gaped open as if he wanted to say something, but then clamped it shut.

"Well, I am sorry to hear of her passing. You have my deepest condolences," he solemnly expressed. "You say your name is Edwards?"

"Yes, Francis Edwards."

"Ah, I see," Mr. Huxley said, returning to the task at hand. He put the tape measure at the top of his shoulder and then ran it down the length of his arm.

"Did you know my mother?" Francis pressed, curious about the man's reaction.

"Yes, I remember her from long ago, but only in passing. I heard she had her hands full with the Davenport children." He grinned with amusement. "They were a handful, and a few still are."

"I'm getting the impression they have reputations in town," Francis shared.

"You could say that," Mr. Huxley replied. "Now stand straight, Mr. Edwards, and don't slouch. I need these measurements to be accurate. It appears what I've started on the other order can accommodate your measurements without making much fuss."

"I'm glad to hear."

"Going to the Howard ball?" Mr. Huxley grinned. "My, my, that is the spring event. Then the garden party will occur in the summer, another ball in the fall, and Christmas where they only open the estate to their closest friends."

"I am more interested in what the ocean has to offer, Mr. Huxley, rather than the estate, to be quite frank." Francis clarified his preference, resisting the temptation to be impressed by aristocratic life.

"Well, good for you then, Mr. Edwards. You have better priorities and goals than others in this town."

As Mr. Huxley finished speaking, the bell above the door jingled, announcing the arrival of Mr. Wilson, who made his way into the fitting room and observed them.

"Will he have new formal apparel for the ball?" he asked.

"Indeed. I can make adjustments." Mr. Huxley glanced at Francis. "You can get dressed now."

"Put it on my account, Mr. Huxley, and I shall pay it forthwith," Mr. Wilson announced. "My gift to Mr. Edwards."

"He tells me he's the son of Catherine Ashby." Mr. Huxley's brow rose above his right eye.

"Yes, he is, and he has a fine young sister by the name of Elizabeth, but she goes by Beth to her close acquaintances and family." Mr. Wilson paused. "She looks much like Catherine."

"Does she now?" Francis couldn't quite catch the gist behind his voice and thought it strange.

"Shall we pass by the dress shop and see how your sister fares?" Mr. Wilson asked.

"Yes, of course," Francis replied. "Good day, Mr. Huxley, and thank you for your time."

"You are welcome, young man."

Mr. Wilson opened the door, and the two walked outdoors. Francis wasn't sure what to make of the conversation with Mr. Huxley and attempted not to overthink the matter.

CHAPTER SIX

Petticoats, Silk, and Lace

As they walked to the dress shop, Celia was on Beth's right and Mrs. Wilson on her left. Squeezed in the middle, Beth could barely stroll without bumping elbows with the two as they made their way into town. Each chatted, sounding like starlings rattling their throats. They expressed thoughts about everything from the weather to the latest fashions.

"It is off-season, so few shoppers will be at the dress shop to hinder our mission," Mrs. Wilson announced.

"We will have to check Mrs. Price's catalog for the latest designs from Paris," Celia noted.

"Paris," Beth repeated in angst. "Surely such dresses must be costly."

"Well, it depends on the fabrics, dear," Mrs. Wilson explained. "A prime silk and handmade lace can add to the expense of course."

"I am not used to such extravagance." Beth furrowed her brow, worried about the money that Francis would have to repay the Wilsons upon their return home. Their father taught them to be frugal and not foolish with hard-earned money. Francis had taken on those characteristics, almost to the point of being a miser when it came to family funds.

"Have you never attended a formal ball?" Celia asked, grabbing Beth by the arm.

"Not at the home of an aristocrat. The assembly hall in town holds its share of dances, but I fear I've only been to a few. Our parents were not prone to social functions but rather reserved."

"Reserved?" Mrs. Wilson said, arching a brow. "That sounds nothing like your mother. I can assure you that she enjoyed her share of dances while here in Aycliffe."

"She did?" Beth gaped at the revelation, finding it difficult to imagine her mother in such settings. "As a governess, I never considered she would be a party to such social assemblies because of her station. Did the Davenports allow her such freedom?"

"They gave her leave to enjoy herself," Mrs. Wilson explained. "As I said, she was well liked by many during her stay here, and allowances were made."

Beth followed as they entered the dress shop, pondering the strange disclosure. A knot formed in her stomach, as she glanced around at the various bolts of fabric, lace, ribbons, and a few dresses already on forms. A middle-aged woman greeted them, and Mrs. Wilson took no time expressing her desire for new frocks for the Howard affair.

"We are looking for ball gowns," she announced, glancing around the shop.

"Of course," Mrs. Price said. "I'm always a step ahead of the spring event, anticipating new orders. I've started a few dresses already, and with a few tucks and adjustments, I shall have a new garment for you in no time. Is it for your daughter?" She smiled at Celia.

"One dress for me and the other for Miss Edwards, our guest," Celia clarified.

"Oh, I see." Mrs. Price walked over and eyed Beth from top to bottom. "I have just the color to accent your fair skin and beautiful golden hair, Miss Edwards."

Mrs. Price walked over to a dress form, showing Beth a silk gown with a bright blue hue that shimmered in the light. The evening frock was an off-the-shoulder fashion with wide flounces that reached to the elbow, trimmed in delicate lace.

"The dress will have a sheer shawl, and white gloves will accentuate it perfectly," she said, looking at Beth. "The color would suit you well."

"My goodness," Celia gasped. "How utterly gorgeous."

"I had hoped on light pink, but now that I see Miss Edwards next to the blue, I'm convinced that color brings out the best of her skin tones. Do you agree?" Mrs. Wilson asked.

"Oh definitely," Celia responded. "I'm almost green with jealousy. I shall have no one to sign my dance card at the Howard affair as all the men will clamor for you."

Beth giggled aloud from nerves as she experienced a flutter of excitement. The affair would test her ability to mingle with society as a young lady, and the notion of strange men asking her to dance sounded petrifying. Regardless of her bashfulness, she determined to overcome her fears.

"Now, for you, Miss Wilson, I have a rather ravishing lavender silk in the backroom that I'm about ready to start," Mrs. Price teased.

"Mother?" Celia cast a pleading gaze.

"Well, your father has given his permission, so a new gown for both of you will be fine. You can bill Mr. Wilson directly, Mrs. Price."

"Splendid." She grinned.

Celia and Beth spent the next hour pinned, tucked, and expertly fitted for their ball gowns. By the time they finished, Beth's fear about the affair had waned. As she looked at herself in the mirror, she appeared beautiful and desirable. Since her mother's death, Beth had not contemplated meeting a young man and getting married. The subject occasionally rose with Francis when he teased her about her shyness. Of course, meeting someone in Aycliffe would never turn into anything of substance since they were only visiting for two weeks. Nevertheless, a brief flirtation would be an enjoyable experience.

As they said their goodbyes to Mrs. Price, the door opened, and Mr. Wilson and Francis entered.

"Well, ladies, how far have you set my budget in arrears?" Mr. Wilson asked with a smirk.

"Once you see how attractive the girls look, you will conclude it well worth the expenditure," Mrs. Wilson assured.

"Enjoying yourself?" Francis approached Beth.

"Yes." She nodded her head in approval but elaborated. "Yet I am yearning to enjoy more." Francis understood her inference.

"Mr. Wilson, if you do not mind, I would like to take my sister for a stroll on the beach. Would you be so kind as to excuse us for the next hour or two to enjoy the ocean view?"

"Why, of course. Do as you please."

"Come along, Celia," Mrs. Wilson said. "Let us give our guests a few minutes of privacy to inhale the sea air." She tugged on Celia's sleeve.

"Have a spectacular time, but watch for sneaker waves. You may come back wet!" Celia warned.

"Don't linger all day," Mr. Wilson said. "Dinner at the Davenports will soon be upon us, and I don't wish to be late."

"Of course not," Beth assured. "We will be back in plenty of time." With those words, Francis led the way, and Beth followed, keen to see the ocean.

After they had sprinted a few yards down the street, Francis exhaled in relief. "At last a moment to ourselves."

"Sometimes I feel smothered by the Wilsons," Beth admitted. "Take me to the beach, Francis. I cannot wait to see it."

With enthusiasm in their step, Francis retraced the path that Mr. Wilson had shown him earlier. As they rounded the corner and arrived to see the view, Beth gasped aloud.

"Oh, Francis, how beautiful!" Beth ran out in front of her brother toward the sandy shore. The gusty breeze kissed her face with a welcoming chill, and she inhaled the freshness of the ocean air. She swung around and yelled back at Francis, who laughed at her antics a few feet away. With her arms outstretched and twirling around in circles, her feet kicked the sand up with her shoes. Not enough to satiate the experience, Beth plopped herself on the beach, lifted her skirt, and untied her shoes. Frantically, she pulled off her silk stockings and drove her toes into the sand, wiggling them with delight.

Francis stood before her, placed his hands on his hips, and sniggered the words, "Having fun?"

"Oh Francis," Beth cooed. "The sand feels glorious between my toes." She stood to her feet and gawked at the ocean. "Do you think the water is cold?"

"It is freezing, and I dare you to stick a toe in it and find out," he challenged.

"I dare you back!"

"All right, if you must." Francis took a mere moment to rid himself of his shoes and socks and grabbed Beth by the hand, pulling her toward the water.

"You rascal, let go of me!" Beth screamed, making

no effort to pull away. A moment later, they halted as a wave broke and sloshed upon their bare skin, wetting the bottom of Francis's trousers and the hem of Beth's skirt.

"My God," Francis screamed. "It's frigid as the Arctic."

"I know! And people swim in it!"

"Not me." He balked, pulling her back from the freezing tide.

They retreated to a respectable distance where the waves could no longer lick at their bare feet. Side by side, they fell into an awestruck silence, peering at the vastness of water and sky.

"I never imagined it to be so stunning," Beth admitted with a sigh. "Why didn't Mother talk of it more? I am sure she loved it."

Francis shook his head. "I am as dismayed as you. The way Mr. Wilson speaks of her, Mother sounds like a totally different woman."

"I know." Beth glanced sideways at her brother. "Mrs. Wilson tells me things about Mother, and I'm aghast."

Francis pondered in silence, and Beth turned her senses to the sights and smells. For a moment, she closed her eyes and listened to the waves breaking on the shore and smiled at the gulls squawking overhead as if they demanded a treat. A pier jutted out into the water, and cliffs rose to heights in the distance. In the opposite direction, a sandy beach stretched until it disappeared around the curvature of the landscape.

"Let us gather our shoes and walk for a while, Francis." Beth dug her toes back in the sand.

"All right, but not too long. I am under the impression the Wilsons are eager for our return so we can prepare this evening to meet the Davenports."

"We won't be late," she assured. "Besides, I have not felt such freedom in so long."

"I daresay, Beth, that this is the most I have seen you smile since Mother left us. It brings me joy watching you," Francis admitted.

They grabbed their shoes and stockings and slowly strolled alongside each other. Beth wondered what it would be like to live in Aycliffe. Though she had no complaint about Dunwich and the townspeople, she experienced an odd tugging at her heartstrings as if she belonged here instead. She would have to see if the sensation remained as the days progressed and what Francis thought of the seaside resort. After all, their home and the business remained elsewhere. Those were their roots, birthplace, and where their parents had planted them. It wasn't unheard of, though, for people to pull up whence they were born and move to another locale.

"Do you like it here, Francis?" she asked out of curiosity.

"For the most part. I am enjoying the scenery."

His rather vague reply gave Beth caution to her own swift desire for something newfangled. Perhaps it was just the setting that caught her fancy, the gentle breeze caressing her face, the warm sun on her cheeks, and the soft swishing of the water to shore that relaxed her soul. They were all sensory invitations to stay and partake. Yet they had only scratched the surface of Aycliffe, and no doubt much more comprised the seaside resort beside the view. Time would tell if roots were meant to be watered or pulled up and planted elsewhere.

CHAPTER SEVEN

The Dinner Invitation

With butterfly jitters in her stomach, Beth entered the grand home of the Davenports. Francis remained close by her side, while the Wilsons followed the butler to the parlor. Celia tagged along behind as if they placed her there to keep Beth from running out the door.

When she first entered the home of the Wilsons, she considered it an exceptional residence. As she stepped into the Davenport dwelling, it barely compared to the opulence and wealth of the mayor's home. From what history the Wilsons had given her and Francis, the Davenports went back generations in Aycliffe, basically as founding fathers of a sleepy fishing village. The Howards, as well, were the local aristocrats, having kept a close relationship with the family lasting for decades.

As Beth entered the parlor, she felt woefully inadequate. Her dress appeared drab compared to the fashions of the family, who all stood in greeting like adorned figurines in a straight line. In a blur of bewilderment, Beth attempted to focus as Mr. Wilson began the introductions.

"Mr. Davenport, please allow me to present Miss Edwards and her brother, Mr. Edwards," he announced, grinning as if he were the proud father of them.

Francis stood by Beth's side, and as soon as Mr.

Wilson spoke the words, Mr. Davenport stepped forward and took her by the hand.

"My goodness, young lady. You are so like your mother that I feel as if she has returned to our home." He paused, and his facial expression turned woeful. "May I offer you both my deepest condolences on the passing of Catherine?"

A bit surprised at the informality in using her mother's Christian name, Beth acknowledged his welcome with a slight quiver in her voice. "Thank you, Mr. Davenport. You are most kind."

"She was a fine woman and taken far too soon. I shall lodge my complaint to the powers that be when I meet her again in heaven, Lord willing." The corner of his mouth turned up in a slight smile.

He dropped Beth's hand and offered his other to Francis, who shook it in return. "Pleasure to meet you," Mr. Davenport said, eyeing him with interest. "I see you have your mother's eyes."

Francis greeted him without hesitation. "Pleasure to make your acquaintance, sir."

As they spoke to one another, Beth noted Mr. Davenport's demeanor that exuded power and confidence. His voice was deep and commanding, although as he expressed his regard for their mother, it softened. Dark brown wavy hair, somewhat grayed at the temples, accented the chiseled features of his face.

He stepped aside and nodded to his family, who stood shoulder to shoulder. "May I present my wife?"

Beth shifted her gaze. An attractive woman stood before her, dressed in a fashionable burgundy gown. Her dark brown hair parted down the middle with flawlessly formed ringlet curls framing her face. For a middle-aged lady, she was stunning.

"How lovely to have you in our home," Mrs.

Davenport recited in a stilted tone. "I am blessed to meet you both and devastated at the loss of your mother."

"Thank you, Mrs. Davenport," Beth replied. "It is a pleasure to make your acquaintance."

Mr. Davenport outstretched his arm toward his children. "May I introduce you to my eldest son, Alexander," Mr. Davenport said with a note of pride in his voice. "I understand, Mr. Edwards, that your paths crossed already."

"Yes, as a matter of fact, they did," Francis acknowledged. "Pleasure to see you again."

Alexander nodded in return, eyeing Beth more than Francis.

Mr. Davenport continued. "My middle son, Edwin, and this is our daughter, Lydia." He paused for a moment and grinned. "And lastly, Richard, our youngest."

Suddenly, Alexander spoke. Beth noted that he had taken his father's appearance in many aspects, from the coloring of his hair to his features. "As the eldest of the group, I can say that I remember your mother vividly, being a boy of six when she arrived in Aycliffe."

"I'm eager to hear about Mother's stay here," Beth announced, genuinely curious.

"If I must say," Alexander boasted with a prideful smirk, "your mother found me always on my best behavior."

"I'm afraid I was a rascal at four years of age," Edwin declared without shame. "I have been told that I drove her to tears on a few occasions."

"Well, I was a perfect little girl," Lydia offered.

"You were terrible at two years of age and into everything," Edwin remarked with a jab. "In fact, if I recall, I got in trouble for some things you did."

Richard interrupted their bantering. "I was not yet born, so I cannot comment on whether I was good or bad under your mother's care," Richard remarked straight-faced. "Perhaps I saved her from additional trials."

"Children," Mrs. Davenport scolded as if they were still fledglings. "You are grown now, so please be adults in the presence of our guests."

For a few moments, the room grew quiet as the six Davenports and three Wilsons eyed Beth and Francis. Beth glanced at her brother, and he shifted in his stance in a display of uneasiness.

"Well now," Mr. Davenport said as if he sensed them floundering like fishes out of water. "Shall we sit and have a chat before dinner?"

"Splendid idea," Mr. Wilson agreed. He motioned to the empty chairs in the room. Alexander stood by the fireplace, while his brother took a stance nearby. Lydia sat next to her mother, and Mr. Davenport took the sizable overstuffed chair that Beth noted must have been his favorite. The Wilsons grabbed empty chairs after Beth and Francis sat down on a two-seat settee.

"Did you have a pleasant trip?" Alexander inquired.

Beth raised her eyes but said nothing. She looked at him, taking in his appearance, now that her bewilderment had subsided. The room focused as the blur of her nerves diminished. Each face became more explicit, and opinions formed in her mind about their hosts.

Francis spoke, apparently noting Beth's repeated hesitancy. "Yes, it was uneventful, although Aycliffe was hidden under a cloak of fog upon our arrival."

"Yes, the fog," Alexander reiterated. "As the air warms and ground remains cold. It is one of the minor drawbacks of living on the coast during the spring."

"Where are you from?" Lydia burst forth in a

squeaky tone.

"Dunwich," Beth answered since she appeared to be directing the question to her.

"I never heard of the place." Lydia's nose wrinkled. "Small village in the country, is it?"

"Lydia," Mrs. Davenport said, giving her a look of disdain.

"Dunwich was Catherine's birth town, was it not?" Mr. Davenport interjected. "She spoke of it often with a twinkle of delight in her eyes."

"Yes, Mother was born there," Francis replied. "Her parents had a small spot of farming land rented from Sir Dutton."

Mrs. Davenport spoke. "It was obvious, though, that Aycliffe became another favorite location of your mother's. She loved the ocean, and the town held a special place in her heart."

"We surmised from her continued correspondence with the Wilsons that a fondness continued long after she left." Beth smiled at their hosts. "Obviously, she valued friendship above all else after her departure."

"Do you have any special plans while you are here on holiday?" Alexander asked, leaning against the stone fireplace.

Beth glanced at him and noted that she enjoyed the sound of his voice. It was tenor in nature and not like his brother's that sounded squeaky, like an irritated mouse. Admittedly, it had a calming quality to it that she enjoyed.

"I will confess that I am enthralled by the ocean after seeing it today." Beth sensed her cheeks flush.

"She is definitely captivated," Francis revealed. He cast a sly grin in Beth's direction. "I am embarrassed to say we both acted like children, taking our shoes off and wiggling toes in the sand."

"The water is so cold that we squealed and ran in the opposite direction after experiencing its chill." Beth chuckled aloud.

Mr. Davenport burst out laughing. After shaking his head at them, he explained his amusement. "Your mother, God rest her soul, was the same upon her arrival at Aycliffe. I think she took the children to the beach every opportunity, whether it be fair climate or foul."

"Oh yes, she loved it," Mrs. Davenport concurred. "Her light complexion easily burned, and I had to give her one of my parasols and a large-brimmed hat to hide underneath." She looked at Beth. "Now, you be careful too, Miss Edwards. On sunny days I daresay you are prone to turning bright pink like your mother with that skin tone."

"I am and will be careful."

The butler stood in the doorway and looked at Mr. Davenport. "Dinner is served."

"Very good," he said, rising to his feet. "Shall we?"

Alexander stepped toward Beth and offered his arm. "May I have the pleasure of escorting you to the dining room, Miss Edwards?"

Beth hesitated and glanced a Francis, who didn't seem to care because Lydia had attached herself to him and was chattering in his ear.

"Yes, of course," Beth agreed, warily taking his arm.

Celia received Edwin's arm. Beth noted that she wrinkled her nose before taking it as if to give him a silent scolding for his character.

As Alexander escorted Beth, he spoke. "I hope, Miss Edwards, that you are not feeling too overwhelmed by my parents' exuberant welcome and by the curious siblings of this household." He paused. "We were all fond of your mother."

"I gather," Beth admitted. "And naturally under-stand."

"Well, you can be assured that we will not over-extend you and your brother too much this evening. It shall soon dissolve into idle chitchat at the dining room table," he assured.

Beth realized that he sensed her unease and consid-ered it kind of him to show his regard for her well-being.

Upon entering the dining room, Beth admired the four tall windows from the floor to the ceiling, covered in elegant draperies. A large crystal chandelier, lit with multiple candles, hung above the long mahogany table that comfortably sat twenty. Beth glanced around the room, impressed by the apparent wealth of the family, the elegant furnishings, and the opulent table setting of fine bone china and cutlery of silver.

Alexander led Beth to a chair, which kept her by his side. They escorted Francis to the opposite side across the table, where Edwin flanked him on one side and Lydia the other. A slight snicker at the arrangement tick-led Beth as she noted Francis's frown by his knitted eyebrows.

Celia, who had been mute since their arrival, sat next to Beth. The Wilsons took their seats near the Davenports at the head of the table. She had almost forgotten their presence and wondered why the change in demeanor after their arrival. Their exuberant personalities had turned into reserved visitors. Beth leaned in toward Celia as they settled into the seating arrangement.

"I am delighted to have you by my side," she remarked in a low tone.

"You need not worry. I shall keep watch over you." Her eyes shifted to Edwin, who Beth noticed curiously stared at Celia.

Two male footmen served, and Beth glanced over the tabletop, noting the setting. Thank God she wasn't a complete country bumpkin with no idea how to behave or what utensils to use in the extravagant environment. Her mother had taken the time to teach her when Beth turned sixteen. For some reason, she believed the education had been intended for her use in snatching up a husband of means rather than becoming the local farmer's wife. To be honest, she held no lofty ideals to further herself in society.

Alexander turned his attention to Beth, taking her away from a wandering mind.

"Do you plan on staying long in Aycliffe?"

Beth looked into his eyes that sparkled from the candlelight. They were gray, almost like the far horizon of the ocean on a cloudy day. The iris was outlined in a dark tint, and Beth deemed his gaze spellbinding in nature. Slightly uncomfortable by his nearness, she pulled away an inch but not so far as to show her unsettled emotions caused by his person.

"Francis and I decided a fortnight would be sufficient," she answered.

"Clearly not enough time to rest and enjoy the locale," Alexander responded. "You have just emerged from a year of mourning and should take care to enjoy yourself."

Beth did not take instruction well from anyone, especially from strangers. The tone of Alexander's voice sounded as if he were charging her to obey his suggestion. She found it vexing because she had formed a favorable first impression.

"And how long would you suggest that I enjoy myself?" Beth asked, tilting her head out of curiosity.

"A month or longer should suffice. I hope that you

and your brother will consider extending your stay in Aycliffe."

Beth glanced at Francis, who appeared sandwiched between two siblings, pulling his attention from one to the other. When a platter of roast duck was offered, she took a small portion and placed it on her plate.

"They have the best meals," Celia said, taking a hefty portion.

Thankfully, Alexander's attention focused on his father's conversation with Mr. Wilson. Rather than eavesdrop, Beth glanced at everyone, wondering how her mother fit into this strange menagerie of people. It was a mystery she had yet to unravel during the short two weeks of her visit.

CHAPTER EIGHT

An Awkward Interrogation

Though Francis had been surrounded by less-than-entertaining dinner guests, he kept a close eye on Beth. Alexander sat to her right, who portrayed more than a friendly and cordial interest in his sister. Men were more apt to notice the subtleties of a look, the grazing of his hand across hers, the tone of the conversation, manner of facial expressions, and the longer-than-respectable gazes upon her breasts. Francis recognized all too keenly that Alexander Davenport had motives.

Naturally, his protective brotherly streak rose like the hairs on the back of his neck. Though Beth was of marriageable age, she remained blind when it came to male intentions. As a young woman, she was pleasant to look at, but her reserved personality and innocent nature made her vulnerable. Beth had not seriously contemplated marriage, nor had there been anyone in Dunwich who pursued her company. Living in a small village, there were few eligible youthful men worth considering a decent catch.

As Francis eyed Alexander, he pondered what he hoped to attain when in a fortnight they would return to Dunwich. They had already been warned about Edwin's possible intentions, who oddly seemed oblivious to Beth's presence altogether. It could be plausible a more cleverly disguised snake in the grass lurked in the Davenport home.

"What is your opinion of our resort town?" Lydia inquired, interrupting his thoughts.

Francis had lost count of how many questions she flung in his direction, most of which were idle chitchat rather than stimulating conversation.

"Pleasant enough," he replied. "But I have only just scratched the surface of what it offers."

"The ocean has much to offer, Mr. Edwards," she announced with a sly grin. "Especially when the menfolk bare their bottoms and dip in the icy waters for their health."

Francis's brow rose over his right eye, and he turned and looked at her in surprise. "You must be jesting, Miss Davenport."

"Not at all," Edwin interjected. "Frankly, I wish the women would try the sport, but alas, it appears only the men may do so in Aycliffe."

Merely contemplating such an activity sent a chill down Francis's spine, and he changed the subject after Edwin's rather bad-mannered remark. Before he could do so, Lydia leaned into his ear and asked in a low tone.

"Do you have a sweetheart back in Dunwich, Mr. Edwards?"

Far too personal of an inquiry, Francis dabbed his lips with the napkin and spoke plainly. "I am far too busy running our family business to court," he nipped in return.

"And what of your sister? Does she have a beau?"

Angry at her invasion of privacy, Francis merely looked at her, frowning to express displeasure at her intrusive question. Not wishing to give her an answer or continue the conversation, he reluctantly turned toward

Edwin. "Mr. Davenport, is it possible to hire a boat and do some offshore fishing?"

"Fishing?" he loudly responded.

His question caught the attention of Alexander across the table. "Do you wish to partake in the sport of deep-sea fishing, Mr. Edwards?"

"The thought crossed my mind," Francis responded, expressing no shame in asking. "I enjoy fishing in our local river for trout occasionally." He paused for a moment and glanced at Beth to see if she felt embarrassed by his confession. After seeing no indication, he continued. "Fly-fishing is a country sport, but deep-sea fishing is something I have yet to try my hand at."

"Fishing?" Mr. Wilson interjected. "You wish to go fishing, Mr. Edwards?"

"If it's not too inconvenient," Francis affirmed.

"I know just the fellow to take you out for a few hours. He can supply the gear and bring you home with a catch."

"Thank you, Mr. Wilson. I believe I shall enjoy the experience." By the facial expressions of most at the guests at the dinner table, they didn't seem to agree that it would be a pleasurable pastime. Regardless of their sentiments, Francis was keen to catch something longer than a twelve-inch trout.

As dinner concluded, the women rose to excuse themselves to the parlor for tea and female conversation. At the same time, the men remained for an after-dinner port. Francis took notice of Alexander's eyes following Beth as she left the room. When the door shut, Mr. Wilson, Mr. Davenport, and his two sons all turned their attention upon Francis. Instinctively, he braced himself, seeing a curious look in their eyes. The elder Mr. Davenport, whose Christian name was James, began the conversation.

"So, Mr. Edwards, tell us about your life in Dunwich. I understand that your father was a watchmaker, and you have continued in his path."

"Yes, I now manage my father's shop. Eight men are in my employ who are craftsmen in their own right," Francis replied.

"I would not think there would be much demand for watches in Dunwich," Alexander remarked. "It is a tiny village, is it not?"

The usual notation pricked Francis's pride. "My father's reputation in clock and watchmaking extends far beyond our village, and demand continues to grow. I sell our watches in shops throughout the county and beyond. However, the London manufacturers give stiff competition," Francis admitted. "I have some concern that our ability to contend with the larger producers may one day severely affect our market share."

"I noticed the chain of your pocket watch," Mr. Davenport remarked, nodding at Francis's waistcoat. "Is that one of your creations, and if so, may I see it?"

"Yes, of course," Francis remarked, taking it from his pocket and unlatching the chain. "My father gave this to me when I turned eighteen, crafted by his hand."

He was proud of the piece as it was as elegant as any aristocrat could afford. It was eighteen-karat gold, with an enamel face and the engraving of a castle. The numbers were Roman numerals, and the hands were gold. When the case was closed, it was an exceptional polished piece. The inside workings bore the name of Edwards & Son, Dunwich. He observed Mr. Davenport examine the watch in awe.

"Fine workmanship," he uttered. "Even my piece from London is no match for this watch." He handed it to Alexander. "What's your opinion?"

Alexander repeated the same examination and

nodded his head affirmatively. "Yes, I agree. Impressive quality and workmanship for a small enterprise."

Francis noted the emphasis on the size of his business, narrowing his eyes in displeasure at the pompous son of the mayor. Perhaps tradesmen, in his eyes, were inferior folk, acting as if his position were loftier. As far as Francis knew, all the man did was cater to his father's edicts.

Edwin took a turn as well as Mr. Wilson, and the watch returned to Francis. "Thank you," he said. "My father was a skilled craftsman. To be frank, I'm not as talented as he, but the business speaks for itself and my workers."

"I may commission you for a new piece," Mr. Davenport announced.

"Well, we can speak of it at your leisure," Francis replied.

The room became awkwardly silent for a moment. Francis sipped his port and glanced at the men, wondering about each of them. The elder Mr. Davenport appeared deep in thought, while Alexander swished the alcohol in his glass in circles. Edwin acted bored and uninterested by glancing toward the window. Richard had not joined them but retired to his room after dinner. As the silence stretched, Mr. Wilson looked at Francis and smiled as if to give him a friendly glance of support.

"I cannot believe your mother has passed away," Mr. Davenport said, frowning. "She brought much joy to our home when my boys were lads, and Lydia was but a toddler." He looked at Francis and knit his brow together. "Did she talk much about her days here in Aycliffe?"

Surprised that he broached the subject in front of his sons and Mr. Wilson, Francis shifted in his chair.

Perhaps they expected him to know everything about his mother's time in Aycliffe. Still, the sad fact remained that he and Beth were ignorant of her engagement as a governess. Rather than avoid the subject, he truthfully responded.

"To be honest, Mr. Davenport, she rarely spoke of her time here in Aycliffe. Beth and I know very little, only to say she kept in touch with the Wilsons over the years." He brought the glass to his mouth and emptied the contents, sensing a gnawing frustration in his gut. "We knew, of course, that she had come here in her youth to be a governess in your home. But beyond that, she never spoke of it."

"Well, my wife and I were very fond of her, and she was very good with the children. Mrs. Davenport was overwhelmed with running the household, and I was far too busy with business matters to help. Catherine brought relief to a household filled with anxious adults and often unruly children," he said.

"He really means unruly Edwin," Alexander laughed.

"And I continue to keep that reputation," he replied with a smirk.

Mr. Wilson glanced at Francis. "Your mother had a very calming demeanor about her. Along with her kind heart and interest in others, she became well liked by so many in Aycliffe." He heaved a sigh after expressing his thoughts.

"Yes, she was kindhearted," Francis concurred. "That trait never left Mother even when she passed from this life to the next."

Francis recalled how difficult it was to see her take her last labored breath and how cheated he felt as she departed the earth. A year earlier, he had lost his father, and when his mother died, a deep void filled his soul.

Those emotions Francis hid from Beth. Instead, he struggled with his profound loss and grief in silence. Perhaps that explained the reason he had become so protective of Beth, fearing that she too would leave him one way or the other. It was selfish on his part, but she represented a constancy that he desperately needed to retain. The thoughts made him uncomfortable as he lowered his gaze into his glass and frowned. Mr. Wilson must have recognized his momentary struggle and sympathetically spoke.

"Well, we should see what the ladies are up to in the parlor," he suggested in a booming voice. "Don't you agree?"

"Yes," Mr. Davenport replied. Everyone else emptied their glass and stood to their feet to join the women.

As soon as they entered, Beth lifted her eyes toward Francis, and he noticed her strained demeanor. She sat tall and stiff in the chair rather than relaxed and comfortable in the presence of the others. Beth's hand clung to an empty teacup, and he walked behind her sitting on the settee and gently placed his hand on her shoulder and gave her a reassuring squeeze.

"What do ladies talk about after dinner?" he asked, grinning sheepishly. "I have always wondered."

Celia giggled. "What do men talk about over port, and why do you always close the dining room doors to be alone?"

Francis raised both his hands in the air. "I am afraid I have no answer to that question. Perhaps I will defer that to your father."

Mr. Wilson took no time to answer. "Manly conversations, Celia. Things that women have no interest in, like politics and newsworthy items of the day."

"Well, we talk about embroidering, the latest

fashions, watercolors, and silly things women speak about," she announced with a smirk.

Lydia chimed in. "She is teasing you, Mr. Wilson. Our conversations are much juicier."

"That's enough, Lydia," Mrs. Davenport said. "We just chat."

Beth covered her mouth, yawned, and blushed. "Oh dear. Forgive me."

"Well, it is getting late," Mr. Wilson said. "It's been an interminable day. Perhaps we should end the evening."

No one objected to his suggestion. Alexander approached Beth and spoke in a low tone. She smiled demurely in return.

"Well, we shall have you for dinner again soon," Mr. Davenport said. "I hope to get to know each of you better."

"And there is the Howard ball," Mrs. Wilson said excitedly. "It will be such a divine evening."

"Yes, divine," Celia repeated.

Francis bid good night to their hosts and watched as Alexander walked Beth to the door. His overt interest in his sister did not sit well with him.

"Until tomorrow," Alexander said to Beth, casting a warm smile.

Beth nodded and smiled, which confirmed Francis's observations. Alexander Davenport was in pursuit of his sister, and he wondered why.

CHAPTER NINE

The Man in the Moon

Beth had taken care to meet Francis for breakfast, as they had agreed beforehand to excuse themselves for a private moment. When she arrived in the dining room, she saw him at the table nearly finished with his meal. Celia had eaten as well and looked as if she was about to leave. Mrs. Wilson buttered a piece of toast, and her husband was nowhere in sight.

"Ah, Beth." Mrs. Wilson greeted her. "Did you have a good rest last evening?"

"Yes, a night of deep sleep on the comfortable mattress." After taking a paltry amount of food for her plate, she sat next to Francis.

"Good morning, Celia," she said. "You look bright and cheerful this morning." Beth noted a sparkle in her eyes and the pretty yellow dress she had chosen for the day.

"Thank you," Celia responded, standing to her feet. "I am off this morning to meet with Susan, a friend of mine."

The announcement caught Beth by surprise. Francis lifted his head as well and regarded Celia. "Well then. I wish you a pleasant day." Beth lowered her eyes in disappointment that Celia had not offered her the opportunity to join the excursion. Of course, she would have declined because she had promised Francis a walk on the beach together. Nonetheless, she felt slighted.

Mrs. Wilson flashed a disapproving look at her daughter but said nothing about her plans.

"I shall be back this afternoon, Mother," she announced. "Susan needs a bit of help with slight alterations to her ball gown."

"Why isn't a seamstress doing that work?"

"You know they cannot afford it," she chided in return.

"Very well. Will her mother be home to chaperone?"

"Yes, her mother will be home," Celia snapped, noticeably irritated by the inquiries.

As Celia sprinted from the room, Mrs. Wilson took a crunching bite of her toast. "You have no other children?" Beth asked. There had been no mention of older brothers or sisters who married and lived elsewhere. Mrs. Wilson swallowed hard and then took a sip of tea.

"No, I'm afraid Celia is the only child the good Lord granted us in life. The birth had been difficult, and the physician told me I could not have any more children."

"I'm so sorry," Beth remarked, embarrassed that such a personal conversation had occurred in front of Francis. "I didn't mean to pry."

"It's a natural question and others have asked. It seems the entire town has large families except for us. Such is the way of things."

"Has Mr. Wilson left for work?" Francis asked.

"Yes, he has gone to the city hall to meet with Mr. Davenport. He is an alderman, you see, and works closely with the city council members."

"Well, Beth and I want to explore Aycliffe and more of the coastline today." Francis dabbed his mouth with his napkin. "Eat up, sister, so we do not waste the morning away."

"Well, give me a few minutes to have a bite to eat." Beth balked, glancing at him disapprovingly with a scowl.

"Did you enjoy dinner last night at the Davenports?" Mrs. Wilson asked, glancing at them.

"Yes, it was fine," Francis replied.

"And what about you, Beth? I saw Alexander say something to you before departing. He is a nice young man." Mrs. Wilson grinned approvingly. "And handsome too."

After shoving down a mouthful of food, Beth lifted her eyes. "Yes, pleasant enough. He asked to call on me at three o'clock this afternoon. I told him we could talk over tea."

"He asked to call on you?" Francis stiffened his posture. "I wondered what he had to say to you before we left."

"Yes, and I saw no harm in it," Beth answered. "It is just tea and conversation, Francis."

"Well, if you don't mind, I'll join you."

His emphatic tone irked Beth, and she arched a brow over her right eye. "Do you truly think I need you to chaperone me over a cup of tea?" She shook her head. "Honestly, Francis, I thought you knew me better."

"Let's not disagree in front of Mrs. Wilson," he chided. "We can discuss the matter on our walk this morning."

"The man is harmless," Mrs. Wilson chimed in. "There is not a roguish bone in his body, unlike his brother."

"I thought his brother was rather docile," Beth remarked.

"As did I," Francis replied. "Alexander, however, was another matter."

"Well, if you would like, I'm happy to join them for tea. We can sit in the library across the way and leave the parlor door open while they chat. Would that suffice?" Mrs. Wilson asked, attempting to bring a solution to the matter.

"Perhaps," Francis relented with a sigh. He looked at Beth, conspicuously irritated by his pursed lips and curt voice. "Are you done yet?"

"Fine." Beth pushed her chair back and rose to her feet. "If I get hungry later on, I will insist you buy me tea and cakes somewhere in town."

"The Olsen Bakery," Mrs. Wilson announced. "They have an adorable tearoom on Main Street."

"Noted. I shall force Francis to take me there. Have a good morning, Mrs. Wilson."

Francis headed for the foyer and grabbed his hat and frock coat while Beth arranged her bonnet and shawl. The crisp morning air greeted their nostrils as they stepped outdoors, reminding them it was early spring.

"A bit chilly, but at least the sun is shining," Beth said, wrapping her shawl tight around her shoulders.

"It must be far more pleasant in the summer." Francis led the way, striding toward their destination with a quick cadence.

The exhilarating trek caused Beth's heart to thump in her chest. Her brother appeared deep in thought, marching as it were to a pounding drum. Perhaps an irritation had raised its ugly head because she had accepted afternoon tea with Alexander. The thought irked Beth, as she feared he would undoubtedly spoil the afternoon with his pithy attitude.

As they turned down Main Street, they noted the townspeople out and about, running their private errands.

"Might we walk the beach rather than the pier?" Beth asked, out of breath alongside Francis.

"Yes. If you prefer to do so, I have no objection. We can take a leisurely stroll and head for the craggy cliffs. Mr. Wilson said when the tide is out, there are interesting caverns underneath."

"Is the tide out?" Beth asked when they turned the corner and faced the expanse of the ocean.

"Indeed, it is. Do you see how far out the water is and the vast beach area?"

Beth's eyes scanned the landscape.

"Look here, sister," Francis pointed. "Do you see the line farther up? You can see how far the waves have washed up on shore when the tide is high."

"Oh, I see." Beth had never noticed. "What causes the tides to come in and go out?"

Francis chuckled as they started their walk in the sand. "I daresay you must not have paid attention during your lessons."

"Such matters are not exactly things that interest most ladies. Nevertheless, I cannot for the life of me remember the reason."

"It is caused by the moon, Beth."

"The moon? What does that celestial object have to do with water sloshing back and forth on a shoreline?" She scrunched her brows together, concluding it a ludicrous answer.

"Well, to be honest, it's the man in the moon," Francis solemnly recited. "He pulls the earth back and forth on a long string and causes the water to withdraw and return."

"Now you jest," Beth grumbled in a deep voice. She narrowed her eyes at him. "I might be ignorant of scientific information, but I'm not that daft as to swallow your explanation." She kicked the sand with the toe of her shoe. "The man in the moon. Honestly, Francis."

Francis bellowed a hearty laugh. As irritating as his answer had been, she enjoyed the fact that he appeared to be more relaxed than minutes ago.

"Well, according to an elite scholar by the name of William Whewell, his great tide experiment indicates that the gravitational pull of the moon is responsible."

"And how do you know such things? Did Father tell you?"

"No, I read about it." Francis paused for a moment. "Father had little interest in scientific matters except for the inward workings of a timepiece. But I, on the other hand, have a more curious interest in reading about recent discoveries."

Beth halted her step and looked at Francis. After studying him for a moment, she shook her head in astonishment. "It never ceases to amaze me how little I know about you even though we are siblings."

"I have little knowledge of your interests too," Francis admitted.

They fell into a digestive silence, strolling down the beach and enjoying the scenery of the sparkling waters and white foamy waves breaking upon the shoreline. A light breeze rather than a strong gale grazed their faces.

"What's your opinion of Alexander?" Francis asked.

"My opinion?" Beth repeated, cocking her head.

"Yes. Has he piqued your interest in some fashion?"

Beth halted her step and looked into Francis's eyes, which radiated his brotherly concern. "He is pleasant enough but carries an air of importance about his mannerism and speech that I frankly find. . . How shall I express it?" She pondered before answering. "Off-putting."

"Is that so?" Francis's tone eased as if he had a weight

lift from his shoulders.

"You need not worry about me, Francis. I have not fallen violently under his spell, nor do I plan on doing so, if that is your concern."

"Well, I noted his interest in minute expressions last evening during dinner, which I found surprising."

"Oh, did you?" Beth scoffed back. "You mean to tell me it surprises you any man would express an interest in me?"

"That is not what I mean," he clarified. "Let me rephrase my comment. I found it curious that he should attempt to express an interest in you when we shall only be here for a brief time. Logically, I questioned the motivation behind his actions."

"Oh, I see." Beth walked again, and Francis followed alongside. "As I ponder it, you have a point."

"Then why did you agree to have tea with him this afternoon?"

"To be polite of course. I could not be rude and tell him that he was not welcome."

"True. You were right to do so." Francis exhaled a sigh. "Nevertheless, be cautious."

"Stop worrying. As I told you earlier, I find Mr. Davenport rather snobbish in character, so the tea and conversation will be boring."

They resumed their walk, and Francis remarked at the landscape ahead. "Those must be the caves Mr. Wilson mentioned." He outstretched his arm and pointed with his index finger down the coastline.

"Do we have time to explore before the tide returns?" The ocean and its wonders were new to Beth, and a seed of fear about its dangers arose.

"I am sure we do," he remarked with confidence.

Beth lagged behind Francis. He stopped at the entrance and turned to wait for her arrival.

"It's awfully dark inside," Beth murmured.

"Your eyes will adjust. Don't be afraid."

They entered side by side and walked a few feet into the dark void. It took some time before Beth's sight adjusted to the dim surroundings. As it did, her ears picked up a rather unusual sound of moaning, echoing off the stone walls.

"What is that noise?"

Before Francis could reply to her question, they halted their step. A couple lay in the sand in a compromising position a few feet in front of them. Beth saw the woman's skirt pulled upward, and the man lay on top of her body. A second later, a female screeched, and to Beth's utter horror, she recognized Celia and Edwin.

Flabbergasted, Beth yelped a quick scream. Francis grabbed Beth by the arm and brusquely pulled her out of the cave.

"Francis, do something! He may force himself upon Celia," Beth demanded, gasping for breath.

"I don't believe he is forcing anything," he insisted, dragging her away.

"But I don't understand. She warned of Edwin."

"Beth, I assure you. . ."

Before he could finish his sentence, Celia bellowed their names. They spun around to see her sprinting in their direction. Edwin emerged from the cave but paused at the opening. Beth glanced at Celia, who noticed her eyes water with tears.

"Wait!" Out of breath and blushing red, Celia halted. "Please, I can explain."

Before Beth replied, Francis answered with disgust. "Please do."

Celia sobbed, and Edwin eventually came to her side, taking her in his arms. In defense, he spoke.

"We are in love."

CHAPTER TEN

The First of Many Secrets

Beth did not realize that her body trembled at the sight of Celia and Edwin standing before them until a moment later. The shock of seeing the two joined as lovers had upset her more than she realized. As she looked at Celia surrounded by Edwin's arms, sobbing from embarrassment, she saw a ruined woman. Recognizing the disgusted look on the face of her brother, Beth knew his sentiments were the same.

"You love her?" Francis scoffed. "You, sir, are a blackguard of the worst sort to take advantage of Miss Wilson."

"No, he has not taken advantage of me," Celia protested, lifting her head off his shoulder.

"Celia, he has seduced you," Beth asserted. "Even you warned me of his poor character upon my arrival."

Celia wiped the tears from her cheeks with the back of her hand. After standing tall, she vehemently defended her actions. "I warned you because I did not wish for you to find Edwin of interest," Celia explained. "Whatever you witnessed between the two of us a few minutes ago occurred by mutual agreement."

"Mutual agreement?" Beth ridiculed. "Do your parents know of this alliance?"

"Perhaps I should explain," Edwin said. He took Celia's hand and held it tight. "My father wishes me to marry money, but the Wilsons are not well off enough to suit his tastes."

"But you have ruined Celia," Beth howled. "You should be ashamed of yourself." Beth lifted her skirt and turned on her heel with a mixture of emotion. Appalled, confused, and embarrassed for having witnessed what she did, Beth didn't quite know what to do except run in the opposite direction. "I cannot bear such a scandal." She remarked, sensing her cheeks burst into heat.

"Scandal?" Edwin squawked, taking an aggressive step toward Beth. He grabbed her by the upper arm. "I find your words an affront, especially considering your mother."

Beth's mouth gaped open in astonishment at his declaration. "I beg your pardon," she spat.

"Edwin, don't," Celia said, coming to his side. "Let her go."

Francis's nostrils flared. "Take your hand off my sister's arm, sir, or I shall respond physically," he growled between his teeth. Edwin submitted and stepped back.

"Edwin, say you are sorry," Celia pressured him. Edwin's demeanor softened at her entreaty.

"I apologize," he sheepishly remarked. "My words are unfounded and rude."

"I think we should take our leave," Francis announced. He nodded at Beth and took a step in the opposite direction.

"Please say nothing to my parents," Celia begged. Her eyes watered further with tears. "No one understands, and my father and Edwin's father will be very cross should they discover."

"I do not understand," Beth admitted. "Despite what you may fear, Celia, I am not a tattletale or gossip."

Francis and Beth retreated down the shoreline back

toward the pier. The leisurely stroll they had enjoyed earlier morphed into a dash of retreat. Filled with shock over what she had glimpsed and the accusation made by Edwin, she felt her throat close. The sprinting steps increased her heart rate and made it difficult for her to breathe. Fearful, she reached out and grabbed Francis by the arm.

"I cannot catch my breath," she gasped.

"Are you having an attack?" Francis inquired with alarm filling his eyes.

Beth nodded, thinking she would soon faint.

"All right, Beth, stay calm. The more you panic, the harder it will be to take in air," he stressed. Beth bent over and placed her hand on her chest. "No, stand up, just like the doctor said, or you will make it worse."

As the intake of air lessened and her chest tightened, Beth did as Francis admonished. She looked at him in horror, deeming at any moment she would die from the lack of inhalation.

"Now, take deep breaths," Francis said, placing his hands on her upper arms to hold her in place. Beth nodded her head. "Think of something pleasant, sister. Close your eyes and listen to the waves near your feet. Do they not bring comfort and ease to your soul?"

When her eyelids shut, Beth tuned her hearing as Francis suggested. The quick gasps subsided, and Beth concentrated on inhaling the fresh ocean atmosphere. Waves in the distance lazily broke upon the shoreline like a calming musical score. It had replaced the vision of Celia and Edwin with something far more pleasant. After a few moments of Francis's hands continuing to hold her upright and the peaceful moment of inward reflection, her breathing returned to normal.

"Feeling better?" Francis asked, giving her a slight squeeze and then releasing his grip.

"Yes, much better." Beth opened her eyes. "I am sorry."

"You had me worried," Francis admitted.

"They always pass," Beth said. "Though not without concern."

"Dearest sister, do not take to heart what just happened," Francis said. "Their relationship is not of our concern, nor should it be."

"But what did he mean about Mother?"

"A harsh word spoken in anger, no doubt, to take our attention off their unbecoming behavior," Francis rationalized. "Come now. We must return so you can ready yourself for tea with Alexander."

"I daresay that I am in no mood," Beth moaned.

"Nor am I," Francis countered.

Alexander did not know what to make of Beth as he sipped tea and glanced at her clutching her cup with two hands. He noted a slight tremble to her fingers and surmised the firm grip had ensued to halt the shaking caused by nerves. Naturally, Alexander attributed her trembling because of female jitters, rather than some physical ailment on her part. Since he hadn't noticed such behavior at the dinner party the evening before, he wondered why she struggled over tea and cakes.

"You must be happy that the weather has cleared," he said. It was not the type of conversation he typically pursued when it came to dialogue with a female. The awkward atmosphere between the two cautioned him to embark on superficial remarks. Beth stared into the liquid, which by now must have turned as tepid as her personality. He cleared his throat, hoping to pull her from her private musings. "The weather?" Her eyes lifted, and her cheeks turned rosy pink.

"Oh my goodness," she blubbered. "Do forgive me. I am ashamed to admit that my mind seems insistent on wandering to the strangest places today."

"Understandable," Alexander said in a sympathetic tone. "I too am prone to periods of daydreaming."

She looked at him wide-eyed. "Oh, I find that hard to believe. I gather from the accolades about your personality expressed by Mr. Wilson that you are grounded in reality."

"Grounded perhaps in my daily tasks. However, I allow myself to fantasize about the unattainable."

"Unattainable?"

Beth cocked her head to one side as if she discovered an ounce of interest in him. He wondered about her inward musings and where they took her as a young female. Did she fantasize about knights in shining armor, or was she more practical and down to earth in her pursuits?

"Well, if you want me to share where my mind leads me, then I think you should reciprocate and share with me your straying thoughts." A mischievous smile curled his lips as he noticed Beth stiffen at the suggestion to disclose an intimate reflection.

"I declare, Mr. Davenport, that you have no shame in tempting me such," she scolded. "Particularly since we are newly acquainted."

Alexander shrugged his shoulders. "How else are two people supposed to become familiar unless they share?"

"Well, it's a gigantic leap from the weather to my private musings," Beth asserted. "I am not inclined to share such familiarity yet."

"Then I must make my own conclusions as to what

pondering thoughts are beneath the beautiful gold locks on your head."

"Now you flatter me foolishly for your own gain." Beth arched a skeptical brow. A moment later she grinned, not insulted by his tactics.

"Yes, guilty as charged. I am prone to praising women for their attributes," he softly chuckled. Alexander took the last sip of tea in his cup and glanced out the window. "I hear that Mrs. Wilson has a fine garden. Would you mind taking a turn through the plot and admiring the rose bushes?"

Beth glanced out the parlor door across the hall where Mrs. Wilson and her brother sat, no doubt eavesdropping on their conversation. He wanted a moment alone and hoped that neither of them would care if they took in the sun for a few minutes. Alexander stood to his feet and stretched out his hand to Beth. Her timidity being near his person continued, reminding him that there were many barriers to breach before he discovered the real Miss Edwards. With a pleading glance, she relented and grasped it.

He released her hand so he wouldn't appear forward. Arriving at the threshold of the library doors, he spoke.

"Mrs. Wilson, we would like to take a stroll through your lovely garden. Do you mind?"

"Mind? No, of course not," she said, grinning with approval.

Francis gave him a cursory glance but made no objection. "I trust the warm sun will do Beth well," he coolly remarked.

An unspoken sentiment of animosity exchanged between them. Alexander instinctively recognized that Francis had concerns. An overprotective brother might pose an obstacle, so Alexander remained cautious in his pursuit. Naturally, at this early stage, he merely enjoyed her company and wished to be congenial during her visit to Aycliffe. The possibility of a romantic connection had been the furthest thing from his mind.

Beth acted cautious and unimpressed. Regardless, Alexander found her company to be suitable in personality compared to the types of women his father had suggested. She possessed no riches nor displayed airs of self-importance. He found it refreshing, along with her pleasant countenance. Beth reminded him of Catherine, which he embarrassingly admitted that he nursed a rather juvenile crush upon as a child.

Familiar with the Wilson residence, Alexander escorted Beth to the veranda doors. They stepped outside into the pristine garden that had bloomed with its array of flowers. Mrs. Wilson had an eye for flora, if nothing else, and her avid garden often garnished local awards. A pebbled pathway led them through the enclosed private property, meandering down various rows of planted bushes and flowers. A few stone benches were situated near flower beds.

"Do you garden at your home in Dunwich?" Alexander asked out of curiosity.

"Oh dear, no. I am ashamed to say that I fail miserably at making anything grow. Even vegetables protest when I attempt to cultivate them." Beth chuckled.

"And what about your mother or father, did they?"

"Mother loved flowers but never tended a lavish garden such as this. A few rose bushes about the house sufficed." Beth paused. "Father, of course, was far too busy with his business."

"And Francis, I take it, has no interest."

"No, he enjoys trout fishing more than gardening."

"I see," Alexander said, strolling alongside Beth.

"And what pursuits do you nurture, if not gardening?"

"Pursuits?" Beth glanced sideways at him as if his question confused her.

"I may not know very much about young ladies, but most pursue some activity to become accomplished."

"Oh, accomplishments," she remarked. "You mean such as playing the piano, singing, or painting?"

"Yes, all of those things." He paused, contemplating a few others. "And outdoor amusements such as archery or riding."

Beth sighed. "I am afraid I shall disappoint you greatly. I cannot carry a tune and have no musical skills whatsoever in either the piano, harp, or zither. As far as sketching or painting, I am dreadfully terrible at art."

"Well, at least you are honest, which in itself is an accomplishment." Alexander grinned in approval.

"Perhaps too honest," Beth admitted. "I love to read and walk. Stimulating conversation interests me, but I realize that society believes that the female population should not be prone to excessive conversation. We should compensate through talent, but alas, I possess none."

"Oh, I wouldn't put too much stock into talent," Alexander countered. "We all are gifted in some way at birth. What do you read? Poetry? Romance?"

"Some poetry." She paused and then jovially admitted. "And I cannot cook, as Francis reminds me repeatedly."

"Neither can I," Alexander remarked with a chuckle. "Alas, we have something in common." Beth snickered at his remark.

As they continued to stroll, Alexander pondered Beth's responses. He didn't care if she could not sing or play an instrument. A woman had to be more than mere talent to interest him. Though he never considered himself a romantic, he knew that he wanted a lady who stimulated him in other ways. A conversationalist would be pleasant if they were prone to enjoying passionate pursuits. As a man, he would undoubtedly enjoy a woman with a flair for intense intimacy, along with a curiosity about the world in which they lived. Any woman that he chose had to have curiosity and courage.

Of course, such wishes were fantasizing, like his foolhearted desires to travel the globe and see far away exotic lands. Regrettably, his industrious personality had coined him as a duplication of his father—destined to run the town and keep the seaside resort prosperous for all to enjoy. Rather than the freedom to choose his destiny, he had become a prisoner of parental expectations. On the other hand, riding a camel in the desert to the pyramids of Giza appeared far more intriguing than town politics.

"Are you daydreaming?" Beth inquired, looking up at him impishly.

Embarrassed that she had caught him in the act, he flashed a lopsided grin in amusement. "You noticed."

"And what do you daydream about, Mr. Davenport?"

Without hesitation, he answered. "A camel."

Beth halted in her step and faced him. "A camel?" she giggled aloud. "My, my, what a bizarre daydream. I would have thought you would ponder loftier ideas besides a large humpbacked beast."

"Does that surprise you?" Alexander asked, curious whether she teased or mocked him. He led Beth over to a small bench. "Shall we sit?"

She obliged and perched herself far enough away from him to maintain propriety.

"It surprises me somewhat. Why a camel?"

Beth appeared intrigued by his confession. "I dream of traveling the world one day, particularly to Egypt," he readily admitted. "My life, though, is anchored in Aycliffe with multiple responsibilities. My father, you see, has expectations."

"Mr. Wilson said that you had entrepreneurial and political interests like your father and that you were ambitious in nature."

"He would conclude that to be the truth because it is the impression I give." Alexander heaved a sigh. "Impressions do not always equate to truth." He scowled. "Now see here, Miss Edwards. It appears you have tricked me into revealing myself to you before you have given me an ounce of knowledge regarding your daydreams."

"Well, one must not divulge everything at once, Mr. Davenport," she slyly indicated. "What would we have to speak about when we meet again?"

"Indeed," he drawled. A small ember of interest in Beth's reserved nature sparked in his heart. He looked forward to getting to know her fantasies and discovering what commonality they might possess. "Then we must meet again," he announced.

"I look forward to it. But perhaps, for now, we should return indoors lest my brother decides to check on my welfare."

"If you insist." He offered his hand. "I sense that he has become your guardian in many ways."

"Indeed, he appears to have taken on that role since the death of our mother." Beth's countenance soured into a downhearted frown. "I often wish that he would grant me a bit more liberty and stop acting like a parent rather than a sibling."

"Then we share something in common," Alexander said. "We both wish to break free of our restraints."

"I suppose we do."

Beth glanced up at him, steadily gazing into his eyes. Perchance she found him of interest.

CHAPTER ELEVEN

Initial Impressions

Francis sat in a leather chair in the library, reading the local newspaper. Mrs. Wilson took a seat nearby, working on a needlepoint project. Their conversation remained sparse as he nurtured a foul mood over the events earlier in the day. He wanted to tell Mrs. Wilson about Celia and Edwin but controlled the urge to do so.

Unknown to Beth, he had taken somewhat of a shining to the exuberant young lady, although they had only interacted briefly. What a fool he had been to consider a closer acquaintance. Now he saw her in an entirely different light thanks to what she described as a mutual agreement between herself and Edwin. The fact of the matter remained that she was no more than a lewd and brazen lady with no morals.

His hand crumbled the corner of the paper that he held, which instantly caught the attention of Mrs. Wilson.

"I wouldn't worry about Beth," she remarked in a calm tone. "Alexander is no threat. In fact, he is a fine young man."

Unlike his brother, Francis inwardly grumbled. "Beth has a good head on her shoulders and can handle herself," he pointed out.

"She is charming as her mother," Mrs. Wilson stated. "It's only natural that men would be attracted and wish to court her to marriage."

"Marriage?" Francis laid the newspaper on his lap. "What can Alexander hope to gain in a fortnight?"

"Oh well, I'm not saying that he will make a proposal," Mrs. Wilson stuttered. "I believe that he is interested in Beth."

"I am not sure that I understand the interest." The tone of his voice clearly revealed his irritation at the thought.

"To be honest, we had hoped that you would extend your stay here in Aycliffe a few more weeks or perhaps a month or two."

"Month or two?" He shot an incredulous look at Mrs. Wilson, questioning her motivation to keep them in town. "I have a business to run, Mrs. Wilson, and such an extended stay would be inconvenient."

"Well, Beth could stay, and you could return to Dunwich for a time to put things in order. Would that not suffice?"

Francis was about to speak in protest when Alexander and his sister returned from their walk in the garden. He stood up, setting the crumbled newspaper on the nearby chair.

"Did you have a pleasant walk?" He glanced at Beth to ascertain her disposition. A smile brightened her relaxed countenance. Alexander grinned as if he had enjoyed their time together, which irked Francis.

"Yes, a fine stroll," Alexander remarked. "Mrs. Wilson, you have outdone yourself in the garden this year. No doubt you will win the annual contest again."

Mrs. Wilson chuckled. "I should feel guilty that I triumph so often in the competition, but my green thumb is my pride and joy."

"The flowers are beautiful," Beth remarked. "The color of the roses is so varied."

"Well, I should go," Alexander said. "Thank you for the delightful tea, conversation, and outdoor enjoyment."

"Let me walk you to the door," Mrs. Wilson suggested.

"Goodbye, Mr. Davenport," Beth said. "I enjoyed our mutual daydreaming."

"You mean you enjoyed mine," he quipped. "Next time, I expect insight into yours." Alexander turned toward Francis, giving him a cursory nod. "Mr. Edwards, I bid you a good day."

"Good day," Francis coldly replied. As soon as they were alone, he turned to Beth. "You seemed to have enjoyed yourself despite your earlier thoughts."

"It took me some time to settle my mind after what we saw earlier today, and I was terribly rude and distant at first. Afterward, I will admit that I found our conversation of significant interest."

"How so?"

"My first impression of his superior attitudes was ill-formed. He is far more interesting, although I sense he is constrained because of his father's expectations. I am not convinced that he wishes to follow in the elder Mr. Davenport's footsteps."

"Interesting." Francis knitted his brows together, although it did not change his cautious opinion of the man.

"Well, I have seen off Alexander," Mrs. Wilson announced, entering the library. "My, my, the afternoon is almost over." She scowled as she glanced at the clock. "Where in the world is Celia? Have either of you seen her today?"

Francis and Beth exchanged a quick glance. Beth

answered, "Not since breakfast this morning."

"Well, her friend Susan must have kept her far longer for something else besides mending a dress." Mrs. Wilson heaved a sigh. "I need to check with the cook about dinner."

Mrs. Wilson swung around and headed for the kitchen. Francis whispered to Beth. "I have been tempted to tell her about Celia and Edwin," he admitted.

"I do not wish to be an abettor to their secret," Beth countered. "But I gave my word that I would not tell her parents and hope you will do the same. Nonetheless, I feel obligated to speak with her privately about her behavior."

"It is a bit late, I would think," Francis argued. "Her reputation is tainted, so what could you possibly accomplish?"

Beth's eyes locked upon Francis as if she read the reasonings behind his harsh words. "Francis, you sound as if you are more upset over her behavior than I am. Why?"

Rather than remain silent so that Beth could assume that he had taken a fancy to her, he replied. "Do as you wish. But what has transpired between Miss Wilson and Mr. Davenport cannot be undone."

She stared at him for a moment but did not pursue the conversation further. Instead, Beth excused herself to rest before dinner and headed upstairs to her room. He glanced at the clock on the fireplace mantel and noted the time and wondered where Celia could be. Perhaps she and Edwin had decided to run off together, creating a greater humiliation. He hoped that the girl possessed more sense than to bring further shame to her family.

Celia had always been prone to extremes when her emotions were involved. After she sobbed for five minutes in Edwin's arms, she tried to pull herself together. Passionate about life and a despairing romantic, Celia had tumbled hopelessly in love with Edwin. Now at the age of four and twenty, she had been frantic to find a husband. No one else in Aycliffe had shown interest in her except for Edwin. As her mother had poignantly remarked, she lingered about town as an eternal spinster.

She admitted that her personality was high strung and a handful at times. Nevertheless, she was not an ugly duckling, unable to turn the attention of the male sex. Her figure was pleasing and not plump like her mother's waistline. Often she received compliments about her expressive eyes and clear complexion. Why she could not snag a husband had been beyond her understanding. To make matters more complicated, Aycliffe was not exactly the bed of social activity either for nine months out of the year. Once the seasonal crowds left, it returned to the status of a sleepy coastal village.

When Edwin Davenport started flirting with her, she naturally fell for his charms even though she knew him to have a reputation. Celia had never imagined, either, that she could snag his attention as a potential love interest. Their families had been close for years. They had played together as children and grown into adulthood side by side, having frequent interaction. Although Celia secretly possessed adoration for him, she never believed he shared the same emotions.

After a few months of clandestine meetings, he attempted to seduce her, but she found the strength to resist until today. Her violent adoration of his handsome persona had gotten the best of her, nearly ruining her completely. If it hadn't been for Beth and Francis entering the cave, she would have tossed away her virtue without a second thought. Although still intact, her reputation teetered on the brink of destruction. By all accounts, after what their guests had witnessed, Edwin should marry her. Although they were of legal age, he, like Alexander, feared to disobey his father.

To make matters worse, Edwin had no means to support Celia, so they would be paupers as soon as they wed. Without the support of his father, Edwin would flounder in trade. He was not industrious like his older brother. Instead, he touted an attitude of entitlement, only working sporadically at clerk-related positions. Regardless of his lack of ambition, Celia overlooked his flaws.

The fact remained. Under no circumstances would Edwin's father agree to a marriage between them. Their family needed money, and he and Alexander were the keys to unlocking new, much-needed fortunes for the struggling resort of Aycliffe and the Davenports' dwindling coffers. Because the town waned in popularity, the crowds that used to come to the city lessened as the resort aged. The burden of the resort's revitalization lay upon the shoulders of the mayor's sons. If Edwin would just choose his life rather than pandering to his father, perhaps they would have a chance of happiness. Even poor Alexander obeyed like a puppy dog in training when it came to his father's edicts. The entire household existed enslaved to the Davenport family greed.

"We should run away," Celia blubbered as they stood arm in arm in the darkened recesses of the cave unnoticed. "We could go to Scotland."

"You know we can't marry," Edwin cajoled. "Besides,

what would we do for money? I have no job and no means to support you. We would end up in a workhouse or worse."

The workhouse. Celia admitted that a comfortable lifestyle was as crucial as a wedding to the person you loved. The idea brought a chill to her spine, and she pulled away. "I suppose we should go. The tide is rising, and soon the cave will fill with water." Times like these Celia almost wished she could drown her sorrows in the ocean.

"What will you do?" Edwin asked. "Do you think the Edwardses will remain silent about what they saw today?"

"I don't know," Celia admitted. "Frankly, I scarcely know them. We can only hope."

"Perhaps while they remain in Aycliffe, we should cease our secret meetings, Celia. If more people see us together, it could get back to my father."

"Oh Edwin," Celia whined.

"If he finds out, there will be hell to pay—not only for me, but perhaps he will take it out on your father. You don't want that to happen, do you?"

Tears rolled down Celia's cheeks as she pondered the horrible possibilities should the truth be revealed about their intimate relationship. As much as she hated to admit it, Edwin was right. Mr. Davenport could behave like a wild bear when riled to anger and might lash out at her father. The situation was hopeless, and a deep sadness burdened her heart.

"Will we ever be together?" Celia threw her arms around Edwin's neck. He drew her into a soft kiss of comfort. Afterward, he stroked the side of her head with his palm. "Be patient, Celia."

"I will try."

"Now wipe your tears and make yourself present-able before you go home."

"When will I see you again?" Celia asked in a begging tone.

"The ball next week, of course."

"And will you dance with me?"

He flashed a sly grin. "Yes, but you must act as if you despise the idea before taking my hand to the dance floor."

"Oh, I shall, since everyone knows you are nothing but a rogue, Edwin Davenport."

He smirked as he knew it to be the truth. "Goodbye, Celia."

Celia blew him a kiss as she walked to the mouth of the cave and disappeared from his sight. They had spent most of the morning and early afternoon together. Indeed, her mother would wonder about her whereabouts. Rather than lying, she stopped by Susan's residence for a few minutes before returning home. The concept of seeing the Edwards siblings put a knot in her stomach that remained until she walked through the door an hour later. It did not take long for her mother to accost her with flared nostrils.

"Young lady, where have you been all day? It is most rude of you to neglect our guests. You have much to learn about being a proper hostess."

"I am sorry, Mama, but the time slipped away from me. Besides, I thought Alexander was visiting this afternoon. Did he not come?"

"He did visit, but that is no excuse for you to disappear for so long. Now, go into the parlor and keep Francis company until dinner. Beth is resting upstairs."

Celia's stomach churned. "Mother, I am exhausted and would like a brief nap before dinner. Might I be excused? Father will return soon and keep Francis company. Besides, I am sure Francis would much rather converse about manly pursuits than the dress affair this afternoon with Susan. What else should I speak to him about?" Her whining and pleading gained a reprieve.

"Fine. But don't be late for dinner," her mother scolded.

With a quick spring in her step, Celia climbed the stairs. As she walked down the hallway to her room, Beth emerged in the doorway.

"Might we have a word?"

Halting, Celia begged otherwise, avoiding direct eye contact. "I am fatigued and would like to rest and refresh before dinner if you don't mind."

"I do mind, Celia, and I think the least you can do is agree to a quick conversation based upon the knowledge I possess."

Celia's eyes darted toward the staircase. Fearful her mother might hear, she relented. "All right. If you insist, but only for a minute."

The door closed, and Celia leaned against it for support. One hand behind her back latched on to the doorknob.

"Have you said anything?" she asked in a trembling voice.

"No, I have not. Neither has Francis."

"Thank you. Edwin and I appreciate your discretion in the matter."

"Discretion?" Beth arched a brow. "A strange choice of words after what Francis and I happened upon this morning. I daresay neither of you used discretion."

Indignant over the remark, Celia let go of the doorknob and took a step forward. "Do not judge me so harshly," she pleaded gruffly. "You know nothing of my relationship with Edwin or other factors that influence our behavior."

"You are correct that I do not." Beth sighed as if to temper her words. "It is not my place to judge. I just wish to caution you that you are putting your reputation in jeopardy if others discover you in such uncompromising situations."

"We are aware of the risk and have agreed not to see one other again for a time," Celia announced.

"Perhaps that is wise." Beth paused. "But have you no shame for your behavior?"

"Shame? What does shame have to do with it? I love him."

"If he loved you," Beth reasoned, "he would not have attempted to seduce you. Do you not see that he planned to use you for his pleasure without the hope of a future together?"

"I do not wish to be scolded," Celia snapped like a turtle. "Especially not by you." She shook her head. "You and your brother are ignorant. From the tittle-tattle around Aycliffe, they caught your mother in a scandal."

"What?" Beth's eyes widened. Her face grew ashen.

"Now, if you will excuse me, I wish to freshen before dinner."

Celia exited the room, trembling from the conversation. She had done the unthinkable and thrown seeds of discord between them while accusing Beth's mother. It was despicable for her to do so even after she told Edwin to remain quiet. Of course, it was all veiled rumors and nothing more. She had lashed out, not knowing anything about Beth's mother except tattle about a kiss. To her shame, Celia had turned defensive to take the pointing finger out of her face and position it elsewhere.

CHAPTER TWELVE

Tea and Cakes

Beth nursed a gnawing uneasiness after her conversation with Celia. Twice in one day, an accusation of the worse sort had surfaced about her mother. Even though Francis thought Edwin uttered in anger, Celia articulated the words as if she knew it to be true. Scandal. The word swirled around Beth's mind for a day, but she spoke nothing of it to Francis, wishing to bear it until she could uncover the truth.

Eventually, Celia returned to her usual gregarious self when in their presence, acting as if nothing amiss had transpired. Francis remained distant but polite to show no disregard in front of her parents. While Beth outwardly attempted to do the same, she found it challenging to forgive Celia for her cruel and thought-less remark.

A few days later, the scheduled afternoon tea at the Howard estate arrived. The guests of honor were Beth and her brother, accompanied by Mr. and Mrs. Wilson and the elder Mr. Davenport and his wife. Celia and the Davenport siblings did not attend. The Wilsons brought them by carriage, and the Davenports followed, so everyone arrived at the same time. As they traversed toward the estate, Beth clutched both hands in her lap, peering nervously out the window at the passing landscape.

"No need to be nervous, young lady," Mr. Wilson encouraged with a knowing grin on his face. "Lord Howard is cordial."

Beth expelled an anxious giggle. "I have never visited a grand estate."

Francis reached over and grabbed her hand. "Beth, they have titles but are people like us. Consider them as such, and you will be fine."

"Well, you may think so, but they are the lord and lady of the county," she asserted. They deserved far more respect than Francis alluded.

"Lord Howard is a widower," Mrs. Wilson clarified. "His wife passed away."

"Oh. I hope they had a long, advantageous marriage with many children."

The Wilsons glanced at one another. Mr. Wilson nodded toward his wife, who explained further.

"Lord Howard is five and forty years of age and not an elderly gentleman," she clarified in a severe tone of voice. "His wife died shortly after giving birth to their firstborn son, who then succumbed to smallpox five years later."

"How dreadful," Beth declared, feeling empathy for another family suffering such untimely grief.

"And he has not remarried?" Francis inquired.

"Not as yet," Mrs. Wilson answered. "His Lordship portrays the picture that he has never recovered from the loss of his wife."

"And you do not believe that to be the case?" Francis inquired.

"It's the impression he gives, but who knows the workings of the man's mind," Mrs. Wilson answered in a bitter tone.

"And he has no one else?" Beth inquired.

"He lives with his niece, Miss Whiting, who just turned eighteen. She came to live with him a few years ago after the death of her parents."

"He has turned into a bit of a recluse and rarely seen in Aycliffe," Mr. Wilson added. "Society appears to bore him of late even though he keeps the tradition of the annual ball each year."

"True, but he enjoys traveling and will leave for lengthy periods to the Continent," Mrs. Wilson clarified. "His niece, however, often remains behind. I fear the girl is neglected and lonely because of his activities."

Mrs. Wilson glanced out the window. "Ah, there is the estate—Rosemont Park."

The grand home of three stories in Elizabethan architecture loomed ahead, facing a large pond filled with ducks. Perfectly manicured shrubs and trees lined the drive as the horses trotted toward an entrance surrounded by an impressive number of steps leading toward the massive oak door at the entrance. As they halted and came to a stop, two footmen scurried toward the carriage. One held out his hand, and Mr. Wilson encouraged Beth and Francis to exit first.

"After you, my dear," Mr. Wilson said, smiling at Beth. She trembled somewhat while grasping the gloved hand of the uniformed footman, who stood void of emotion, gazing ahead. Francis exited and stood next to her, lifting his eyes at the facade with too many windows to count.

"Impressive." He crooked his neck backward. "Fine stone workmanship."

"Yes, a splendid building. It was built in 1642 by the first earl," Mr. Wilson remarked as he gazed at the Bath stone facing.

The Davenports exited their carriage and joined the group, following the footman up the twelve stairs to the large double doors of the estate. Beth cursed herself inwardly for her childish jitters, hoping not to make a fool of herself in Lord Howard's presence. They were escorted into a grand sitting room off to the left, filled with gilded gold-framed paintings of ancestors. Fine furnishings, the like of which she had never seen, adorned the room embellished with the wealth of English aristocracy.

A table garnished with teapots of fine china and finger foods awaited the group. Another footman stood nearby, ready to wait on the guests. Beth glanced around, but the lord of the manor had not yet arrived. A large portly man with graying hair entered the room, obviously the butler.

"His Lordship will join you momentarily," he announced in a low and authoritative voice. "Please make yourself comfortable and help yourself to the refreshments at your leisure."

"Thank you, Clifford." Mr. Davenport eyed the spread of treats.

"He is such a dutiful servant," Mrs. Davenport added. "Been with the family for two generations. It's a wonder His Lordship keeps him on rather than letting him retire."

"Good servants are hard to come by, my dear. The man is loyal," Mr. Davenport asserted.

Beth glanced at Francis, who obviously had fallen into a contemplative silence. She wondered if he felt out of place as he looked around the room. Mr. and Mrs. Wilson obtained a cup of tea, but Beth waited lest her trembling fingers shake the cup and saucer. Instead, she walked toward Francis and invited him to take a seat next to her. Before she could do so, a man entered the room whose presence immediately commanded everyone's attention. By his side stood a petite young lady, whom Beth assumed to be his niece.

"Your Lordship," Mr. Davenport said, standing and bowing at the waist.

"Mr. and Mrs. Davenport, a pleasure to see you again." He reached out and shook hands with Mr. Davenport and smiled warmly at his wife. "Mr. and Mrs. Wilson," he said, nodding at them.

The tone of his voice was smooth as velvet to Beth's ears. She stood unmovable upon seeing his appearance, never having witnessed such a handsome, fair-haired man in her life. Impeccably dressed, at least six feet in height, and athletic in appearance, he exuded charisma.

"Your lordship, may I introduce to you Mr. Edwards and Miss Edwards," Mr. Wilson announced.

Lord Howard fixed his gaze upon Beth first. He took a step forward, reached out to her clutched hands in front of her waist, and took one, tenderly holding it in his palm. His bold and unwelcomed action unsettled Beth, but she did not protest.

"My dear, you look so much like your mother that I am in awe. It grieved my heart to hear of her passing. A great loss to everyone." He brought her hand to his lips and kissed it. Afterward, he moved in front of Francis.

"It is a pleasure to make your acquaintance, Mr. Edwards," he said, offering his hand to shake. "My condolences."

"Your lordship," Francis said, reciprocating with a nod and taking his hand.

"May I introduce to you my niece, Miss Whiting, who resides with me at Rosemont Park?"

"A pleasure to make your acquaintance," she said, acknowledging the introduction.

Beth noted the young lady. Dressed in a beautiful day dress of fine lavender-colored silk, Miss Whiting appeared elegant, like a porcelain doll.

"Please, take refreshments and have a seat," he offered. "I am most eager to get to know the two of you."

Beth's mouth felt like a ball of cotton, so she opted for a cup of tea but nothing to eat. She sat on a two-seat settee, which she had hoped Francis would join when he had received refreshment. However, as soon as she did, to her dismay, the earl sat next to her instead. Afraid to inch over, she remained motionless but glanced at Francis, looking for his support. He merely grinned at her uneasiness and took a seat next to Miss Whiting instead.

"How has your stay in Aycliffe been thus far?" the earl queried, looking directly at Beth.

She gazed into his eyes that were blue as the ocean, and for a moment, she thought she would drown in the depth of his stare. Even after a sip of tea, her mouth remained dry, and her hands trembled slightly as she held the cup. It was disquieting to be so close to his person that radiated a magnetism she could not deny. Men such as he could easily seduce any weak-willed woman with a simple touch of his hand.

"It has been pleasant." She responded with a calm tone despite her nervous jitters. "Francis and I have enjoyed the ocean immensely."

"And this is your first time to Aycliffe, I take it?" he asked.

"Yes, the first."

"You must forgive my curiosity," the earl said, "but did your mother speak of her time here at our coastal resort many years ago?" He glanced over at the Davenports. "I remember how well she handled your children, Mrs. Davenport, especially the rambunctious Edwin."

"Yes, she managed them well," she noted.

"And I take it you are now acquainted with

Alexander, Edwin, Lydia, and Richard."

"Yes, I have made their acquaintance."

Beth glanced at Francis, pleading with him with her eyes to enter the conversation. Lord Howard had obviously fixated himself upon her person in nearness and conversation.

"Our mother rarely spoke of Aycliffe," Francis announced. Lord Howard pulled his eyes away from Beth and looked at Francis, appearing somewhat downcast at hearing it. "We were, of course, aware of her continued correspondence with the Wilsons these past twenty years."

"Really? How admirable that she thought so well of them to maintain a friendship over the years. I was unaware they corresponded."

"Might I inquire how you were acquainted with our mother?" Francis asked. "If you do not mind me asking."

Mr. Davenport shot Francis a disgruntled look, and Mr. Wilson stiffened his position in the chair. Beth noted that Mrs. Wilson's mouth gaped open, and her forehead crinkled with worry lines. As she looked at the earl, she saw no outward reaction to the inquiry. He merely smiled and spoke in an even tone.

"I met your mother at our annual family ball," he explained. "Mrs. Davenport asked if Miss Ashby might attend. Everyone was welcome back in those days. I remember my father took a shining to her beauty," he chuckled. "And even danced with her a few times. My mother was not too pleased."

"Yes, it was the finest affair she had ever attended, and she expressed her gratefulness for the invitation," Mrs. Davenport interjected.

"You see, I was but a youthful man of one and twenty myself, and if I remember right, I took your mother for a spin around the dance floor. I would have danced with her more often, but I had already engaged myself to my late wife, Lady Margaret. Nevertheless, your mother was sought after by many men that evening. Beautiful woman," he remarked. "Not shy at all but a delightful conversationalist and warmhearted."

"It's hard to imagine Mother in such a light," Beth admitted. "I wish that I could have seen her then."

"You will attend the ball next week with your brother?" Miss Whiting asked.

The earl looked intently at Beth. "Do tell me you will be here."

"Yes, we plan to attend," Beth said with a faint smile.

"Splendid," he remarked. "Perhaps you will allow me to dance with you at least once to honor your mother's memory."

"It would delight me," Beth nervously responded.

The earl's pleasant countenance faded into a reflective one as he stared out the window of the parlor for a moment. Beth didn't know what to make of it but wondered if the conversation had stirred memories. Miss Whiting sat quietly, watching her uncle's reaction.

Mr. Wilson brought up the subject of bird hunting on his estate, and the three men conversed about the next excursion. Francis appeared interested, and Lord Howard included him into the conversation, inviting him to partake in the festivities.

The hour passed, filled with chatter. Miss Whiting appeared to hang upon Francis's words with interest. At the same time, Beth noted the earl emulated a vast array of emotions. His laugh was contagious, and when he smiled, his eyes brightened like the sparkling waters of the ocean. Then something would catch his mind, and the smile would slowly fade as if it were the sun setting on the horizon. A momentarily painful expression would replace it. Aware of the reflective mood, he would clear his throat and replace it with a slight grin or glance with interest at Beth, making her feel self-conscious of his attention.

As they rose to leave, he extended his hand toward Beth to help her from a seated position. At first, she hesitated, looking at his upturned palm and the warm smile on his face. He observed her with a glint of affection, and she grasped it.

"Thank you, Your Lordship," she said.

"My pleasure, Miss Edwards."

The earl followed everyone outdoors and insisted on attending Beth, helping her into the carriage. By the look in Francis's eyes, he noted the earl's attentive bid for Beth's well-being but said nothing in front of the Wilsons.

"It was a pleasure, Lord Howard," Francis said in parting. "I am keen to hunt with you next week."

"Excellent sport and fresh air. We shall have a time of it, I am sure," Lord Howard said cheerily.

The carriage door closed, and the driver urged the horses down the pathway toward Aycliffe.

"He appears to be an affable man," Francis remarked.

The Wilsons glanced at one another, and Beth noted a slight look of contempt in Mrs. Wilson's eyes. She wondered why but did not press the matter further.

"Yes, he is an agreeable man," Mr. Wilson concurred, failing to express further accolades.

Their odd responses caused Beth to pondered the meaning. Then the words of Celia raked across her mind in an unwelcomed assault. Scandal. The whimsical sensation that she had cherished a few moments earlier vanished into dark thoughts of speculation.

CHAPTER THIRTEEN

Game of Hearts

Upon their return to the Wilson residence, Francis and Beth took a moment alone in the garden for a quiet and reflective stroll. The afternoon had turned to dusk, creating a relaxing golden hue among the varied flowers. A gentle warm breeze continued to rustle the leaves. It had been the warmest day since their arrival.

"Finally, a moment of privacy," Francis said, sighing in relief. He walked a few steps and then glanced at Beth who appeared deep in thought. A pout turned her lips downward.

"My, my, sister, you seem to turn the heads of all the men in Aycliffe, including that of an earl, no less." He hoped a slight teasing poke might bring about a smile.

"Oh, don't be ridiculous." She dismissed him with a flip of her hand.

Francis noted the blush in her cheeks. "Well, you must be blind if you failed to detect the man's interest in you. If it hadn't been for Mr. Wilson bringing up hunting, I daresay he would have fixated upon you for the entire hour."

"All right," Beth admitted. "I will be frank that I noticed and felt uncomfortable with his attention. It is a mystery why he should take any interest in me."

"Perhaps your appearance reminds him of Mother,"

Francis concluded. "And he finds you as attractive. He noted Mother's youthful loveliness." Francis did not consider the possibility of the earl's sentiments to be a foolish conjecture.

"Francis, I have no dowry, no title, no impressive resemblance to Mother. Surely, he would wish to pursue someone in his class." She strode slowly past the rosebushes and let out a moan. "Besides, the man is over twenty years my senior. If I marry, I would prefer someone closer to my age."

"A minor sacrifice for riches and the title of countess. You could do no better anywhere else." Francis smirked and gazed intently at Beth to determine her thoughts. "And do you find him affable?"

A nervous giggle rumbled in her throat. "Well, Lord Howard has certain merits I find captivating."

"Then there is Alexander Davenport." Francis reluctantly brought up the name. "You apparently are pursued by him as well."

"For what purpose, I have no idea. Did not Edwin say that Mr. Davenport wanted the brothers to marry for money? I have no inheritance worth pursuing."

"Yes, I find that odd," Francis agreed, pondering Alexander's motives. "Perhaps he has decided to defy his father's wishes since he indicated to you privately that he wanted to seek other interests."

"Possibly." Beth kicked a few pebbles with the toe of her shoe in frustration. "But to be honest, Francis, I am not inclined toward either Alexander or the earl, for that matter. Instead, I am deeply disturbed by other concerns."

"About what?" Francis halted in his step, and Beth did too. They faced each other, and her brow furrowed. When she brought her hands together to wring them in worry, he knew it to be serious.

"Do you remember the odd comment about the scandal and our mother that Edwin made?"

"What of it?" Francis asked, perturbed Beth had brought the matter up again.

"Celia spoke rashly to me privately when I talked to her about Edwin. She was sputtering mad, so perhaps she said it to hurt me rather than there being any truth to it." Beth lowered her eyes.

"What did she say?" Francis scowled at the thought of it.

"Something to the effect that we were ignorant of scandal and insinuated that our mother was well acquainted with it."

"What the bloody hell is that supposed to mean?" Francis spat with anger rising in his gut over the sordid gossip.

"Oh dear," Beth grimaced. "I should have said nothing."

Francis's nostrils flared, fuming that Celia would stoop so low as to make an implication regarding their mother. What possible scandal could she have been involved in at Aycliffe? As he ruminated over the foul prattle, he determined to flick the idea away like a hornet intent on stinging his flesh.

"Brother, you look ashen as the whitewashed wall behind you," Beth remarked. "Are you all right?"

"No, I'm not," he muttered. "The thought of it upsets me."

"Oh, Francis, you cannot believe that she had some sordid affair while here at Aycliffe."

"I don't know." Francis shook his head, hoping it was mere conjecture on their part.

"But who? Mr. Davenport?"

Francis remained silent, pondering the possibility. He observed Beth, seeing if she had any intuition on the matter when to his dismay Mrs. Wilson came outdoors with Celia at her side.

"We have company," he muttered.

Beth swung around when they arrived in their midst, and Francis adjusted his posture.

"Now, what are the two of you doing out here? The sun has set, and it is practically dark. Come inside, dears, as dinner will be served soon." Mrs. Wilson reached out and patted Beth on the arm.

"Mother insists that I am a terrible host," Celia admitted. "Won't you join me in the parlor for a game of cards before we dine?"

"Cards?" Francis's brow arched.

"Yes, how about a game of hearts?" Celia suggested. "You do know how to play hearts."

"He's rather ruthless when it comes to hearts," Beth announced. "My brother has a competitive streak in him, so if you wish to play, I warn you it could get unpleasant."

Francis pulled his mouth at Beth's statement, knowing full well she wanted to egg him into embarrassing himself for sport. It was just like Beth to change the seriousness of one conversation and then make light of another to take their minds elsewhere.

"The problem, you see, Miss Wilson, is that my sister is a sore loser. She would rather poke at my competitive streak than admit that she hates me beating her at anything." He looked a Celia and grinned. "Sibling rivalry."

"Well, come inside," Mrs. Wilson said. "I will fetch the cards."

They returned indoors to the parlor. Mr. Wilson sat in front of the fireplace, reading the newspaper. He lifted his head to note their entrance.

"I heard Celia suggested cards to pass the time. Have

you agreed?"

"Yes, they agreed, Father." Celia took a seat at a small card table, and Beth and Francis followed suit. As soon as she received the deck from her mother, she handed it over to Francis.

"Would you care to deal?"

"Gladly." Francis snatched the deck from her hand. After a few shuffles, he meted out the cards, discarding the two of diamonds and setting it aside. Each received seventeen cards, and Beth grasped them, determined to beat him.

The game started in silence, but Mr. Wilson appeared entertained watching the three of them play and intent on drawing them into a conversation.

"What is your opinion of Lord Howard?"

Francis played a card and then spoke. "Impressive estate and interesting man. He appeared fascinated with Beth."

Celia let out a soft chuckle, playing a card. He couldn't tell whether it was because of her move or the comment.

"Well, look at her," Mr. Wilson remarked nonchalantly. "She is a beauty in her own right, and believe me when I say that she looks much like her mother did twenty years ago."

"That is true," Mrs. Wilson agreed, fiddling with her cross-stitch.

"That may be true to some extent," Beth remarked. "But I felt unworthy of such attention."

"Nonsense," Mr. Wilson remarked. "Francis, you shall have more time with His Lordship after the ball when we go hunting for fowl. He owns the best dogs in the county, and his land is filled with plump birds for the taking."

"I look forward to it," he mumbled, pondering the

next card to lay down.

"All this talk is making me lose track of how many hearts we have played," Celia remarked with a huff.

Francis bellowed a laugh. "Save your energy, Miss Wilson, because you will not beat me at cards."

"See what I mean, Celia? He is far too competitive for my taste," Beth complained.

The game continued in silence, and before long, Francis declared himself the winner.

"I do not understand why I cannot beat you at this infuriating game!" Beth glowered at Francis.

"See, what did I say? Sore loser," he snickered.

"I shan't play another." Beth rose to her feet and walked over to the settee and plopped herself next to Mrs. Wilson, whose eyes widened at her behavior. Francis attempted to make light of it.

"I think Beth is somewhat frustrated and tired from the day's activities," he remarked. "Perhaps another game after dinner, sister, and I will let you win. Will that suffice?"

"I will let you know later," she grumbled.

"What about that deep-sea fishing excursion?" Mr. Wilson asked. "Are you ready to try your hand tomorrow if the weather holds?"

Francis smiled at the thought of it. A day away fishing might give him a reprieve. "Yes, I am ready."

"Capital," Mr. Wilson said. "I shall make arrangements on the morrow for you with Mr. Cranston, who has already agreed to take you out on his boat."

"Oh, and there is a luncheon at the Davenports tomorrow," Mrs. Wilson remarked. "I almost forget to tell you. Mrs. Davenport sent an invitation to Beth, Celia, and myself to partake with her, Lydia, and a few other ladies from town."

Francis noted Beth's countenance cringe at the thought of another social function. No doubt she would rather spend her day wandering the beach than having lunch with society.

"Do I have to go, Mother?" Celia whined.

"Yes, you have to go," Mrs. Wilson ordered. "She will be offended if you refuse to attend." She glowered at Celia and remarked in a huff, "Honestly, young lady. You astound me with your manners of late."

Francis hated to admit the fact that he enjoyed Celia receiving a reprimand of some sort. Between her dealings with Edwin and slandering their mother, he thought she deserved far more. An urge to throw her over his lap and give her a good spanking caused him to grin.

Their servant announced that dinner was ready. Francis came to Beth's side and whispered in her ear. "I hope you enjoy your luncheon tomorrow."

She glared at him and whispered back. "Enjoy your fishing. I might use the opportunity to do a little fishing myself."

Francis nodded approvingly, understanding her intent.

CHAPTER FOURTEEN

The Fishing Expeditions

A flower arrangement decorated the table that wasn't too high to obscure faces on the opposite side. Beth glanced at the ladies, attempting to remember their names during the introduction. Mrs. Davenport sat at the head, Mrs. Wilson to her left, Lydia to the right of her mother, and then Celia.

They had placed Beth next to Mrs. Wilson but touched elbows with Trudy Beecham, the wife of the chief constable. Next to Lydia sat Rosemary Winters, the wife of one of the city aldermen. When they chat, the room sounded like a cackling henhouse, and Beth attempted to restrain her laughter over the scene. To make the gathering more amusing, chicken was on the menu.

Celia, despite not wanting to come, became perky and animated as ever. Lydia kept staring at Beth with a lopsided grin, as if she were the keeper of all the gossip she wanted to glean about her mother. With that purpose in mind, she determined to engage in conversation regardless of what Celia warned when they first arrived. No doubt Celia merely wanted to protect her reputation, and Beth wondered if Lydia was privy to Celia's affair with Edwin.

"I hear that you met Lord Howard," Mrs. Winters remarked. "May I inquire of your impression of him?"

Surprised at the question, Beth swallowed the mouthful she had been chewing, took a quick sip of tea, and dabbed her lips with her napkin. The pause gave her time to deliberate.

"I thought him to be a very gracious host," she remarked.

Lydia smirked. "Mother said he could not keep his eyes off of you."

"Lydia!" Mrs. Davenport said in a reprimanding tone.

"You are quite right," Beth admitted. "My only complaint about the visit was his overt attention made me uncomfortable." She glanced around the table, and all eyes stared at her. "Why did he act in such an obvious manner?" She had hoped that everyone would respond with an opinion. Instead, they merely looked at her with a blank stare. Only Mrs. Wilson gave the same overused response.

"As I said yesterday, dear, you look very much like your mother. It undoubtedly surprised His Lordship, and he found it—how shall I put it—mesmerizing."

"Well, it makes no sense to me," Beth replied. She looked directly at Lydia. "What do you think?"

"Me?" she squawked. "Yes, Lydia, you."

She glanced at Mrs. Davenport, whose eyes widened as if to be cautious.

"I have no idea," she said. "Having not seen the look in His Lordship's eyes, it is hard to say what he thought about you."

"And you, Celia? Do you have any idea?"

Celia narrowed her eyes at Beth, giving her a cautionary glance. "I agree with Lydia. Since I was not there to observe the interaction, I cannot guess."

"Well, it's a mystery to me." Beth sighed. She had expressed her thoughts and gained nothing in return.

"I wouldn't worry about it," Mrs. Beecham cajoled. "His Lordship is a fascinating man, and many people conclude that he is lonely."

"I have heard rumors about his younger days, that he—"

Mrs. Wilson cut off Mrs. Winters in the middle of her sentence without an apology. "Let us not gossip about Lord Howard, ladies, as it wouldn't be polite."

"Yes, I agree," Mrs. Davenport sternly added. "Let us not sin and become a group of busybodies, slandering individuals during lunch."

"He insists that I dance with him at the ball," Beth remarked, refusing to let the conversation die. She had never been so tenacious to fish for answers.

"Oh, then you should do so by all means," Mrs. Beecham chimed in. "I hear he is a splendid dancer. You surely wouldn't want to offend His Lordship by dismissing his request."

"Perhaps I will step on his toe, and his infatuation with me will wane," Beth chuckled. The ladies laughed with her, which seemed to lighten the mood around the table. Everyone returned to idle prattle and chicken.

When they finished luncheon, they all retired to the parlor for tea and finger cakes for dessert. Beth made it a point to latch on to Lydia and sit next to her. When she joined her on the settee, she appeared surprised. Ignoring her reaction, Beth spoke.

"I feel bad that we have not had the opportunity to get to know one another better since I arrived in Aycliffe."

Lydia spoke in a low tone. "I surmised that was because Celia told you to stay clear of me, telling you I was the town gossip."

"Indeed, but I don't always take to heart the opinions of others. I would much rather form my own thoughts by getting to know people. Don't you agree that approach is more productive?"

"Absolutely." Lydia glanced at Celia.

An unfriendly narrowing of the eyes exchanged, and Beth instinctively knew they hated each other. She wondered why there was so much animosity.

"How much do you remember about my mother?" Beth asked, innocently starting the subject.

"Very little," Lydia admitted. She took a cup of tea in hand. "I was far too young to remember details. Alexander and Edwin have more memories of her than I possess." She looked at Beth. "Do you remember your time as a toddler?"

"Oh, goodness no," Beth readily admitted. "I remember, though, when my brother teased me relentlessly and attempted to get me in trouble."

"Brothers are rascals. I had two constantly poking at me. Now that they are older, I pester them in return in other ways more annoying than a physical jab with a finger." She flashed a prideful grin as if she enjoyed the revenge. "Not so much Alexander, however. I'm fonder of him than of Edwin."

"Well, I must admit that my mother's stay here in your home as a governess is mostly a mystery to Francis and me." She frowned, taking a sip of tea, wishing that she had a more private moment with Lydia. Unfortunately, the ladies in the room were also clamoring for her attention and conversation.

"Tell us about your dress for the ball," Mrs. Davenport asked. "Mrs. Wilson just told me it's ready for the final fitting."

"Oh, the dress," Beth said. "I almost forgot."

"I have a new dress too," Celia interjected. "We shall both be the belles of the ball."

"And I will not?" Lydia chimed in, raising a brow for

the obvious exclusion.

The next few minutes, everyone jumped into the conversation as if they had leaped into a refreshing pool of water, speaking of new ball gowns and shoes. Lydia leaned into her and whispered during Celia's recitation of the lace and ribbons on her dress.

"I am sorry that I can tell you nothing more about your mother."

"It's quite all right." Beth wondered how her brother fared with his fishing expedition since hers had been a failure.

The moment the boat left the dock, Francis believed Poseidon had bestowed a blessing. He could not have asked for a more perfect day of weather or calm seas as it glided across the shiny surface of the ocean. The small schooner's skipper, Mr. Cranston, stood by his side, while the other two mates manned the ship's sails and rudder. Occasionally, Francis struggled with bouts of nausea, having never set foot on anything bigger than a wooden fishing punt on the local river. When the sensation passed and he regained his sea legs, he took full advantage of the experience.

"You feelin' better now, lad?" Mr. Cranston asked, looking at him with a bit of amusement in his eyes.

"Do you ever get seasick?" Francis asked.

"Nah, not even when the winds are blowin' and the seas are as choppy as me wife in a bad mood," he chortled. "Love the ocean like me dad and granddad before me."

"Has it changed much since your father fished these waters?"

"Aye, the town wasn't a highfalutin' resort until the Davenports got their hands on it. Was a small fishin' village with men folk makin' their livelihood from the ocean." He wiped a bead of sweat from his brow and readjusted his oilskin fishing hat. "Just a handful of us left now, sellin' fish to the townsfolk. What goes around comes around, they say. Guess that's true. Heard them Davenports got money problems since the town isn't as popular as before."

"Is that so?" Francis listened intently.

"Mr. Wilson tells me you're Catherine Ashby's boy," he remarked. "Them Wilsons done invited you and your sis to Aycliffe?"

"Yes, I am, and yes, they did. We arrived a week ago."

Mr. Cranston appeared to be ruminating in thought, staring out at the horizon. "Good weather," he remarked.

"Did you know my mother?" Francis asked, hoping to stir his recollection.

"Who me?"

Francis nodded.

"Not really. Seen the young lady 'bout the town with the Davenports' young'uns," he said.

"Well, my sister and I know very little of her stay here in Aycliffe. It's a mystery."

"Is it now," he said, keeping his eyes averted. "Don't go in for chin-waggin' at all. Especially 'bout those dead and buried."

Francis wanted to pressure him for more, but instead, Mr. Cranston barked an order to drop anchor and set up the lines. They were a respectable distance offshore now, and Francis could barely see the town any longer.

"Now you be fishin' for sea bass," he explained. "You might get a cod or haddock in the mix."

"As long as it is bigger than a trout," Francis snickered. "I will be satisfied."

"You gonna cook 'em?"

"Well, not me, but I'm sure Wilson's cook will do a fine job."

Francis enjoyed the next two hours, euphoric over the catch of fish he reeled in. Mr. Cranston said he must have had a lucky streak to be so fortunate on the number of large bass that he managed to pull on board. The crew enjoyed a merry laugh watching his excitement.

Fishing gave Francis time to contemplate. He enjoyed fly-fishing on the river near home. It was quiet and nothing to fill his mind except the greenery along the shoreline, the birds in the trees, and what trout would next nibble at his bait. Deep-sea fishing was vastly different, especially since he had the company of the crew nearby. Nevertheless, just looking at the expanse of the ocean while waiting for a bass to take the bait brought a soulful peace.

When he had caught his fill, they sailed back to port. Francis noted off in the distant hills behind the town Rosemont Park. It commanded a rather eye-catching view of the horizon that he had not seen upon their visit.

"Amazing how you can see the Howard estate from offshore," Francis noted.

Mr. Cranston turned his head and took note. "Aye, the big house."

"What do you know of Lord Howard? I met him the other day. He seemed agreeable."

Mr. Cranston frowned. "They say he's a fine fella, but I never spoke to the man. Lots of twaddle and speculation about his life floats about the town gossips. Ladies love to talk about rich folk."

"What kind of twaddle?" Francis pressed.

Mr. Cranston pressed his lips together in a straight line and averted a direct gaze into Francis's eyes. "Not sure," he brusquely dismissed. "We best be packin' those fish for you to take back to the cook at Wilson's kitchen."

By the uncomfortable look on Mr. Cranston's face, Francis knew better than to push him further. He could only presume that somehow the talk that roamed about town had to do with another, and he wondered if it was his mother. The thought of it made him ill at ease.

"Thank you, Mr. Cranston, for the enjoyable excursion," he remarked. "I am sure that fishing for trout will no longer excite as much as deep-sea fishing did today."

"You are more than welcome, lad. More than welcome indeed."

Francis watched as the shore approached and wondered how Beth had fared with her luncheon. Perhaps she received more information to either confirm or deny the innuendos being dropped by Celia and Edwin. He hated the unknown and the secrecy surrounding their mother's time at Aycliffe.

Upon Francis's return from his excursion, he found Beth had just returned from her luncheon with Mrs. Wilson and Celia.

"Well, did you catch any fish or get seasick?" she teased.

"Almost lost breakfast, but finally found my sea legs after a while. And yes, I have returned with quite the catch."

"Fine job," Mrs. Wilson remarked, smiling.

"I have given the fish to your cook, and it delighted her to receive the bounty of the sea."

"I'm sure Miss Princeton will find whatever you caught useful for a few meals," Mrs. Wilson said. "Now, if you will excuse me, I'm afraid that I'm going to take a short nap after that rather rich lunch and sweet cakes."

She patted her tummy with her palm.

Celia remained in their midst, and Francis wanted to shoo her away so he could talk privately with Beth. Unfortunately, no matter how many scowls exchanged between the two, Celia remained steadfast.

"What did you and Lydia talk about?" Celia asked, looking directly at Beth.

"Nothing in particular."

"Oh, I find that hard to believe. Did she mention Edwin?"

"Edwin?" Beth repeated the name with a tone of disdain. "No, nothing about Edwin."

Celia mused silently for a moment. "You asked about your mother, didn't you?"

"That is enough, Celia," Francis interjected, agitated at her insistence to poke at Beth. "Would you mind giving us privacy? You look as if you could use a nap too."

A huff left Celia's lungs. "Fine," she spat, pushing past them, and running upstairs. After a rather loud bang of her bedroom door, Beth sat down, overcome with emotion.

"I feel like I'm wandering around a dark room and cannot find my way," she moaned.

Francis sat down next to her. "How was your luncheon?"

"I dined on chicken in a room of cackling hens," she expelled. "Truthfully, it was fine. I tried to befriend Lydia, but it was difficult to find a private moment to talk about anything." She reached over and patted Francis on the arm. "Did you enjoy your fishing expedition?"

"Indeed." He beamed, remembering how satisfying the trip had been. "I am proud of myself. It was an exhilarating experience on the schooner. We were far enough out to sea that the shoreline almost vanished completely."

"How exciting," Beth remarked.

"Mr. Cranston was a fine skipper. He told me that he recollected Mother around town with the children."

"So many years ago?"

"Yes, his family has been fishing in Aycliffe for generations."

Francis glanced around to make sure no one was nearby. He lowered his voice and leaned in toward Beth. "He said that the town is not as popular as it once was, and the Davenports are having financial problems."

"Really," Beth drawled, narrowing her eyes at the tidbit.

"We also talked about Lord Howard."

"What about him?"

"That a good deal of townspeople gossip about him, but he wouldn't go into details."

Beth's countenance soured. "Oh Francis. I am so tired of these inferences and comments about Mother's time here in Aycliffe. Truthfully, I just want to go home and let whatever happened here stay buried." Beth reached out and grabbed his forearm. "Tell me you agree, and we can forget about all this chatter from Edwin and Celia."

Francis nodded his head affirmatively. "Though I am intrigued and wonder if there is any truth to it, I am inclined to agree with you that, for Mother's sake, we should let the matter remain." He reached out and took her hand, patting it softly. "I can tell this has upset you, Beth. Let us forget about it, attend the ball, and then make arrangements to make our way back home."

Beth heaved a sigh of relief. Although Francis knew he made the right decision, inwardly the unsolved mystery gave him cause for concern

CHAPTER FIFTEEN

Looking Through a Glass Darkly

The evening of the grand ball at Rosemont Park arrived. As Beth descended the staircase to meet the Wilsons and her brother, they appeared pleased with her appearance. Celia stood adorned in her new lavender silk ball gown, looking stunning in her own right.

"You look wonderful," Mrs. Wilson said, stepping closer and gushing at them approvingly.

The candlelit room caused the light to shimmer in waves against the blue silk. Even though it was an off-the-shoulder fashion baring more skin than Beth dared to show in her entire life, she felt beautiful. She could tell by the look in Francis's eyes that he approved, albeit with a bit of reservation over the daring fashion.

"Delicate lace trim," he remarked with an arched brow. "A bit revealing."

"It's the latest of fashion," Celia said, coming to Beth's rescue.

"Well, I admit that you look stunning, which only means that I shall have to keep an eye on you this evening."

"And look at you, dear brother. Handsome as well in your new garments. Do not forget to dance with the wallflowers."

"Yes, fine tailoring," Mr. Wilson grinned. "All the ladies of the household are beautiful, as far as I am concerned." He gave Mrs. Wilson an approving peck on the cheek. "Even you, dearest, in your new frock."

"You flatter me, Mr. Wilson." She gave him a tap on the arm with her fan. "I must say that I am looking forward to this evening."

Beth's heart raced in anticipation as she drew a shawl around her shoulders and went outdoors to the waiting coach. As they journeyed to Rosemont Park, Mr. Wilson stared at Beth approvingly.

"You remind me of your mother twenty years ago, taking the same trip. Oh, what an impression she made upon every one that night."

Beth wanted to forget about the mysterious past of her mother, but apparently, that would not happen.

"It was her first formal ball, just like you," Mrs. Wilson revealed. "She was so excited and giddy. Of course, fashions twenty years ago were far different from what they are today."

"I much prefer today's gowns," Celia remarked. "The empire waistlines did nothing to advance a woman's figure."

"That was the point," Mrs. Wilson remarked. "Dresses were far more modest."

"What did Mother wear?" Beth asked in curiosity.

"Now that I recall, the color was close to what you are wearing this evening. Catherine's hair was up in a beautiful coiffure. Mrs. Davenport lent her earrings and a necklace for the evening out of the kindness of her heart." Mrs. Wilson recalled.

"And a rather large ostrich feather," Mr. Wilson added. "She looked like a princess."

Beth's eyes caught sight of Rosemont Park. Multiple torches lined the roadway and illuminated the estate.

Every room glowed with candlelight, and a line of carriages with attendees arrived one after another.

"My goodness, what a sight," Beth remarked, wide-eyed.

"The estate looks divine," Celia remarked. "Every-one of importance in Aycliffe—and the county, for that matter—attend. It has always been the event of the year."

"Yes, and plenty of food and champagne, so pace yourself." Mrs. Wilson flipped her fan open, giving her reddened cheeks a cooling.

The horses slowly made their way and finally stopped. A footman opened the door and stood at attention.

"Oh look. The Davenports are right behind us," Mrs. Wilson remarked as she exited.

Mr. and Mrs. Davenport emerged, and then the carriage behind them held the three siblings, Lydia, Alexander, and Edwin. As soon as Beth saw Edwin, she glanced at Celia, who looked forlornly in his direction but made no outward indication of any hidden amorous affections. No doubt they had agreed to keep their secret hidden.

Everyone followed two by two into the double-door entrance, greeted by footmen and maids who readily took overcoats or wraps. Lord Howard stood alone, greeting guests upon their arrival. He smiled warmly, shaking hands with the gentlemen and exchanging pleasantries with the ladies. As they approached ahead of the Davenports, Beth found her emotions arouse with a mixture of intrigue and caution. The room disappeared into a haze as Lord Howard focused his attention upon her.

"Miss Edwards," he said, reaching for her hand again. He took her gloved fingers to his lips and kissed them. "I am delighted to see you this evening."

Beth gave a curtsy. "Thank you, Your Lordship. I am delighted to be here, as well."

"Mr. Edwards, welcome." He turned his attention to Francis after letting go of Beth's hand.

"Thank you for the invitation," Francis said.

"My pleasure."

Beth stepped away, and Francis followed. She did not turn to watch Lord Howard welcome the Wilsons or the Davenports. Instead, her feet propelled her forward into the residence and toward the music. Couples climbed the grand staircase, which led to an enormous assembly room on the second floor.

"Quite the affair," Francis remarked, observing the crowded room.

"It is beautiful." Beth gazed, mesmerized by the sights and sounds. Music permeated the air, couples danced, footmen held trays of champagne, and the atmosphere filled with excitement. While staring at the awe-inspiring scene, Alexander arrived at her side.

"Miss Edwards, would you grant me the honor of being the first to dance with you this evening?"

He held out his white-gloved hand, and without hesitation, Beth clutched it. "It would delight me," she replied, giddy with enthusiasm. A moment later, she found herself in his arms, spinning around in a waltz that made her head dizzy. It was the most glorious moment of her life being adorned in an elegant dress, feeling beautiful as a woman, and in the embrace of a handsome man.

"May I compliment you on your gown this evening, Miss Edwards? You are ravishing," Alexander remarked with a sincere and deep voice. He looked into her eyes, expressing a hint of admiration.

"Thank you. May I return one and say that you are proficient in the waltz?"

"Well, it is easy to lead a woman across the dance floor, especially when your partner follows so skillfully." Alexander's smile remained fixed.

"So true." Beth pondered the remark. "I much prefer a man who sets the example in all things that I can admire and follow if I am so inclined." Alexander gazed curiously at her for a few moments and then asked a surprising question.

"If I traveled to the ends of the earth, Miss Edwards, would you be inclined to follow me?"

His inquiry caught her off guard because it insinuated marriage, or at least she thought it did.

"To the scorching deserts of Egypt?" Alexander inquired and gave Beth an aggressive twirl in his step.

"I am not sure that I can envision myself riding on a camel, frankly." The idea had never entered her head.

"And why is that? Do camels frighten you?"

"Not at all. They are just odd-looking creatures."

"Yes, I suppose they are," he agreed. "Humped backs, skinny legs, long necks, and a rather ugly face."

Beth giggled. They were quite unsightly. "I wonder how a person gets on top of that large hump. It would be a most unladylike position."

"True, but I believe the camel comes down to the rider's level by getting on their knees so you can mount them. They wear saddles of sorts," Alexander clarified.

The current piece ended, as well as their odd topic of discussion. Alexander hesitantly released Beth, slipping his hand from her waist and letting go of her hand. She had been so immersed in the waltz and camel conversation that she had paid little to anything else. His touch was firm but tender, and admittedly, she enjoyed the closeness of his person.

The attendees clapped after the number, and Beth felt parched from the exercise. "Would you mind fetching me something to drink? I am afraid all this talk about the desert has brought on a thirst."

"It would be my pleasure," he said, stepping away.

Beth went to the side of the dance floor and patiently waited for Alexander's return. She glanced around at the attendees, admiring the beautiful ball gowns and handsome men that filled the room. To her surprise, Francis stood by a young woman whom Beth did not recognize, apparently in a conversation. While watching her brother, who looked rather dapper in his new clothes, her eyes caught sight of Lord Howard approaching in her direction. The musicians commenced another waltz, and Beth knew what would come next.

"Miss Edwards, I believe this is the dance that you promised me," he announced in an authoritative tone.

Before Beth could reply, Alexander arrived with two flutes of champagne in his hand.

"Your Lordship," he said, looking clearly miffed by his clenched jaw.

"Mr. Davenport."

Beth immediately sensed a bid for her attention that would not be denied by either of them.

"I am here to dance with Miss Edwards. Please excuse us." He extended his hand, obviously expecting her to take it.

Beth glanced at Alexander and mouthed "sorry" while being led to the floor. Lord Howard placed his hand upon the small of her back, and Beth placed her left on his shoulder. After he closed his fingers around hers, she quivered at his touch.

Oddly, he remained silent but kept his eyes upon hers as they waltzed around the room. Beth noted that Francis had taken the hand of the young lady he was speaking with and began waltzing. When her eyes returned to Lord Howard, he smiled warmly at her.

"Are you enjoying yourself, Miss Edwards?"

"Oh, immensely." Her quavering voice exposed her uneasiness. Even though she attempted to pull her gaze away from him, she felt helpless to do so.

"Will you be staying long in Aycliffe?"

"I am afraid that we will leave next week as my brother must return."

Lord Howard remained silent for the remainder of the dance, maintaining eye contact. When the musical piece ended, he released her and stepped back.

"Will you take a walk with me, Miss Edwards, or would you prefer another dance?"

"A walk?"

"Yes, I find the air in the room somewhat stifling. Perhaps some fresh air on the balcony would give us a few more minutes to converse."

Beth's eyes darted around, looking for Francis and Alexander. They both had disappeared, and the invitation sent a nervous chill down her spine. He looked at her forlornly as if any refusal would severely offend him, so Beth relented.

"Yes, a breath of fresh air would be good."

He offered his arm, and Beth took it. They departed out the glass double doors that led to an overhanging balcony above the garden. Eyes followed their departure, and Beth worried about how it appeared. As they stepped into the night air, she inhaled a shaky breath, attempting to calm her nervous jitters.

"Ah, much better," Lord Howard remarked. "Don't you agree?"

Beth nodded, forced a smile, and prayed Francis or Alexander would come to her rescue.

CHAPTER SIXTEEN

His Lordship

Beth remained attentive but often glanced through the double doors, seeing couples spin by as the music played. She wondered why Francis wasn't out looking for her. Indeed, by now, he must have noticed her disappearance. Even Alexander didn't seem to pay attention that she had disappeared onto the balcony with the earl. As anxiousness continued to gnaw her inwardly, Francis came into her peripheral vision. He stood by the doors with Miss Whiting at his side. A sense of relief flowed through her body. The earl's niece put her finger to her lips, signaling Beth to remain silent while they eavesdropped.

"As much as I love opening my home for this annual event, I find it taxing," Lord Howard admitted.

Beth turned her attention to him, hesitating to make eye contact. "Why?"

"People say I have become somewhat of a recluse since my wife died. If it wasn't for Annie coming to live with me, I probably would have gone mad from grief over the past."

"Well, she appears to be a delightful young lady." Beth thoughtfully paused and continued.

"I would not enjoy being a recluse. I'm too fond of company and pleasant conversation."

"Then you take after your mother."

"In some ways, I do but not in all things." Beth felt the urge to disagree.

"I have a matter to discuss with you," he announced.

Apparently, Annie had heard enough and walked onto the balcony, interrupting the conversation.

"Uncle, you are rude," she scolded him. "You have a room full of guests, and I find you outdoors instead with Miss Edwards."

Francis stepped alongside Miss Whiting and gave Beth a raised brow of disapproval for having a moment alone unchaperoned. Lord Howard looked at him directly and then back at his niece.

"Perhaps you are right, my dear." He turned toward Beth. "Thank you for the dance, Miss Edwards. I hope you enjoy the remainder of your evening here at Rosemont Park."

Before Beth could reply, he turned on his heel and left her standing in the presence of Miss Whiting and Francis.

"You should be careful, Beth," Francis scolded with a sly grin. "You could ruin your reputation if caught alone with a man."

"Oh, my uncle is no threat. Do come back inside and enjoy yourself."

Beth followed them indoors, and to her surprise, Alexander approached holding a flute of champagne for her to drink. He looked mortified by the awkward situation.

"As requested, your drink," he said, handing her the glass.

"Thank you, Alexander. I apologize for keeping you so long." She brought the glass to her lips and took a sip of the refreshing liquid.

"Francis, why don't you ask Miss Whiting for a

dance." Beth hoped to regain a moment alone with Alexander.

He arched a brow but couldn't say no. "May I have the pleasure?"

"I would be delighted," Miss Whiting replied.

They excused themselves and left Beth alone with Alexander in the crowded room. Unable to help herself, she let her gaze rove over the area, looking for the earl, but he had disappeared.

"Would you like to dance again?" Alexander asked. "When I saw Lord Howard take you onto the balcony, I worried that I would never see you for the remainder of the evening."

"Whatever do you mean?" Beth asked, cocking her head at him, surprised by the remark.

"I just meant that I feared he would gain all of your attention, and I would lose precious moments by your side." Alexander shifted in his stance as if his admission embarrassed him.

A sudden rush of sympathy rose in Beth's chest as she realized he would be disappointed to lose another dance. "Frankly, I don't understand why he pays me so much attention. I find it somewhat disconcerting." Beth hoped that he might clarify the mystery for her. Instead, he avoided it entirely by gulping the rest of his drink.

"Shall we dance again?" Alexander set the flute down on a nearby table.

"Isn't it considered rude to give your attention to one woman at a ball?" Beth glanced along the sidelines. "I see a few wallflowers that might enjoy a waltz from a handsome man as yourself."

An instant smile spread across his face. "Oh, you consider me handsome, do you?"

"I shall neither affirm nor deny that remark lest your ego swell." Beth put her glass down next to his.

"One more dance, but then I expect you to do the honorable thing and ask the lonely women pining along the sides of the room."

"Very well. I shall obey your request but reserve the right to ask you again later this evening."

Alexander offered his gloved hand. A new piece had started, and he swirled her effortlessly around the room. Her gown swished around her hips, and her step matched his to near perfection. A few times they came near Miss Whiting and Francis, who were enjoying another number together. By the smile on her brother's face, she wondered if he had taken a shining to her. A bold move on his part, but they would soon both be back home, and these brief flirtatious moments for everyone would fade into obscurity.

As the dance ended, Beth wandered toward the balcony door to inhale a breath of fresh air. A few other attendees were doing the same thing as the room grew warm.

"Do you mind me asking what His Lordship spoke to you about?" Alexander inquired.

Beth lifted her eyes and noted Alexander's concerned frown. "Nothing of consequence, but he mentioned he wanted to speak with me about something."

"About what?" Alexander pressed.

"I have no idea because Miss Whiting and my brother interrupted the conversation before he could speak of it." Beth thought for a moment. "It must not be crucial since he did not pursue the matter."

"Oh, he will pursue it if it is important to him," Alexander snidely remarked.

Beth looked at him and scowled. "You sound as if you dislike Lord Howard by the tone of your voice. Why is that?"

Alexander did not reply. Instead, Francis and Miss Whiting wandered over, imposing themselves upon the conversation. Bothered by the lingering mystery, Beth decided to ask Miss Whiting.

"Might I ask you a question?" Fully aware her course of action was impertinent on her part, she proceeded without an air of caution.

"Why yes, of course," Miss Whiting answered, taking a step closer.

"Your uncle indicated that he had something to speak to me about, but the opportunity did not present itself. Do you know what might be on his mind?"

Miss Whiting lowered her eyes for a moment as if the inquiry embarrassed her. After heaving a sigh, she regained her composure.

"He would like to ask you to stay here in Aycliffe, live at Rosemont Park, and be my companion until he finds a suitable match for me."

Francis's eyes widened as he sputtered without hesitancy. "I am afraid that is out of the question."

Shocked at the declaration, Beth didn't quite know to react. Alexander, nonetheless, made known his thoughts on the matter.

"Frankly, it is a grand idea."

Francis spun his head around and scowled at Alexander. "You only assume that because you wish to court my sister." His nostrils flared. "I am not ignorant of your motives."

Beth's mouth gaped open at her brother's insolent remark.

"What motives?" Alexander shot back, clenching his jaw in anger.

Aghast that the two sparred in public, Beth sternly interjected, "Gentlemen, stop this now before you make a scene." She glowered at them, shifting her eyes to each.

"Neither of you have a say in the matter as far as I am concerned. I am old enough to decide myself."

"I disagree," Francis remarked. "You are my responsibility, and I won't leave you behind in Aycliffe and return home without you."

"You are smothering her," Alexander rebuked Francis. "Let her be her own woman."

"I beg your pardon?" Francis took an aggressive step toward Alexander, who refused to flinch at the intimidation.

Miss Whiting wrapped her arm around Beth as if to shield her from the onslaught of domineering male behavior.

"I judge we need to take a stroll together to defuse the situation. Don't you agree?"

"Wholeheartedly," Beth said. Following Miss Whiting's lead, they walked away, leaving Alexander and Francis behind to make fools of themselves. The temptation to accept the invitation churned in Beth's brain with each step they took. Living at a grand estate such as Rosemont Park would be glorious, but she barely knew Miss Whiting or Lord Howard. On the surface, they seemed good-natured enough, presenting no thought for concern.

"Do you want a companion, Miss Whiting?" Beth asked as they continued to stroll the ballroom in circles.

"Oh, do call me Annie when we are alone," she insisted. "And I shall call you Beth if you don't mind."

"I have no objection."

"Well then, to be honest, it would be convenient to have another lady my age to converse with. I am afraid that my uncle doesn't understand me very well or my female emotions, for that matter. Uncle often travels and leaves me here to fend for myself."

"Well, that is inconsiderate," Beth remarked. "Why

does he behave that way?"

"It's just his nature. He prefers to be alone."

"I admit that I find him mysterious," Beth said.

"Oh, there is nothing mysterious about him, I assure you. He does very well in displaying his emotions more than he ought."

"Well, you must be of great comfort to him since he has no wife or children of his own." Beth assumed that to be the partial reason behind his character traits.

"He also fills a need in my life since my parents are dead. My mother was his sister, and I am an only child. My father died when I was only ten years of age. When Mother passed, Uncle took me in to care for me. It was the best for us both as we filled the void in each other's life."

Annie took a few more steps, and Beth reflected upon her situation. The death of her mother and father had left a void in her life. Francis had taken on far too much responsibility to run the family business. Now he acted as if he had some parental responsibility where she was concerned. She was of age and able to make her own way in life. His constant oversight was getting on her nerves. Perhaps staying at Rosemont Park would be a delight and relieve him of worries.

"You know, I will speak to Francis about it," Beth said. "I am inclined to accept but will wait until your uncle asks me himself."

"Shall I prod him?" Annie halted in her step, seeing the earl close by.

"No, let him ask me on his own accord." Beth caught his eye, and he nodded at her and smiled. A few moments later, Francis arrived at her side with Alexander.

"Have the two of you calmed down?" Beth asked.

"I would like to waltz with my sister," Francis

proclaimed.

"And you?" Beth asked, looking at Alexander.

"Miss Whiting, may I have the pleasure of this next dance?"

"Why Mr. Davenport, I thought you would never ask."

Beth considered Annie's reply to be slightly flirtatious in nature, and it pricked her heart with a seed of jealousy. Surprised by her reaction, she noticed Mr. and Mrs. Davenport standing nearby. They took quick note of them on the dance floor, smiling approvingly. Beth surmised they had plans for Alexander as, no doubt, Miss Whiting would be the sole heir to Lord Howard's fortune. Francis grabbed her hand.

"Are we dancing or not?"

"Don't step on my foot," Beth warned.

"I shall endeavor to keep away from your toes."

They waltzed, and Beth watched as Alexander and Annie spun past them, smiling at one another.

"What is it?" Francis inquired, noting her sour facial expression.

"I think the Davenports are hoping Alexander will court Miss Whiting."

Francis glanced at the two swirling by. "Makes sense if they want him to marry for money."

"But is it right? Why can he not marry for love?" Beth moaned.

"Do you believe he loves you?" Francis asked in a tone of irritation.

Beth looked at her brother directly in the eye. "I have no idea, and I do not love him if that is what you are worried about." Although she questioned her emotional response a few moments ago that showed affections had seeded in her heart.

"Good, because next week we leave for Dunwich,

and that will be the end," he reminded her in a stern tone.

Would that be the end of it? Beth didn't want to return home with Francis. She wanted to stay at Rosemont Park. It might allow her to discover secrets about her mother. On the other hand, she might even fall in love. With those thoughts in mind, she determined to take the offer seriously should Lord Howard ask her to stay.

CHAPTER SEVENTEEN

A Snake in the Grass

Celia wandered around the ballroom, refusing to stand along the sidelines like a wallflower. As far as she knew, her dress accentuated her attractiveness, but no one seemed to notice. Throughout the evening, she had desperately attempted to keep her eye upon Edwin, not looking as downhearted as she felt. He appeared to be having a splendid time dancing with a variety of women, but he failed to ask her as promised. In fact, everybody in the grand hall appeared to be enjoying themselves, waltzing with smiles on their face.

Two men asked her to dance, no doubt because they were sorry for her, standing by her parents looking desperate. Francis gave her a quick whirl out of pity, but that was the end of their short attachment. Lord Howard obviously enjoyed Beth immensely, as he could not keep his eyes off her the entire evening. Alexander had done his best to impress Beth too, and she saw the spark of interest in his eyes. All the attention Beth received irked her, adding to her irritability.

She was about to plop herself on a chair somewhere and sulk when Miss Whiting and Beth came walking past her, arm in arm like bosom friends. They nearly passed by without a word before she took a step directly in front of them. Her abrupt move caused them to halt, wide-eyed with surprise.

"What are you ladies up to?" Celia hid her underlying frustration with a sweet tone.

"Just taking a turn around the room," Beth remarked.

Apparently more sensitive than Celia gave her credit, Beth looked at her kindly with a hint of sympathy in her voice.

"Would you care to join us? Miss Whiting was about to show me a few of the rooms at the estate so we could get a breath of fresh air."

Ecstatic by the opportunity, Celia replied. "Thank you. I would like to join you if Miss Whiting doesn't mind." She judged it only polite to ask.

"I don't mind a bit," Miss Whiting replied. "I'm sure the menfolk will wonder where we have disappeared to in the crowd. Frankly, I think it would do them good to worry about it. Don't you agree, Beth?"

"Wholeheartedly."

"What menfolk?" Celia asked, looking puzzled.

"Alexander Davenport and my brother were having a tiff earlier," Beth announced, obviously miffed by their behavior. "I would rather not go into details. Needless to say, it proved embarrassing." They took a few more steps and wandered down a long hallway. "And what about you? Are you enjoying the evening?"

Celia's stomach muscles tensed from anxiety. No, she was not enjoying the evening but wondered if she should be honest about her disappointment. After heaving a sigh, she lied. "Oh yes, it's a wonderful ball, although I haven't danced as much as I would have liked."

"I am sorry to hear that," Miss Whiting remarked. "There are some men who just do not understand how to behave at social gatherings and dance far too much with the same woman."

"You are right," Beth agreed. "However, I am guilty of dancing far too many times with Mr. Davenport. I told him to ask other women like a gentleman should."

As they took a few more steps, Miss Whiting stopped at tall double doors. "Would you like to see the library? It is one of the finest rooms in the estate and boasts of many books you are welcome to read."

"I would love to," Beth remarked.

Celia held her tongue, not caring one way or the other if they went to the library or the servants' quarters. She just wanted to pass the time and not ruminate about how miserable she felt.

Miss Whiting pushed open the double doors and led them into an enormous room lined with shelves of books from the floor to the ceiling. The interior was dimly lit with a few candles, and it took a moment for her eyes to adjust to the surroundings. There were tables where one could sit and read. Single chairs were placed by the windows, and a large brown leather davenport sat in the middle of the library, the back of which was toward them. No sooner had the three entered when they heard moans and halted their step. Celia stood rigid at the familiar sound.

"Who is there?" Miss Whiting demanded in a gruff voice. "Show yourself."

A second later, Edwin's head popped up, and a woman rose from underneath him. Celia froze in horror and shrieked aloud.

"Good God, Edwin, what are you doing?"

He jumped to his feet, and a young lady did too, whom Celia did not recognize. She adjusted her dress, rearranged loose strands of hair into place, and stood next to Edwin. A blush burst upon her cheeks. Celia's eyes noticed Edwin's undone pants. A spear of betrayal stuck in her heart, knowing full well exactly what he had lodged in the other woman.

"Mr. Davenport," Miss Whiting wailed in disdain. "This room is my uncle's private library. How dare you trespass and perform such lewd acts!"

Beth, obviously unable to control her tongue, jumped into the conversation. "I think it's apparent what he is doing here," she coldly announced. "He is ruining the reputation of another woman without an ounce of remorse."

Edwin's eyes shifted over to Celia, and she noted the terrible truth behind his unrepentant gaze. Realizing what he had done, she choked out the words, "Once a snake, always a snake. Edwin Davenport, I hate you!"

Without forethought, Celia strode toward him and slapped him hard across the face. She had hit him with all her might, but he did not flinch. Instead, the woman who stood next to him came to his rescue with outrage in her eyes.

"How dare you hit my future fiancé," she sneered.

"Your—your what?" Celia sputtered, unable to believe the declaration.

"You heard me. Mr. Davenport, and I are soon to announce our engagement."

Celia's body trembled with rage. "He promised to marry me, not you—you hussy!"

"Whatever do you mean?" The lady glowered at Edwin with eyes that demanded an answer.

"Oh dear," Miss Whiting remarked. "Should we leave these three alone, or would you rather stay and look at the books?" she asked Beth, stifling a giggle.

"I would rather stay and support Celia and perhaps peruse a few titles later on for more entertainment." Beth smirked at Edwin. "Mr. Davenport, what do you have to say for yourself?"

Edwin swallowed hard, and Celia's anger grew as he refused to look her in the eyes. Then to her deep pain, he reached out his hand and grabbed that of the unknown woman at his side.

"It is true. Lady Ellen and I are to be married," Edwin admitted. "Father has approved our match, and a formal announcement is forthcoming in a few days."

"There, I told you!"

Celia bore a hateful stare at Edwin and spoke with a trembling voice. "You are a ruthless rake who nearly seduced me, and now you toss me away as if I am nothing!" She looked at the woman at his side. "And you, Lady Whoever You Are, you are no lady to let him take you. You will be next on his long list of conquests, thrown aside like fish guts!" It sounded repugnant but got her point across.

Unable to control the searing anger coursing through her veins, Celia clutched her fists together like two hard rocks, stepped forward, and pounded Edwin repeatedly on his chest. Edwin turned his head as if she were about to hit him in the face, receiving multiple blows before he attempted to step out of her reach. He ran around the other side of the davenport, and Celia followed like a madwoman with flaying arms.

"Do something!" Lady Ellen screamed.

Celia heard Beth and Miss Whiting laugh aloud. "Do something? The man deserves every blow and much more," Beth uttered.

As Edwin backed into a table and knocked over a tall vase, the crash reverberated throughout the room. Shards of porcelain flew everywhere. A moment later, Lord Howard stormed into the library with flaring nostrils, demanding answers.

"What is going on here!" With one quick swoop, he

gathered Celia in his arms from behind and stopped her advancing attack against Edwin. His grip was too tight for Celia to break, although she gave a rather impressive attempt to wiggle her way out of it, kicking her feet as he lifted her up from the floor.

"He almost ruined me, and I am going to kill him!"

"Not in my library," Lord Howard declared. He shot a glaring glance at Edwin. "What is going on here?"

His niece offered an explanation. "I was showing Beth and Celia the library when we came upon Mr. Davenport and Lady Ellen in a compromising position on the davenport. It appears that they were—"

"I understand," he interrupted. Lord Howard glared at Lady Ellen. "And what do you have to say for yourself, young lady?"

"I humbly beg your pardon, Your Lordship," she entreated with flushed cheeks.

"Do you now?" He looked at her with distaste and shifted his glare to Edwin. "I suggest, young man, that you and your lady friend remove yourself from this room immediately. You can be assured that I will be having a stern word with your father regarding this incident."

Upon hearing that the earl decided to speak to the elder Mr. Davenport about Edwin's behavior, Celia fell limp in Lord Howard's arms. With one swoon from weak legs, she found herself unable to stand any longer. The hurt and anger coursing through her veins had drained all strength from her body. Instead, unabashed tears streamed down her cheeks.

"How could he do this to me?" she blubbered.

Edwin did not answer, but in a quick step left the room with Lady Ellen in hand.

The earl carried Celia to a chair and set her down. Thankfully, he did not lay her upon the davenport where Edwin had been caught up the skirts of another woman.

"Now calm yourself, Miss Wilson," he entreated.

Celia brought her hands to her face and covered it with shame.

"Beth and Annie, would you mind tending to her while I take care of business at hand?" Lord Howard asked.

A flood of panic rushed through Celia's heart. "Oh please, do not tell my parents that Edwin has ruined my reputation! I beg you to spare me the disgrace."

"I will say nothing to your parents. However, I believe you should be frank with them about your situation so they may do what is necessary to protect your name."

"We will watch over her," Beth offered.

"Thank you."

Lord Howard departed the library, and Celia broke down into uncontrollable sobs. Beth and Annie came to her side, bending down and giving her a hug.

"I am so very sorry," Beth said. "I feared this would happen."

Afraid that Beth would start with demeaning platitudes about having no one to blame but herself, Celia pulled away. Embarrassed, frustrated, and unable to face anyone after what she had just witnessed, she lost control of her emotions.

"Do not look at me with such condescension," she ranted. "You have judged me harshly ever since you discovered me with Edwin."

"Celia," Beth tried to cajole her, but she would have none of it.

"I heard rumors they caught your mother in a compromising position with another man. That is why she left Aycliffe, so don't judge me," Celia shouted, taking the attention off her misguided judgment.

"My mother has nothing to do with your mistakes with Edwin," Beth said, standing erect and hovering over Celia. "As far as I'm concerned, you are spewing hateful lies about others to take the focus off yourself."

Perhaps that was precisely what she was doing. Anything was better than admitting what she had blindly done with Edwin.

"I hate you both," Celia spat.

She pushed past the two and ran out the door of the library, gasping for air. She didn't know where she was going or where her feet would take her next. All she knew is that she didn't wish to go back to the ballroom to face anyone—especially not her parents or Edwin. After seeing the front entrance, Celia ran out of doors and disappeared into the shadows of the night.

CHAPTER EIGHTEEN

The Aftermath

Once again Celia had thrown a fiery dart, accusing Beth's mother of hideous things. By the time Celia had left the library, Beth's heart pounded in her chest with such fury that she grabbed a nearby chair and sat down. Afraid that another attack would ensue, Beth attempted to calm herself. Annie had not noticed her state because she busied herself cleaning up the stand knocked over by Edwin. The vase was a total disaster, shattered on the floor with pieces strewn across the hardwood floor and onto the nearby carpeting.

"What a shame," Miss Whiting moaned. "It was such a marvelous piece." She swung around and saw Beth's ashen countenance. "Oh dear. Are you all right?"

Beth didn't reply but inhaled a deep breath to calm her nerves. Annie walked over and put her hand on Beth's shoulder.

"It's the horridly cruel statement that Celia flung about your mother that has upset you, isn't it?"

Beth could not deny her astute observation. "I will be honest that I am tired of the innuendos thrown about regarding my mother. Ever since I arrived with my brother, people have spoken either accolades or ill will."

Annie sat down next to Beth and grabbed her hand. "I confess that I know nothing about her."

Beth glanced at the library door and saw Francis

arrive with a flustered countenance.

"Are you all right?" he asked, approaching Beth with a quick step.

"Yes, yes, I'm fine." Beth rose to her feet.

"Have you seen Celia?"

Miss Whiting answered. "No. She left here in a rather upset state of mind, I'm afraid."

"Mrs. Wilson is complaining of a painful headache and wants to leave. Why has Celia run off?"

"Miss Whiting, myself, and Celia walked into the library and discovered Edwin up the skirts with another young lady."

"Goodness," Francis exclaimed. "He is a blackguard of the wickedest sort."

"Someone by the name of Lady Ellen also declared their impending engagement," Beth added.

"I am afraid that Celia did not take it very well. My uncle caught her in the act of practically beating the poor chap to death." Miss Whiting barely hid the smirk on her face, and Beth found it amusing. "As you can see, she ran Edwin into a rather fine vase which toppled to the floor."

"Then do you know where she has run off to?" Francis asked, not amused by the news.

"I have no idea," Beth answered. "She just darted out of the library."

"Rather distraught, I would add," Miss Whiting interjected.

"Well, help me find her, will you? The Wilsons are eager to leave." Francis headed for the doorway, and they followed.

"Has anyone bothered to ask one of the footmen if they have seen her?" Beth inquired. "She may have run outdoors for a breath of fresh air." After seeing a slight panic in her brother's eyes, Beth wondered why he bothered to care what happened to Celia. Perhaps he felt sorry for her, which frankly eluded Beth's emotions.

"You check indoors," he barked like a general giving orders, "and I'll check outdoors."

As he ran off, Miss Whiting gawked at his quick departure. "He appears to be overly concerned about her welfare."

"I noticed. We better look as well."

They wandered back to the ballroom, surprised to see that the remainder of the guests continued to dance as if nothing appeared amiss. The Davenports were nowhere in sight, but Beth caught the worried glances of Mr. and Mrs. Wilson and made her way to their side.

"Oh, dear Beth," Mrs. Wilson said, grabbing her hand. "Have you seen our Celia anywhere? I am so sorry to cut the evening short, but I have a violent headache from this stuffy room and loud music."

"We were with her earlier, but she appears to have disappeared. Francis is looking, and I'm sure he will find her soon."

"That girl is always wandering off somewhere," Mr. Wilson remarked. His eyes continued to scan the ballroom. "I swear I'm going to put her on a tether."

"Mr. Wilson, how uncivilized to suggest such a thing," she scolded.

He shook his head. "This evening has been rather odd if I do say so. Why, did you see how the Davenports suddenly upped and left after His Lordship spoke to them? I wonder what that could be about."

"One never knows," Miss Whiting remarked, attempting to make light of it. "Sometimes my uncle gets started on political conversations that rile the feathers of his best friends. It can be rather off-putting."

Beth appreciated that Annie had made light of the situation. "Well, we will look around for Celia," Beth announced. "Perhaps she went outdoors for air. Francis is checking."

"Good lad," Mr. Wilson remarked, appearing somewhat relieved.

To Francis's dismay, a footman confirmed that Celia had sprinted out the front entrance and into the dead of night. He mentioned that her loud sobbing had lifted the heads of a few horses in the lengthy line of waiting carriages and nodded in the general direction of Celia's footsteps. Francis followed the path blindly into the vast grounds of Rosemont Park. Thankfully, though not a full moon, enough of the celestial object shone on a cloudless night to illuminate his path. The farther his footsteps took him, the closer he came to a line of trees that jutted into a wooded area, making it challenging to see.

"Celia!"

He called her name, hoping that she would respond but heard nothing. The more he walked, the angrier he became at Edwin. If he ever saw the scoundrel again, he would undoubtedly strike him in the jaw and send him flying for his insolence. He had nearly ruined poor Celia and apparently another foolish woman. Whether he was genuinely engaged to this Lady Ellen was another matter. Regardless, his evil guise of confessing his love for Celia was unforgivable.

"Celia!"

He called again but received no response. Turning around, he realized that the giant facade of Rosemont Park diminished into the night. His footsteps led him to the tree line, and he halted, yelling her name again.

"Celia, it's Francis. Answer me!"

An owl hooted in response, and then an eerie silence followed. When Francis caught the sound of a twig snapping, he turned his attention to the left. He followed the sound and came upon Celia lying on the ground. She had pulled her legs up into a fetal position and softly sobbed into the grass as if she were muffling her shame.

"Thank heavens," Francis groaned. "I was worried about you."

"Leave me alone," she begged. "I just want to lay here and cry all night long and let nature take me to the grave. There is nothing to live for now."

Moved by her sorrowful state, Francis knelt by her side but refrained from touching her. "All is not lost, Celia," he said, attempting to encourage her. "Will you let me take you back to the estate? Your parents are worried and wish to leave for home."

Celia shot upright. "Leave for home? Do they know about Edwin?"

"No. Your mother has a headache."

"Are you sure?" Celia reached out and grabbed his forearm, giving it a tight squeeze.

"As far as I am aware, nothing has been said. The Davenports have left Rosemont, so you need not worry about facing them upon your return."

"Good, because I do not wish to look upon Edwin's face ever again," she said, sticking out her lower lip like a child.

Francis shook his head. He really liked Celia for some odd reason, and it was quite a shame that she had not the sense to keep herself from a scoundrel like Edwin. The man had used her without scruple, and Francis hoped that she could find redemption despite having discovered her in an uncompromising position.

"Come, let me get you back to the estate before they release the hounds to find us." He offered his hand, and with a weak grasp, Francis hoisted her up to her feet. She brushed off her dress, which now bore stains of grass and dirt. With her hair in disarray and her clothing soiled, he knew her parents would surely question where she had been. A small twig clung to her hair, and he gently pulled it away.

"I'm afraid, Celia, you are quite the sight," he grinned. "What shall we tell your parents?"

"Oh dear." She touched her stray and dangling curls. After noticing the state of her gown, she moaned. "Father shall be so cross with me for spoiling this dress."

After reflecting for a moment, Francis offered a solution. "I suppose you could say that you needed a breath of fresh air, took a walk, and tripped and fell off the garden path. Perhaps clumsiness on your part might hide the reasons behind your disappearance."

Celia looked into Francis's eyes and fluttered her lashes as if she noticed him for the first time since he arrived in Aycliffe. It was a surprising gesture.

"You are very kind despite my poor behavior," she remarked solemnly.

"I am behaving no different than any gentleman should." He offered his arm. "Now, please let me escort you back to your parents. I'm sure your mother is yearning to go home and nurse her headache."

They slowly made their return, finding the Wilsons anxiously standing in the foyer. As they entered, Mrs. Wilson caught sight of her daughter and squealed.

"Celia! Where have you been?" After eyeing her appearance up and down, her father made his displeasure known.

"You look a fright, and that fine gown is ruined! What have you been up to?"

Celia trembled, so Francis dropped her arm and waited for her response. He could tell by the quivering of her lower lip that there were no words to describe how she really felt. No doubt the shock of discovering Edwin with another woman loomed in her mind rather than coming up with an excuse about her soiled appearance.

"If I may be so bold as to answer for your daughter, sir. It appears that she came outdoors for a breath of fresh air, and as she was walking in the garden, she tripped and fell."

"Yes," Celia's voice quivered. "I tripped and fell."

"Oh, this does my headache no further good," Mrs. Wilson moaned. "I need to go home and lie down. All this excitement tonight has been too much for my nerves."

As they were about to leave, Lord Howard approached along with Miss Whiting. "I hope you are better, Mrs. Wilson," he remarked. "I see you have found your daughter." He glanced at her disarray but said nothing.

"Your Lordship, I apologize that we are leaving this fine ball so early," Mr. Wilson remarked. "I hope you can forgive us."

"Nothing to forgive," he said, smiling warmly. "Take your wife home and tend to her. I'm sure we will have other occasions to see each other again."

Surprisingly, he took a step toward Francis. "It was good of you to come."

"Thank you."

"And you, young lady. I am afraid that I still have a question to ask of you, but that can wait until another time." He took Beth's hand and gave it a quick kiss. "Until then."

"Of course. Another time." Beth glanced at Miss

Whiting.

"Goodbye," Miss Whiting said. "I so enjoyed our time together."

"I did as well," Beth replied. "It was an entertaining evening."

"Are we ready?" Mr. Wilson prodded everyone to move along as Mrs. Wilson stood at the door, yearning to leave.

Francis was more than ready to depart, and the notion of returning to a peaceful life in Dunwich brought comfort.

CHAPTER NINETEEN

The View from on High

Francis sat at the dining room table, occasionally glancing at Celia while nibbling on a piece of toast. Her usual exuberant personality lay shrouded by the grief she nursed inwardly. As much as her behavior had disgusted him, he could not help the empathy stirring in his heart. After glancing at the Wilsons, who appeared subdued, and his sister, who barely spoke a word, the morning had turned into an oddity of stifled emotions. It should have been a lovely evening for everyone who attended.

"Mrs. Wilson, I trust your headache is gone?" he asked.

"Thankfully, yes, but I do feel as if my brain is in a fog this morning and am tempted to go back to bed." After making the remark, she yawned. "Oh dear. Excuse me."

Francis glanced over at Mr. Wilson, who had picked up the morning newspaper and hid behind the front page.

"Anything of interest in the news?" Francis inquired, trying to start a conversation.

Beth glanced at him as if she wondered why he was poking at everyone. Mr. Wilson peeked over the top.

"Huh, a bare-knuckle boxing match. James McGinty from Glasgow won after seventy-one rounds. Good

Lord, what a fight." He grinned. "I would have enjoyed watching that athletic feat."

"Feat?" Mrs. Wilson squawked. "How can you call it a civilized athletic event? My word, Mr. Wilson, two men beating each other to death with bloodied fists?"

"Well, I don't know," Celia remarked, lifting her head and glaring at everyone at the table. "There are times I would like to bare my knuckles and hit someone!"

Obviously unable to hold her anger in any longer, she shoved her chair back, threw her napkin on the table, and stormed out of the room.

"My word. What has her in such a tizzy?" Mr. Wilson frowned as Celia stomped in the other direction. "Did some young man spurn her at the ball?"

"Mr. Wilson, she is at a delicate age and no closer to finding a husband. Do be kind and understanding," his wife said.

"If you would like, I will talk with her," Beth offered.

"Would you?" Mrs. Wilson asked. "Very kind of you to offer."

"Of course. My pleasure." Beth took a sip of tea and, after setting her cup down on the saucer, glanced at Francis. "Let me befriend her."

Her glare told him to stay put, and he nodded in agreement. When she left the room, he took advantage of his time alone with the Wilsons to steer the conversation elsewhere.

"Might I speak about something in confidence with you?" The Wilsons gave him their attention. "I need your advice."

"Of course. Happy to oblige," Mr. Wilson stated, folding the paper.

"It has come to my attention that Lord Howard has it in his mind to ask Beth to stay in Aycliffe and be a companion to Miss Whiting. He means to have her live at Rosemont Park." Francis noted both sets of eyes widen at the announcement. After a quick glance between the two, he continued. "Beth is considering the proposition, but as her elder brother, I have my concerns. Naturally, I take it upon myself to watch over her until she is wed. Then that responsibility will fall to her husband."

"Oh my," Mrs. Wilson said, revealing a trace of alarm in her tone. "Well, as I mentioned before, Mr. Wilson and I think it would be a fine idea for you both to remain a bit longer at Aycliffe."

"Yes, of course," Mr. Wilson chimed in. "However, I'm not sure that staying at Rosemont is the answer. You are welcome to stay here with Beth as long as you wish."

"I cannot stay," Francis reiterated in frustration, shaking his head. "There is the business that I must attend to and other matters at home. I cannot uproot and abandon my life in Dunwich." After hearing the rather sharp tone of his voice, Francis could tell he had offended the Wilsons by the dismay on their faces. "I— I apologize," he stammered. "As you can tell, I am frustrated and fear that Beth will accept this invitation whether or not I agree to it."

"Well, she barely knows Miss Whiting, although I have no objection to the young lady as a whole," Mrs. Wilson remarked. "Perhaps they won't get on, and Beth will change her mind."

"I can only hope," Francis admitted.

"It might not look proper either for Beth to live at Rosemont Park with Lord Howard in residence. I daresay that would give me cause for concern if I were her mother," Mrs. Wilson remarked. "I doubt Catherine would approve if she were still alive."

"Well, he means to travel while Beth is there.

Nonetheless, I fear others have motives with my sister," Francis admitted, scowling.

"Who would that be?" Mr. Wilson asked.

"Alexander Davenport pays far too much attention to her and is eager for her to remain."

"Oh, I wouldn't put much stock into his interest," Mr. Wilson replied, as if the matter were nothing to fret about. "He's a young man, but his father wants him to marry money."

"Like Edwin, so I hear," Francis mumbled. As soon as the comment left his mouth, he regretted a slip of the tongue but pursued the thought.

"They are an upper-middle-class family, which has standards like any other," Mr. Wilson defended. "Why, I even have standards for Celia as to whom she should wed."

Mrs. Wilson sighed. "Oh, how I wish Celia could meet a nice man and settle down. I do so worry about the girl. We are far too lax with her altogether, allowing her to leave home without a proper chaperone. Her flitting about town by herself harms her reputation."

"I've told her time and time again that the practice is questionable, even if she is four and twenty years of age," Mr. Wilson said, flaring at the nostrils. "I swear if she ever gets herself in trouble, I shall send her to a nunnery in France."

"Oh, Mr. Wilson, don't even suggest such a thing," Mrs. Wilson groaned.

Francis had unknowingly stirred a bee's nest with his question and regretted bringing Celia under scrutiny. He wondered if the Wilsons would disapprove of his interest in their daughter, judging him socially unacceptable. Suddenly, the insinuation of being judged as undesirable caused him to push back his chair, rise, and excuse himself in a tiff.

"I beg your pardon, but I wish to check on my sister," he announced. Rather than wait for an answer, he turned heel and headed out the double doors. He heard the Wilsons speak to one another but could not catch their words. No doubt they wondered about his abrupt departure.

He found Celia and Beth together in the parlor, sitting next to one another. They both appeared calm in demeanor, as Celia's hands rest in her lap. Beth had placed her right hand on Celia's forearm, he surmised as a means of comfort.

"I trust things are going well." He entered the room and halted in front of them. "Do you mind the interruption?"

"Not at all," Beth replied.

"You know, it's a pleasant morning. Shall we all go for a walk on the cliffs? I would love to relish the view from up on high."

"That sounds delightful. Celia, what do you think?" Beth squeezed her hand for encouragement.

She lifted her eyes to Francis and forced a slight grin. "Yes, perhaps a breath of fresh air would do me good."

As they congregated in the foyer together, Mr. Wilson came out of the dining room. "We are off for a walk on the cliffs," Francis announced.

"Well, it's a splendid day." Her father looked at Celia with a frown of concern. "Just be careful you don't walk too close to the edge. It's a long drop to the craggy rocks below."

"We will be careful," Celia said, assuring him in a firm voice.

After grabbing hats, bonnets, and shawls for the ladies, the three left for their destination. Barely a word exchanged as they traversed their way through town and headed up the path that hugged the cliffs of the shore. A gusty breeze spun around them like a whirlwind, making it hard for Francis to keep his hat from blowing off his head.

"Blustery, to say the least," he remarked. The ladies' frocks, ribbons, and shawls twirled from the wind.

"Indeed, it is." Beth agreed, chortling a laugh.

"You must be used to this, Miss Wilson," Francis said, hoping to draw Celia into a conversation and erase the morose look on her face.

"Yes, sometimes it could actually blow one off the cliff if the gale is powerful enough." She glanced over the edge.

Concerned by the cynical comment, Francis came to her side and offered his arm. "Here then, you better let me walk cliff side while you take my arm on the other. I shall not see you blown away. You are far too pretty to be lost at sea."

"Well then, I shall take Celia's other arm," Beth announced, "so I won't blow away."

The three of them walked arm in arm, enjoying the scenery of the dark blue ocean. Francis heard the pounding waves on the rocks below and enjoyed the various fowl circle overhead. After spotting a hawk riding the air current above, he halted and pointed upward. "Look at that fine bird. What a view he must enjoy. If only men could fly," he remarked, wishing for wings.

"He's probably looking for a field mouse to eat," Beth said. "Or some other poor critter."

"I did not realize you were such a dreamer, Mr. Edwards," Celia remarked.

"Yes, somewhat, but I never have much time to dream about anything except keeping time. It appears my focus is always on the passing second of one's life rather than being able to savor the moment for any length as I do now."

"Then you should stay in Aycliffe and enjoy it much longer," Celia suggested.

"I am considering staying," Beth admitted.

"Whatever do you mean?" Celia spun her head at the remark.

"Apparently, Lord Howard wants to ask me to stay and be Miss Whiting's companion."

"You mean to live at Rosemont Park?" Celia pulled everyone to a halt and turned toward Beth.

"I see you do not care for that idea," Beth remarked.

"Nor do I," Francis added, making his thoughts known.

Beth scowled at Celia. "Before I decide, I want you to tell me the truth about my mother and the horrible things you have been insinuating."

Shocked that Beth brought up the subject, Francis interjected, "This is neither the time nor the place to speak of it."

"We are alone," Beth vehemently objected. "It's the perfect time and place."

Celia's facial expression changed to one of mortification. She dropped her arm from Francis and took a step back.

"I only know rumors about your mother," she replied, lowering her eyes. "I said those horrible things to you to hurt you. That is all."

"What rumors?" Francis pressed. Celia remained silent, glancing back and forth at them. She bit her lower lip as if she were keeping the words locked away.

"Well," Beth insisted. "What rumors?"

"That your mother had an affair with Lord Howard," she blurted. Celia wrung her hands together.

"The younger or elder?" Beth asked, scowling.

"The former earl."

"I don't believe a word of it," Francis said, shooing away the idea with a flick of his hand.

Beth scowled at the thought. "I am so sickened by all these statements and shrouded comments about Mother that I'm ready to scream."

As the three of them stood there together, a carriage approached down the cliff-side trail. Stepping out of the way of the oncoming horses, Celia groaned.

"Oh my. Speak of the devil, it's Lord Howard's carriage."

"How can you tell?" Beth asked.

"By the crest on the door. And look, it's slowing."

Francis watched as it came to a stop, and it was Lord Howard and Miss Whiting traveling away from Aycliffe.

"Out for a healthy walk?" he asked, opening the carriage door.

Francis stepped back, and His Lordship exited. His niece remained inside but poked her head out, smiling.

"Hello! Beautiful day, isn't it?"

Beth answered. "Yes, indeed. We are taking in the scenery and fresh air."

"Annie and I are off to visit friends for the night but will be back on the morrow." Lord Howard glanced at the three of them and then turned his attention to Beth. "If you don't mind, Miss Edwards, I would like to invite you to tea again."

"Oh, do come," Annie pleaded with a bright sparkle in her eye.

"And you, Mr. Edwards, are welcome too," Lord Howard added.

"We would be pleased to join you for tea," Beth answered.

His Lordship glanced over at Celia and stepped forward, taking both her hands in his. "You appear much better today. Please forgive me for being gruff with you last evening. I did not intend to harm you."

"You did not hurt me. Perhaps it turned out to be a good thing that you hindered me from doing more bodily damage to Mr. Davenport. I believe that I could have committed murder," she chuckled.

"Yes, Mr. Davenport. I gave his father an earful about his uncomely behavior in the library. I'm afraid he took offense. Nevertheless, I kept my promise not to mention the incident to your parents." He dropped Celia's hand.

"Thank you. I am very appreciative."

"You know, if it is true that Mr. Davenport has done what you say, I could make a ruckus that he should marry you. As far as I'm concerned, a man who takes advantage of a lady should pay for his misdeeds."

Celia inhaled a sharp breath of alarm. "That is very kind of you, Your Lordship, but I fear I do not wish to marry the blackguard. Should I make him pay for his misdeeds, it would only make me miserable. Some other lady can deal with his deceitful ways, but I shan't."

"Then you are a wise woman," he remarked. He turned to Beth. "Well, I hope to see you tomorrow at three o'clock. And Miss Wilson, please join as well."

The earl climbed back into the carriage, tipped his hat, and then banged on the roof, signaling the driver to leave.

Francis watched the carriage as it pulled off into the distance, pondering the man's motives for what would surely be an invitation to be Miss Whiting's companion. "I don't like it," he muttered.

Beth instantly objected. "I think he is very kind to us, and I am still inclined to accept his invitation."

"But Beth," Francis moaned. "There are a thousand reasons for you not to stay in Aycliffe. What about the household in Dunwich?"

"Oh, the household?" Beth pulled her mouth to one side. "Hire a maid and cook for goodness' sake. You can afford the expense. I need not remain tied to our parents' home to clean and cook as if I'm your wife." She put her hands on her hips and snarled. "Better yet, why don't you find yourself a wife to run the household and settle down while I pursue my interests?"

"Brother-and-sister spats." Celia snorted a giggle, obviously entertained. "I have never had the chance to spar with an overcontrolling brother."

"If you would just do what I say," Francis grumbled. "Honestly, you frustrate me to no end."

"Well, you must admit, Mr. Edwards, that your sister has the right to her own mind. She is of age," Celia remarked, coming to Beth's defense.

Francis stomped down the pathway ahead of them, needing a moment to cool down. As he proceeded in a huff, he glanced over his shoulder. "Are you coming?"

Beth and Celia walked arm and arm as if they were both against him. "Women," he muttered under his breath. He heaved another sigh and tried to enjoy the scenery, pondering how he could talk Beth out of this infernal idea to remain behind.

CHAPTER TWENTY

The Arrangement

Beth had spent a better part of the prior evening arguing with Francis about the impending question Lord Howard would ask. At an impasse, she made the decision regardless of her brother's objections. After all, she was of age, and although she appreciated Francis's concern, she needed to live her life. In the end, Francis made no promises that he would not make his objections known once the earl broached the subject. Celia decided not to accept the invitation, wishing to remain a respectable distance while they worked out their disagreements.

As they arrived at the Howard estate, Beth enjoyed the exhilaration of being back at the residence. The grounds were beautiful, and as they exited the carriage, she glanced around.

"Oh look, Francis. I didn't notice before, but you can see the ocean from here," she said, pointing at the horizon.

"Yes, I noticed Rosemont when I was out on the fishing boat. You can see the impressive building from quite some distance." At least the tone of his voice had returned to a civil one.

The two were escorted into the sitting room, where Lord Howard and Miss Whiting waited for their arrival. It didn't take long for Beth to feel smothered in greetings by His Lordship.

"So good of you to come," he said. "Please take a seat and make yourself comfortable."

Beth sat next to Francis on the settee while the earl, thankfully, took a chair next to his niece.

"Miss Wilson decided not to join you?" he inquired.

"No, she decided against it," Beth answered.

"I hope she is not feeling too embarrassed about what happened at the ball," he remarked with concern.

Francis answered, "Candidly, it will all work out for the best now that she knows Mr. Davenport's genuine character."

"I've heard about his personality although I take little stock in the town gossip," Lord Howard admitted. "Young ladies need to be careful, which brings me to the topic I wish to discuss with you."

Miss Whiting sat quietly, as if she had spoken to Lord Howard beforehand, giving him full control over the conversation. Beth wondered if she had told him that she had mentioned his intention. Unsure whether she had, Beth decided not to say anything but demurely act slightly surprised at the suggestion.

"As I have confessed to you before, Miss Edwards, I am rather a recluse of sorts. Since my wife died, I have enjoyed the freedom of bachelorhood and relish coming and going as I please."

Beth glanced at Francis, who listened intently to his confession.

"Society seems to think I should remarry, but I would rather travel instead. I do not do well dealing with disappointment and grief." He paused momentarily and lowered his gaze. "Nor do I wish to seek a replacement for my wife."

"Travel is a worthy pursuit," Francis remarked. "It helps take the mind off unpleasantries."

"My selfish activities, however, leave my niece alone far too often in this large, rambling estate. Although my staff does an excellent job of keeping Annie in comfort and safety during my absence, it leaves her without proper companionship."

Beth witnessed a hopeful glint in Annie's eyes, even though she remained silent while the earl delicately handled the subject.

"Which brings me to you. I would like to know, Miss Edwards, if you would extend your stay at Rosemont Park as my niece's companion. I plan to go to Scotland for a month and do not wish to abandon Annie for an extended period."

"A month?" Beth repeated. A bit surprised he didn't want a long-term commitment brought a sharp pang of disappointment. She had hoped that it would be indefinitely.

"Do say yes." Annie encouraged Beth, speaking her mind.

Francis remained quiet while Beth pondered the invitation. Even though she did not know Annie very well, she had an innate sense that they would be bosom friends if she accepted the offer. It would be an enjoyable experience living at such a grand estate. Her eyes shifted over to Francis, who said nothing. Obviously, he had decided to forgo a stern objection based on the short duration, at least for the moment.

"Francis, it's only for a month," Beth reasoned aloud. "You can return to Dunwich next week for business's sake, and I will return four weeks later. Does that sound agreeable to you?" Everyone looked at Francis.

"I can assure you, Mr. Edwards, that your sister will be safe here at Rosemont. The young ladies will have each other for company while I am in Scotland on business." Lord Howard attempted to allay any fears.

"I might consider agreeing to the arrangement if I know that the Wilsons will check on Beth periodically," Francis remarked.

"Splendid idea," Lord Howard agreed. "Miss Wilson can visit anytime as well."

"Hmm," Francis mused aloud. "Three young women alone in a large estate. Do you think they will get into any mischief?"

"You do have a point," Lord Howard replied, bringing his hand to his chin in a thoughtful gesture. "There should be ground rules, naturally, about entertaining men without a proper chaperone."

"You can be assured," Annie remarked, "Clifford, Uncle's butler, won't allow anyone through the front door he doesn't deem safe. The man is a guard dog."

"Well, the only young man I am acquainted with is Alexander Davenport," Beth advised. "He's somewhat harmless."

Lord Howard frowned. "Harmless, perhaps, but his father seems to think my Annie here would be a good match. The man wants the family inheritance, and I shall not allow him to weasel his way into her heart. Harmless or not."

The staunch pronouncement shocked Beth, and she literally gawked at his harsh remark. He appeared quite irritated at the possibility of Alexander pursuing his niece. A part of her felt as if she needed to defend him in some manner, so she spoke her mind.

"From what I gather, Mr. Davenport has other desires in life. He wishes to travel, much like yourself. He appears more adventurous but perhaps restrained because of his father's expectations."

"He has spoken to you as much?" Lord Howard inquired. "If so, then it makes me think such intimacy on his part regarding his private goals tell me he may be interested in courting you instead."

Beth straightened her spine at his comment. Perhaps Alexander showed interest in her, but she had not fallen into any state of unabashed adoration. Neither had he made any attempt to become familiar with her in that fashion.

"I have surmised the same," Francis remarked, using an irksome tone of voice.

"He is congenial and an excellent conversationalist." Beth continued to defend his actions. "I have no reason to suppose his intentions are otherwise than being friendly. He has made no romantic overtures. After all, I will not be a permanent resident at Aycliffe, will I? What purpose would there be in pursuing me when I am soon away to Dunwich?" Beth expelled her remarks with such vehement objection that she was out of breath. "I wouldn't think too badly of him, Your Lordship."

"I have no interest in Alexander Davenport," Annie assured her uncle. "Although I do agree with Beth. He has only been a gentleman in my presence."

"Well, I beg to differ," Francis argued. "I don't trust him."

"My goodness," Lord Howard remarked, widening his eyes. "I apparently stirred a bee's nest of opinions about this young man, haven't I?" He paused and then admitted. "Perhaps I judge him too harshly because of his father's intentions that may not be his goals."

"I believe you have," Beth concurred.

"Well now, it appears, Miss Edwards, that you are not afraid to express your opinion and rightly so. Nevertheless, what is your answer? Shall you stay and be Annie's companion for the next month? I leave in five days and wish to do so without hesitation or worry that I am abandoning her again."

As much as she hated to admit it, she should ask Francis his opinion. She looked at him straight in the eye, with a hopeful gleam he would relent. "Do you agree to this arrangement? I see no cause to refuse."

Rather than torture her with hesitation, he readily answered. "Yes, I agree, as long as the Wilsons remain in contact with you to check on your welfare. When His Lordship returns from Scotland, then I shall expect your immediate return to Dunwich."

Expect. His demands annoyed Beth, but she was grateful Francis made no blatant objection to the arrangement. His tightening control incited her to never return to Dunwich. The restraint he placed upon her behavior and life choices was smothering, just as Alexander had pointed out.

"Well, it's settled then," Lord Howard proclaimed.

Annie displayed a broad grin of approval. "Oh, Beth, I am so looking forward to having you by my side," she gushed.

Their discussion had taken preference over tea, and the footmen served them. Lord Howard took Francis aside, and Beth heard his inquiry regarding his watch-making business. While they chatted about timepieces, Beth sipped her tea. As she glanced around the room, excitement filled her soul.

"Uncle, do you mind if I show Beth her room?" Annie asked.

"No, of course not."

After turning his attention back to Francis, Annie grabbed Beth by the hand. "Come with me upstairs. You will love the view from your chamber window."

With exuberant steps, Beth followed Annie up the grand staircase of red carpet. After traveling along a hallway, Annie opened a door.

"This suite will be yours, Beth. It's like mine, with a

sitting area, desk, fireplace, and windows that face the ocean."

As they entered, Beth's eyes widened in delight. The decor of light green and rose overwhelmed her senses. The windows illuminated the interior. A beautiful mahogany writing desk with a matching chair sat against one wall. A velvet settee caught her eye, looking inviting and comfortable, and a grand four-post canopy bed sat in the middle. The furniture appeared fit for a queen.

"Oh my, such opulence." Beth attempted not to act like a silly child having received a new toy.

"Come here and look out the window. It's a beautiful view."

Annie pulled back the drapes so Beth could see the scenery. "Lovely."

"I am so thankful that you accepted Uncle's invitation. You know, he's going to Scotland to meet the Duke of Montrose's eldest son."

"Why?" Beth asked innocently.

"To arrange my marriage, of course."

"With someone you have never met?"

"Yes," Annie replied without a hint of concern. "I have always known that it would be an arranged marriage. Frankly, he's keen to marry me off so I am no longer a burden."

Astonished at Annie's announcement, Beth stared at her in disbelief. Yet, it was a familiar manner of circumstances.

"I feel that I am a burden to Francis and should marry. However, I have no earl to arrange my marriage for me." Beth giggled aloud, contemplating how ludicrous it would be for Francis to choose her husband. On the other hand, she never doubted he would voice his opinion on any potential match. He had shown that to be true with his less-than-amicable comments regarding Alexander.

"Well, perhaps the duke's elder son has a younger brother," Annie suggested. "How delightful would that be?"

"In a fairytale, perhaps," Beth scoffed. "We are of different classes, Annie. You know that I could never marry into the aristocracy. Who would have me?"

"Fiddlesticks," Annie said. "I think it makes no difference. You are a beautiful and wonderful young lady."

"Besides, I would rather marry for love than convenience," Beth clarified.

"My mother always told me that love would come later and not to entertain romantic thoughts about marriage. Arranged marriages appear to be financial choices rather than romantic ones."

"Then I feel sorry for you," Beth admitted. "Really, I do." With a pleasant smile, she continued. "I hope the duke's son turns out to be a very handsome and kind gentleman."

"I do too," Annie admitted. "I have told Uncle if he was to arrange anything for me, it should not be with anyone as old as him."

"Oh dear. Did he take offense?"

"No, he bellowed a hearty laugh and promised to find a younger gentleman of title and means."

Beth experienced a pang of guilt, leaving Francis alone with the earl too long. "I should rejoin my brother, as I'm sure he is eager to depart."

"Very well, I can let you go for the afternoon, knowing that soon we shall be companions to each other for an entire month."

When they returned to the sitting room, Francis appeared at ease as they chatted about the upcoming hunt in a few days.

"Is the room to your liking?" Lord Howard asked.

"Very much so. I will be comfortable indeed."

"Good then."

"Francis, we should get back to Mr. and Mrs. Wilson in time for dinner," Beth said.

"Yes, we should go." He turned to the earl. "It's been a pleasure. Thank you for the afternoon."

"And thank you for allowing your sister to stay with Annie while I am away. It is most kind of you to agree to the situation."

After saying their farewells, Beth and Francis climbed into the carriage.

"He's a delightful fellow," Francis remarked.

"Annie is a delightful young lady," Beth responded. "Thank you for allowing me this opportunity, Francis. I know it is not easy for you to let go of the leash."

"Yes, it is difficult for me to give you free rein, Beth."

Happy to hear that Francis had no concern, Beth glanced out the window at the ocean in the distance. Their trip to Aycliffe had become more than she could ever imagine. Despite its pleasantness, there still lay a shrouded mystery surrounding their mother. She wondered if staying at Rosemont Park would shed any light upon the past. Only time would tell.

CHAPTER TWENTY-ONE

The Hunt Begins

Brandon Howard sat leisurely in a wicker chair in his garden, sipping a refreshing glass of lemonade. The hunt had been a success, with his guests having returned with multiple braces of fine fowl. His retrievers fetched the fallen birds, and groundskeepers went before the four of them, beating the thick brush and dense patches of grass to scare the fowl into flight. The pheasant population on his estate barely diminished, as an abundance of birds remained to hunt on another day.

Francis appeared slightly out of his element, admitting that he had never hunted game before, being inclined to fish for sport instead. Brandon thought him to be an amicable fellow but noticed the overbearing hand of protection that rested on his sister. In retrospect, he could not blame him for guarding her reputation. She was a beautiful young lady and could fall victim to male flirtation. Grief had a way of making a woman vulnerable. Until Beth recovered from the loss of her mother, she would have a weakness.

Even though he had invited everyone to the estate for the day, Brandon would have much rather remained alone. Social interaction drained him emotionally. Although he did his best to be friendly and welcoming to others, he fought a raging battle for a solitary life. He hadn't always been such a recluse, but life's losses had left him bitter and broken. Perhaps it had been his punishment for the reckless days of his youth and carefree attitude that nothing ill would ever befall. Instead, he lost his wife after childbirth and his only son to smallpox. Annie would receive a wealthy inheritance upon his demise, but it saddened him deeply that he had no legitimate heir to call his own.

He was sure of one thing though. Eliminating the need to worry about his niece's welfare while he escaped would ease his conscience about his selfish pursuits. Although he loved having Annie around, he had ulterior motives to arrange a match now that she had turned eighteen. One less person in the household would ensure his privacy but also allow him to travel. Brandon grinned, thinking about his particular lady friends that he had waiting for him in Paris and Rome. They were always willing to provide him comfort in their beds and a splendid time.

"Your Lordship?" Mr. Davenport poked him out of his musings. "Will you be having a fall hunt for fallow deer?"

Brandon raised his eyes to his guest, who always enjoyed the benefits of the estate when it came to fowl and venison. "Yes, if I am not planning a wedding." He shot a sly smile at Davenport, knowing it would poke his interest.

"Wedding?" His brow scrunched together.

"Yes, I'm in the process of arranging a match for my niece. The Duke of Montrose's eldest son is now of age, and I'm off to Scotland in two days to settle the contract."

Mr. Wilson wandered over and stood nearby, listening to the conversation. "Did I hear you right?" he inquired. "Annie is betrothed?"

"Yes, very soon," the earl announced, making sure to smile in approval. Davenport's countenance grew pale, which the earl took satisfaction in watching as the blood drain from his face. His ancestors might have rejuvenated the sleepy fishing village to one of a fashionable resort. Nevertheless, the Davenports irked him because of their snobbery and control of the town's affairs. As the buildings and streets aged, so had its popularity. More than once, Mr. Davenport displayed the brazen audacity to darken his door to ask for an investment of funds to shore up the dwindling seaside locale. Brandon would hear nothing of it, as his father had more than amply invested his fair share in years past toward its growth. If he had been half the businessman he boasted to its residents, he would have shored up enough funds to make repairs as the buildings aged. It only confirmed to Brandon what a pumped-up peacock of a man Davenport was behind closed doors.

"And what of your children, Mr. Davenport?" Brandon asked, to stir the pot of discontent. "I heard a rumor that Edwin is soon to be engaged."

"He was, but I'm afraid his recent behavior has led to a severing of the relationship," he solemnly answered. Davenport averted his gaze and took a sip of his drink.

"Shame," Brandon remarked. "Well, I am sure there are plenty of young ladies in Aycliffe who will gladly consider Alexander an agreeable match. Edwin, I am afraid, has a rather roguish reputation he may not overcome." Brandon knew it was a slight insult, but the truth his father needed to face. Of course, he was once a rogue himself but had the sense to put away his wildness when he wed. He grimaced inwardly at how hard it had been to do so, but he found love with Margaret, which tempered his wandering lust.

"Perhaps," Davenport remarked. "But like Your Lordship, I have a vested interest in whom my sons marry." After a curt nod, he stepped away to seek refreshments.

Brandon walked over to join Beth, Francis, Alexander, and Annie, curious as to their discussions. "What is the topic of conversation?" he asked, innocently standing among them.

"Alexander was boasting of his hunting success, while I'm afraid Francis didn't do as well," Beth remarked. "They are both slayers of fowl," Beth jested. "Such pretty birds too, and now they will be someone's dinner."

"I did not realize you had an aversion to hunting," Alexander noted.

"I hate to see anything killed for sport," Beth explained. "Although I certainly understand the need to do so for food."

"But men love sports," Annie teased. "It's one of their favorite pastimes." She giggled. "That and chasing the ladies."

Brandon returned a raised brow at Annie's tongue-in-cheek comment.

"Rightly so," Alexander chimed in. "I enjoy a good hunt now and then."

"You mean the hunt of birds and not ladies, I'm assuming," Beth clarified.

Alexander lowered his head while stifling a smirk. Then he glanced at her with a noticeable spark of affection. "The ladies too, when warranted."

A slight irritation rose in Brandon's gut at Alexander's interest in Beth. Perhaps it was true that he had shown no desire toward Annie, or at least felt an aversion to his father's prodding to pursue her fortune. Not wishing the discussion to degrade into the female sport, Brandon stirred the conversation elsewhere to test Alexander's motives.

"Have you heard, Mr. Davenport, that Miss Edwards will stay in Aycliffe for a month as my niece's companion?"

Alexander's countenance brightened at the news. "No, I had not," he replied, shifting his eyes back to Beth. "Is this true?"

"Yes, but I'm afraid that His Lordship's butler shall keep watch at the door when it comes to bachelors who attempt entry." Beth invoked a slight despairing tone.

"Oh, then I am not welcome to visit," he commented, straight-faced.

Francis appeared to enjoy Alexander's disappointment as he watched the discussion.

"It's not that you are not welcome," Brandon clarified. "A visitation from a bachelor to two young women unchaperoned might taint their reputations. Annie is soon to be engaged to Lord Montrose from Scotland. It's a matter of appearances, Mr. Davenport. Nothing personal."

"Engaged?" He glanced at her with a broad smile. "I offer my hearty congratulations, Miss Whiting."

"Thank you."

Brandon took notice of his sudden change in demeanor, as if it had released him from a burden.

"Also, it complicates the matter that I shall return to Dunwich, leaving my sister behind. It is only wise that you do not visit." Francis added his thoughts with cold regard.

Alexander's countenance swiftly changed as he narrowed his eyes at Francis. "I'm sure you do."

After a brief hesitation, the air electrified between the two gentlemen. "Please excuse me." Alexander turned on his heel and walked toward his father and Mr.

Wilson.

Brandon watched Alexander stride dejectedly in the other direction. "He is enamored with you, Miss Edwards," he concluded, turning toward Beth.

"And is that so terrible that he regards me as pleasing?" She pressured him for an honest response.

"Not in the least," Brandon replied. "I too find you pleasant company. You have the qualities of your mother, who was a flame attracting many moths during her time in Aycliffe." He noticed Beth's countenance sour and instantly realized that his comment had brought offense.

"Such a comparison insinuates that as a flame, she tempted and led others to their downfall." Beth scowled agitated by his remark. "It makes me question whether you are asserting that Mother led someone in particular to their disgrace while here."

"I don't think His Lordship intended for that analogy," Francis intervened. "Our mother would never intentionally do such a thing."

"Perhaps, but it is adding to the lengthy list of ambiguities spoken regarding her since we have arrived. I wish the commentaries to cease."

Astonished at Beth's outburst, Brandon attempted to allay her fears. "Miss Edwards, I apologize for my poor choice of words. I would never say anything derogatory regarding Catherine Ashby. On the contrary, I can only sing praises about her character."

Francis reached out and gently touched Beth's forearm as if to calm her and bring assurance. Obviously, since they had arrived in Aycliffe, the wagging tongues had caused some damage to the memory of Catherine. It angered Brandon, although the fact remained that over twenty years ago, an incident occurred. One that he wished to forget.

Perhaps the opportunity had arisen to paint the picture he wanted Beth to see and sweep away the speculation once and for all.

"Mr. Edwards, would you mind if I took Beth for a walk in the garden alone? I would like a word with her in private."

Annie intervened. "Francis, you can keep me company. I have heard nothing about your village where you live or your business for that matter."

Francis hesitated momentarily, apparently glancing at Beth for an indication of her preference.

"I will be fine," Beth assured her brother.

"Yes, of course, Your Lordship. Your gardens are worth the stroll," Francis agreed.

The earl offered his arm to Beth, which she took. He felt a slight tremble in her gait when he led her along a pebbled pathway.

"Please accept my apology," he said with heartfelt sincerity. "I have obviously offended you by my thoughtless comparison, which was never my intention. I assure you."

Beth remained silent for a few moments and then spoke in a low tone. "Accepted. Nevertheless, I owe you one as well for my curt and disrespectful reply a few moments ago. I am mortified at the anger that rises up within me when it comes to my mother's memory."

"It sounds as if you have been the victim of Aycliffe gossip. Is that true?"

"A few comments have been slung like mud, all of which I have found confounding."

"I see. And these comments have led you to believe that something occurred during your mother's time here in Aycliffe?"

"Yes, they have," Beth remarked.

Brandon halted in his steps and took Beth's hands

in his, which were cold to the touch rather than warm and inviting. The poor girl was wrought with nerves. After concluding that an opportunity had presented itself to tell a story, he took full advantage of the moment.

"If I tell you what happened, it may bring you even more distress."

Her brows knit together with concern.

"The truth is rarely simple, my dearest Beth. It sometimes carries barbs that can harm us when revealed." He squeezed her hands tighter. "Is that what you wish?"

Purposely he had called her by her Christian name, but she did not flinch at his forwardness. Her hands remained clutched in his, and she lowered her eyes, staring at their joining.

"Is it very terrible?" she asked with a quivering lip.

"Love is not terrible, my dear. However, sometimes it is highly inconvenient and ill timed. Such were the affections that my father held for your mother."

"Your father?" She lifted her eyes curiously to his.

"Yes. As I said before, he had taken quite a shining to your mother. Unfortunately, it became much more than that during her stay at Aycliffe. I'm afraid he fell despairingly in love with her."

"But wasn't he married to your mother?" Beth squeezed his hands in return.

"Yes, indeed, he was a married man. My mother, still very much alive, became devastated by his change in affections."

Beth pulled her hands away and brought one to her brow. "I am afraid I'm slightly dizzy," she admitted.

"Take my arm," he insisted. "There is a sturdy bench ahead." He led her to the granite seat and assisted her as she sat down. They faced the rose bushes, and he could see the hunting party off in the distance. Francis stood speaking with Annie, and the Davenports and Mr. Wilson occasionally glanced in his direction, undoubtedly wondering about the conversation.

"Are you all right? Shall I continue?"

"Continue?"

"Do you wish to know the truth, or shall we leave it shrouded in the fog?"

CHAPTER TWENTY-TWO

Clarity or Perplexity

As soon as he mentioned the fog, Beth's mind went to the shoreline on the day they had arrived. She remembered the dense midst and how difficult it was to make out any landscape or buildings as they approached Aycliffe. When she recognized anything with clarity, it was only after they had closed the distance.

At that moment, she wanted the truth about her mother. It, too, had been hidden from view. Now, the individual who knew what happened could tell her everything. The Wilsons or Davenports had not offered to clear the air, but the earl appeared ready to do so. All she had to do was ask.

The questioned loomed before her as she searched Lord Howard's eyes for an answer. Did she really want to know? Would there be barbs, as he said, to scratch the memory of her mother? She feared that the woman who had raised and loved her and Francis might not be who she knew all along.

"You hesitate," Lord Howard said. "Shall we let the affair rest with them?"

"Affair?" Beth asked, frowning at his word choice.

"Beth, I use the word not in a sordid sense," he clarified. "By an affair, I mean the matter that happened between them."

Before she could ponder it further, she blurted out. "Yes, please. I wish to know."

The earl smiled warmly at her response. "Very well then."

He glanced over at the guests before starting, and Beth concluded he wanted to maintain privacy.

"My father had a weakness when it came to the ladies, which my mother tolerated throughout their marriage. Although I was not privy to any of his indiscretions, there had been rumors of other women."

"Oh, I see," Beth remarked, embarrassed for him by the confession.

"When your mother came to Aycliffe, it was as if he lost his moral senses. He took every opportunity to cross paths with your mother and unabashedly seek her attention in return."

"And did she give it?" Beth asked, wanting to know if she encouraged it.

"As far as I know, she did not. Nevertheless, it did not dishearten my father's pursuit of her affections."

"I believe she would never do such a thing," Beth boasted in confidence.

"Yes, but unfortunately, my father put your mother in a compromising position. On the night of the ball, he had convinced her to walk in the garden with him alone." He lowered his eyes and remarked thoughtfully. "Perchance, she had been naive to do so without careful thought about how it would appear to others. My father, experienced in the art of seduction, embraced and kissed your mother. Another couple, who observed their shocking behavior, interrupted them."

"Oh dear," Beth groaned.

"Father told me he wanted to make her his mistress, but I quickly put an end to his ill-conceived idea."

"Did rumors swirl around Aycliffe perpetrated by

the couple who discovered them together?"

"Like wildfire," the earl admitted. "It became such an embarrassment that not long after, your mother resigned from her position and left Aycliffe."

"I see," Beth pondered. "But then why did she maintain such a long relationship of correspondence with the Wilsons?"

"Friendship or perhaps curiosity," he surmised. "To be honest, I have no idea."

"Did your father love her, or was it merely. . ."

"Lust?" he asked, concluding her words with a slight smirk that surprised Beth.

"Yes."

"I think in his way, he believed it to be love. Whatever he concluded, it was inconvenient and ill timed; of that, I am convinced."

"It must have been a terrible blow to your mother," Beth said.

"Yes, but nothing she had not experienced before," he replied indifferently. The earl reached over and took Beth's hand. "Now, there. Are you satisfied that it solves the mystery?"

"Relieved," Beth admitted. "I had pondered the most terrible things, speculating upon the comments."

The earl stood to his feet and offered Beth his hand. "We should rejoin my guests lest our time alone brings scrutiny."

Beth stood to her feet and walked alongside the earl as they made their way back, thankful that he had revealed what occurred. Naturally, knowing what his father did, Beth wondered why the earl had taken her out onto the balcony alone the night of the ball. Regardless, her mother must have been mortified over what happened, and Beth wondered if she had attempted to resist his advances. If it appeared as scandalous to ignite such gossip, perhaps she had a moment of weakness overtake her good sense.

The day progressed toward late afternoon, and Beth's anxiousness to depart stirred. It appeared the others felt the same.

"We should be getting back to town," Mr. Wilson announced. "Mr. Davenport and Alexander are preparing to leave."

"Yes, that sounds agreeable," Francis said. "Your Lordship, thank you for the morning hunt. I found the new sport of interest, and I may pursue it when I return to Dunwich."

"Very good. You are always welcome here, Mr. Edwards. Feel free to send a post next time you come to Aycliffe, and we can go out together."

"I would like that very much," Francis said.

Annie gave Beth a hug. "Just a few more days, and we shall have the month together. I cannot wait for your company," she gushed with excitement.

"Neither can I," Beth admitted.

The Davenports bid their goodbyes, but Beth noted they acted aloof. Alexander looked distraught with a tense jawline, avoiding eye contact with her. It pricked her heart with disappointment. As they departed in the carriage, Mr. Wilson and Francis returned to Aycliffe together with their bagged pheasants.

"We shall have a good deal of fowl to eat between the two of us," Mr. Wilson boasted as they settled in for the return trip.

"Indeed," Francis replied. "I am sure your cook will do a fine job of roasting one bird before I leave."

"So it's all set then, is it? You shall return to Dunwich while Beth will be a companion to Miss Whiting for the next month?"

"Yes, that is the arrangement," Beth acknowledged.

"Shame," Mr. Wilson remarked. "Mrs. Wilson and Celia would have enjoyed you staying at our home. But nonetheless, one must not disappoint the earl if that is what he wants."

"I am looking forward to the experience. Mrs. Wilson and Celia are more than welcome to visit often while I'm at Rosemont Park." Beth glanced at Francis, who seemingly remained uninterested in the conversation by staring out the window. She was about to say something when Mr. Wilson interjected.

"Naturally, we could not help to notice the stroll you took in the gardens with the earl. Was the conversation to your liking?"

Beth's inhaled a sharp breath at his straightforward question. She hesitated to answer and thought it best to hold what she had learned for Francis's ears only.

"Oh yes. Lord Howard is a good conversationalist and is eager for me to spend time with Miss Whiting."

"I must say," Mr. Wilson began, "that I was aghast when he announced he had all but arranged his niece's marriage."

Francis swung his head around, joining the discussion. "Is it true that Mr. Davenport hoped Alexander would win Miss Whiting's affections?"

Beth could not believe Francis had pursued the topic and had no qualms about having a sibling spat in front of Mr. Wilson. "Francis, I daresay that is none of our business. Apologize for your forwardness."

"I shall apologize for nothing," he retorted. "It's an honest question."

Beth glanced at Mr. Wilson, who appeared shocked, by the crinkle in his forehead. "I consider Mr. Davenport to be a close friend," he tersely replied, scowling to show his disapproval. "Whatever intentions there may have been, I am not liberty to confirm or deny."

"See, you have offended Mr. Wilson," Beth pressured.

Francis shifted in his seat as they neared the Wilson residence. "Yes, perhaps I spoke out of rude curiosity. I offer my apology, sir."

It took a few moments before Mr. Wilson responded, remaining agitated about the query. "Accepted, young man. Perhaps it's been a long day, and our patience is frayed."

The carriage came to a halt, and Beth exited the interior as soon as the door opened. There was much to think about regarding her mother and the days ahead. She hoped to have a few moments alone with Francis to discuss what Lord Howard had conveyed, which hopefully would put all speculation to rest once and for all.

Celia and Mrs. Wilson were in the parlor doing cross-stitching, having no interest in coming to the estate for pheasant hunting. As they entered, Mr. Wilson became the first to boast of the day's success by dangling a brace of dead birds in front of the ladies.

"The hunters have returned," he proudly announced.

"Good gracious, Mr. Wilson," his wife exclaimed. "Take those to the kitchen at once and out of my sight."

Francis had a good chuckle as he held up his three dangling dead birds. "Not as successful, but indeed a good time had by all."

"Did you have fun?" Celia asked Beth, smiling at her. "Was Alexander there with his father?"

"Yes, he came, but the other brothers did not." Beth answered Celia's question, knowing full well its purpose was to determine if Edwin had taken part.

"I knew Alexander would not give up the

opportunity," Celia remarked. "Edwin, I'm sure, has other pursuits." She pursed her lips together, frowning at the thought of him.

"Well, if you would excuse me," Beth remarked, "I would like to rest before dinner." She glanced at Francis and nodded toward the staircase. He instantly understood her meaning.

"I shall clean up as well," he announced. "If you will excuse us."

"Here, let me take those birds from your hand, young man, and deliver them to the cook," Mr. Wilson offered.

Francis handed them over and then retreated upstairs with Beth by his side. "I'm assuming you wish to speak with me about your conversation with Lord Howard," Francis remarked in a low voice.

"Exactly." They reached the landing, walked toward Beth's room, entered, and closed the door. She had much to convey and felt relieved the mystery that had plagued them had been solved.

CHAPTER TWENTY-THREE

The Departures

Francis neatly folded his last item of clothing and placed it squarely in the middle of his travel case. After he closed it tightly, he stood staring at it with a frown crinkling his forehead. The thought of returning home and to the business tasted bittersweet. The trip to Aycliffe had been relaxing and puzzling, and the idea of leaving Beth behind created a seed of doubt he could not shake.

He walked to the window and took a last glance at the gardens behind the house, realizing that he would miss the greenery and the blue ocean. Having no interest in gardening or a green thumb to speak of, he wondered if he should hire a gardener to tend to their property in Dunwich. A few flowers here and there, with trimmed hedges, might make the home look more presentable. A wave of guilt flowed over him as he realized he had neglected their residence since the death of his mother. His father would not be pleased, but running a business to provide an income had been a daunting task. The craft of keeping time for others had given him no time to enjoy life.

When he realized that his mind wandered, he walked over to the edge of the bed and sat down. Francis heaved a sigh, lowering his head into his hands. If business wasn't enough to drain him, there was the matter of his sister's care that weighed heavily upon his conscience. He should have never allowed the companion arrangement with Miss Whiting. What did he think when he agreed to leave Beth behind among strangers? It was ludicrous and a dereliction of his duty to care for his sister's well-being. Supposedly, he could trust the Wilsons to check on her periodically up at the grand estate perched on the hill. He worried that Alexander Davenport would take advantage of the situation too, despite Lord Howard's demand that he not call upon the ladies during his absence.

Perhaps these illogical worries were a waste of effort. Beth would still return home to Dunwich, and any pursuit that Alexander would attempt would come to naught. Francis wanted Beth to meet someone in the village and remain close to their childhood home. His parents would have wanted it, and he was determined to keep what he had left of the family together.

As far as his bid to find a wife, one day he would meet someone who would catch his eye. Although Celia had done so at one time, he concluded that her parents would not approve of any match except one that provided ample social advantages or perhaps wealth. If he had been honest with himself, it had been a momentary attraction that eventually faded. His interest in Celia as a potential mate ended because of circumstances and her questionable judgment. She was pleasant enough as a young lady but lacked qualities he wanted in a wife.

Then there was the matter of his mother's stay in Aycliffe and the surprising revelation from Lord Howard about the incident involving his father. The explanation on the surface appeared plausible, and Francis admitted that such behavior twenty years ago would have caused the town's tongues to wag with gossip. If that had indeed been the case, Francis wondered why the Wilsons had not openly discussed the matter with them. There remained a shield of secrecy. As a knock came at the door, Francis halted his useless brooding.

"Francis, the carriage is waiting," called Beth.

He grinned at the familiar turn of events when he balked at his sister's lateness two weeks ago. He rose to his feet and opened the bedroom door.

"I will admit you sound more pleasant in your call than I did."

Beth grinned. "I am more patient than you."

"Come in for a private word," he said, grabbing her hand. Francis pulled her forward and closed the door.

"You will miss the coach back to Dunwich," she protested.

"I worry about you, Beth," he moaned. "Are you sure you want to pursue this arrangement at Rosemont Park?"

"Very sure." Beth placed her palm on his right shoulder and patted him. "Stop your worrying. I will be fine."

"Promise me you will return home if you are unhappy."

"Of course." She cajoled him with an assuring grin. "I will be home in a month."

Francis searched her eyes, and having convinced himself she would, he turned and picked up his suitcase. "Very well then."

Beth opened the door and headed downstairs. He followed behind, seeing the Wilsons and Celia standing in the foyer, waiting for him.

"Well, this is goodbye," he said, glancing at the Wilsons. "Thank you for your hospitality."

"You are more than welcome," Mr. Wilson replied.

"We expect your return for another visit. Our home is always open to you."

"Indeed," said Mrs. Wilson.

Celia stepped toward Francis and stood in front of him. "May I write to you?"

"Write?" Francis repeated, bewildered by her suggestion.

"Yes, you know. It's an activity that involves a pen, paper, envelopes, and Her Majesty's postal services." Celia smirked, and her sparkling eyes were welcome.

"If you would like to write, I am happy to receive your correspondence. Nevertheless, I must warn you, I'm not prone to writing letters," Francis admitted.

"He isn't, Celia, but when I get home, I shall make sure he answers you."

"Who knows, we may end up corresponding for twenty years like your mother and my parents," Celia jested.

"If you must write, let me know that my sister is behaving herself," Francis commented, glancing at Beth.

"Give me a hug goodbye, brother, and stop recruiting spies." Beth threw her arms around him and gave him a tight hug. "Don't worry about me," she whispered in his ear. "I will be fine."

After a flurry of farewells to his hosts, Francis climbed into the carriage. As it pulled away, the horses trotted down the lane, taking him away from Aycliffe, the sea air, the sparkling ocean, and the secrets of the past. He took his last glimpse of the shimmering waters, knowing how much he would miss the sights and smells of coastal living. His life, however, did not allow him to consider anything beyond the confines of Dunwich and timekeeping. Fate had dealt him a far different hand, so for the meantime, Aycliffe would simply remain a place to visit.

As much as she loved her brother, Beth let out a sigh of relief when he departed. A sense of freedom and excitement washed over her as it was now her turn to start a fresh adventure. She had packed her bags early in the morning, and the Wilsons had readied their carriage to take her to Rosemont Park.

"Well, time to say my goodbyes," she said, turning toward the Wilsons.

"I promised your brother that I would check on you often," Mrs. Wilson remarked.

"No doubt he begged you to do so," Beth said, smirking. "I hope that you and Celia will visit Rosemont occasionally, as I would like to see you."

"Well, I will often visit if Miss Whiting doesn't mind," Celia announced. "Either way, I do hope that your time at the big house, as we call it, is pleasurable."

"I know it will be," Beth said. "Take care."

After giving a quick hug to everyone, she concluded her farewells and began the journey to the estate. The time with Annie would be an adventure. Beth hoped that they would continue to get along and forge a close friendship. A part of her wished that she could see Alexander, but that did not seem to be possible with all the precautions placed to keep him away during the earl's absence. She wished that Francis didn't hold such adverse feelings about Alexander either, as she doubted that he deserved such disdain.

The carriage traversed toward Rosemont, and Beth noted clouds forming along the horizon. They were dark, puffy, and tall in nature, appearing as if a storm formed offshore. Undoubtedly, Francis would tell her the scientific name of the cloud patterns, surprising her with his knowledge. She grinned, remembering his man-in-the-moon explanation about the tides. A fondness rose in her heart for her sibling, understanding how difficult leaving her behind would be for him.

Beth's thoughts gave way as they crested the hill and Rosemont Park loomed ahead. The impressive estate spoke of wealth and position in English society. It would be educational to see how the household ran with its many servants, including a butler, head housekeeper, footmen, maids, and kitchen staff. Beth wondered how involved a woman would have to be in overseeing such an elegant estate. The carriage slowed and came to a halt. A footman exited and opened the door, helping her out.

"I will see that they deliver your bags to your room," he said.

As she approached the door, she recognized Clifford, the butler, waiting for her with a smile. He was an older gentleman with a full head of silver hair, and Beth thought him to be in his sixties. Even though elderly in appearance, he radiated a spryness about him. The years served at the Howard estate etched in his forehead with layers of wrinkles, resembling the rings of a tree. Perhaps he possessed knowledge of secrets and scandals, but Beth surmised that his loyalty probably outweighed any temptation to speak of them.

"Welcome to Rosemont Park, Miss Edwards. Might I take your shawl and bonnet for you?"

"Yes, thank you," Beth replied.

"Miss Whiting is waiting for you in the parlor. If you follow me, I shall announce your arrival."

When Beth entered the parlor, she found Annie

standing by the window. Dressed in a dark blue day dress, she appeared absorbed in deep thought. Clifford cleared his throat.

"Miss Edwards has arrived."

Annie spun around and instantly smiled at Beth. She walked toward her and gave her a tight hug in greeting.

"Oh, Beth, I'm so glad you have arrived. Uncle left yesterday, and I have been dreadfully bored."

"Well, we will have to rectify that emptiness," Beth said. "I'm so happy to be here."

She took Beth by the hand and dragged her to a nearby chair. "Sit and let us talk. Did your brother leave for Dunwich?"

"Yes, this morning."

"Will you miss him?"

"Miss him?" Beth chuckled. She paused, wondering if she should tell Annie the truth about the freedom that she experienced upon his departure. "To my shame, I am relieved."

"I get the sense that he is overly controlling when it comes to his little sister," Annie surmised with a grin.

"I tolerate it because I love him. Nonetheless, I feel giddy that for the next month, I am on my own."

"Well then," Annie mused, bringing her finger to her chin, and tapping it mischievously. "What trouble do you think the two of us can get into?"

"Oh dear. Do you have any ideas?"

"Well, I deem it sad that Alexander has been barred from Rosemont. Perhaps we can nonchalantly bump into him on the pier while taking a stroll. I sense that he likes you and you like him."

Beth's cheeks flushed with embarrassment. Francis would be beside himself if he ever found out their devious tactics. The idea sounded sinfully tempting.

"I would like to see him again," Beth admitted. "I find his company enjoyable."

"Well, since Uncle is matchmaking my future, I thought I would try my hand at matchmaking yours while you are in Aycliffe," Annie admitted. Her eyes twinkled with enthusiasm. "Shall I write him an invitation to meet us tomorrow afternoon at the pier?"

Beth couldn't believe that Annie had such a wicked streak in her. She appeared so innocent in nature. Regardless, it was kind to care, so Beth gladly agreed to the rendezvous.

"Yes, that sounds delightful. No one will think anything of it if we are together, and Alexander greets us like he would anyone else. It will appear as a happenchance meeting."

"There would not be a hint of scandal in such an innocent arrangement." Annie walked over to a small writing desk, opened a drawer, and pulled out a piece of writing paper. "Now, what shall we say?"

Beth rose to her feet and stood beside Annie as she thoughtfully stared at the blank sheet of paper. A second later, she penned his name, "Mr. Davenport. . ."

"Shall I tell him you wish to take a leisurely walk?"

"Oh dear, no," Beth gasped. "Make it sound innocent." She thought for a moment. "Why don't you say that we plan on taking a stroll on the pier tomorrow afternoon at two o'clock and that we hope to cross paths."

"A bit vague, don't you think?"

"Well, I don't wish to sound like a hussy." Beth crossed her arms in front of her waist.

Annie burst out laughing. "If you insist, then I shall pen these few words. Hopefully, he will understand its meaning." After doing so, Annie folded the paper, sealed it with wax, and wrote his name on the front. "There, I shall give it to one of the footmen to make sure it gets delivered before day's end."

Excited that she might spend a few undisturbed moments with Alexander, Beth tingled with girlish jitters. "Thank you, Annie," she said. "You are kind to do this for me."

"Think nothing of it," she replied. "What are friends for?"

"Yes, what are friends for?" Beth repeated, thankful that she had gained one in Annie.

Chapter Twenty-Four

The Happenchance

Alexander stood in front of his father's enormous oak desk in the mayoral office, observing the sour expression upon his face while he perused papers. Since the day they returned from the pheasant hunt, his father had been in a foul mood. Even his mother received the brunt of his short temper over the simplest conversation of late. Edwin suffered his rage over a broken engagement with Lady Ellen. When he heard the news that Miss Whiting would wed the son of a duke, it nearly caused a stroke. The sad fact remained. James Davenport teetered on the brink of bankruptcy.

"I will be glad when June arrives," he muttered, perusing another bill. "We need the summer months to bring money back into the town."

"Are things that bad?" Alexander asked, knowing full well they were. For once, he wanted to hear good news. His father's latest demand weighed on his shoulders as a heavy burden.

"I have been thinking about Lord Dunley's daughter in the neighboring county. Rumors have it she has come of age. Perhaps we can entice His Lordship to Aycliffe for a family holiday."

"Perhaps you could speak to Lord Howard to extend an invitation," Alexander half-heartedly suggested.

"I'll be damned if I ask that egotistical man for another favor. He continually refuses me, whereas his father was far more generous in nature," James spat vehemently. "I don't wish to endure another rejection from his cold, hardened soul."

Alexander pondered about how they could rekindle the resort's popularity. The fact of the matter was that the town had aged. Buildings were outdated, and many facades needed painting. Streets were strewn with potholes, and some businesses had closed because of poor sales. Even the hotel accommodations were less than posh, and not one restaurant could boast of a decent cuisine.

The bathing machines were old and in need of repair. The pier held firm, but so many community matters needed attending to that it was beyond his father's ability to revive the ailing location. They needed a miracle, and in his father's eyes, only money to reinfuse into the town would save it. The fact of the matter remained: they could invest heavily again in its revival, but would the crowds return? Other resorts were far more fashionable these days, drawing essential figures in society. Aycliffe did not hold any enticement to make it attractive.

"Then I'm not sure how you can encourage Lord Dunley to Aycliffe. The resort doesn't lure crowds as it used to."

"Don't you think I damn well know that! I've sunk half of our family fortune into keeping the town afloat. Sometimes I wonder if we should up and leave this godforsaken place and settle elsewhere. Then the village can sink into oblivion like it was before my ancestors raised it from a stinking fishing hamlet."

"Father, your bid for me, or Edwin to marry into money is ill thought. The aristocracy wishes to marry within its ranks. What do I have to offer? Absolutely nothing."

"I do not think it impossible. Edwin caught the eye of Lady Ellen. If he hadn't acted like such a blackguard with Celia, he would still be engaged."

"Perhaps, but she was far from becoming an heiress, and her dowry was a pittance since her father is also in financial straits."

"Yes, but with a foot in the door of a titled house-hold, more opportunities are open to us."

Alexander let out an exasperated sigh, hating the connotation of being an upstart. "My marriage is not the answer to your problems."

"You will do what I expect of you, damn it," his father roared. "There is money with daughters of wealthy industrialists too. We should broaden our search to the north."

Acutely aware that nothing would calm his father today, Alexander glanced at his pocket watch. It was a quarter to the hour, and he needed to excuse himself for a more pleasant engagement.

"If there is nothing further, I would like to take my leave." He hoped his father had no more errands for him at the present time.

"Fine, be gone with you," he said, shooing him away in irritation. "I have more important matters to attend to than to argue with you."

Perhaps Alexander should have been offended by the cold disregard of his father's words, but he had grown accustomed to his rudeness. Without a second thought, he retreated and closed the office door behind him, thankful for a moment of reprieve.

Yesterday afternoon he had received a surprising invitation from Miss Whiting. It was short but purpose-ful in words, appealing to him to partake in an innocent stroll on the pier. The insinuation of crossing paths would appear as a simple chance meeting. He smiled, wondering if this had been Beth's idea to find a way to keep in touch now that her brother and Lord Howard had departed. If so, Alexander considered it ingenious since they had barred him from visiting Rosemont Park. He feared that he lost forever his chances to spend more time with Beth.

Even though he took a brisk walk from the office to the pier, he was five minutes late arriving. It was a warm, sunny day, and the townspeople were taking advantage of the weather after yesterday's rain squall. Alexander slowed his pace lest he appeared too anxious. After walking a few feet, his eyes scanned the long pier, but he did not see Miss Whiting or Miss Edwards. A slight fear shot through his heart that they might play a ruse upon him for sport, and he scowled at the thought of it.

"Why Mr. Davenport, is that you?" came a female voice from behind him. "Imagine running into you on this sunny day."

Recognizing Miss Whiting's voice, Alexander spun around, delighted to see Beth standing by her side. In like fashion, he took off his hat and greeted the ladies. "Miss Whiting, a pleasure to see you today." He glanced at Beth. "And Miss Edwards, how fortunate it is to cross paths."

"Fortuitous indeed," Beth said with a broad smile. She twirled her parasol around once as if she were implying her excitement.

"Would you like to stroll with us along the pier? It's such a beautiful day," Miss Whiting suggested.

"Indeed, it is." He offered neither lady his arm for propriety's sake. A few people nodded at them as they passed by, but the pier was not crowded so that it would bring unwanted attention.

"The weather is a welcome reprieve after yesterday's afternoon storm," Alexander mentioned, attempting to make small conversation. He glanced at Beth and smiled at her, enjoying the sun, kissing her cheeks as she hid underneath the parasol. No doubt it was because of her fair complexion she found it necessary to protect her beauty from the rays. Even so, he could tell that her skin was flushed, and he hoped it was because of him.

"Yes, I saw the storm clouds offshore as I was traveling to Rosemont Park yesterday," Beth noted.

"So you have settled in then with Miss Whiting?"

"Yes, I have."

"And Lord Howard, has he left already for his excursion to Scotland?"

"He has." Miss Whiting announced. "He may return with my future husband."

"Again, I congratulate you on your impending engagement, Miss Whiting." Alexander noticed no hint of concern about an arranged marriage. The idea of his father arranging his nuptials put his stomach in knots.

"I am surprised that you have not yet found a wife, Mr. Davenport," Miss Whiting commented. "By all accounts, I would have thought you would have chosen a nice young lady by this time in life."

"My father keeps me busy," he said, using it as an excuse. He grimaced at the tiring errands he ran, listening to his complaints about Aycliffe's woeful financial problems and the Davenport fortune dwindling. They were far from being out on the street as paupers, as much as his father complained.

"Oh look! There is Miss Fisher. I must say hello to her."

Suddenly Miss Whiting sprinted off a few feet away and spoke with a lady. She appeared surprised when Miss Whiting accosted her for a conversation.

Alexander knew instinctively it was for Beth's benefit.

"Well, it appears that she has abandoned us," he smirked.

"Apparently," Beth said, looking up at him with bright eyes. "I hope you don't mind, Mr. Davenport, about the rather outrageous invitation we sent."

"Not at all. I am delighted to take a walk on the pier this afternoon." He fiddled with the brim of his hat. "I have wanted to continue our discussions about your daydreams."

"Oh yes, daydreams. If I remember right, you shared with me your wishes to visit exotic locations."

"Yes, and as I recall, you shared nothing with me."

"That is true," she mused aloud. Beth glanced down the long pier. "I do not think Miss Whiting would mind if we kept strolling. I am sure she will catch up with us when she finishes with Miss Fisher."

"If you're sure we won't offend her, leaving her behind."

"In all honesty, this has been her plan all along," Beth admitted.

"How very clever of Miss Whiting."

As they slowly walked down the wooden pier, the ocean remained calm with gently rolling waves. Alexander felt at peace next to Beth as she had a soothing effect upon his muddled mind. His heart stirred in her presence, on the brink of falling in love.

"I wanted to apologize," she said, rousing his attention.

"Apologize for what?"

"For my brother's rudeness toward you." Beth heaved a heavy sigh. "He is overly protective of me as no doubt you have noticed."

"Yes, it's quite obvious." Francis irked him, and there was no question her brother thought him to be disagreeable. "Why is that, do you think, Miss Edwards?"

"He fears that you will trifle with my affections while I'm in Aycliffe and sees no possibility of a future between us since I will eventually return to Dunwich."

Alexander halted in his step and faced Beth. "Do you believe that I trifle with your affections?"

"Not in the least," she acknowledged.

"I'm glad to hear of it because I would never trifle with you. On the contrary, if I offered my heart, it would be on the sincerest of terms."

Beth smiled warmly at him and searched his eyes as if she wondered whether he had already offered his heart. One question remained unanswered—did she feel the same? He glanced around and, after seeing no individuals watching their interaction, reached out and took her right hand, clad in a leather glove. After lifting it to his lips, he kissed it softly, wishing he could touch her flesh instead. Although such intimacy did not present itself, he hoped that his actions would speak what emotions he harbored at that moment.

"Mr. Davenport," she whispered, fumbling at his movement. "I fear that I am ignorant of the ways of the heart."

Alexander could no longer contain his affections. "I will admit that I am enticed by your beauty, drawn to your kind and gentle spirit, and find great comfort when in your presence." She looked at him, nervously batting her eyelashes.

"Then I shall confess to you," she began in a quavering tone, "that you fill my daydreams."

"Ah, at last!" he chortled. "I am flattered, Miss Edwards, that I fill your fantasies."

Beth blushed profusely, and he was about to say something else when Miss Whiting arrived at their side.

"My goodness," she gasped. "Miss Fisher can talk

your ear off when given the opportunity. I thought I could never drag myself away from her gabbing lips." She glanced at them keenly and then grinned. "Am I interrupting anything of importance?"

"Miss Edwards and I were just speaking of daydreaming," Alexander divulged.

"Oh, anything of interest?"

"Camels," Beth sputtered. "He daydreams of camels."

Beth's quick response in putting the attention upon him had been a ploy not to reveal her daydreams, so Alexander played along.

Miss Whiting wrinkled her nose. "What on earth is there to daydream about camels?"

The door opened, and Alexander took a moment to spout his wishes to travel the world and see its wonders and exotic lands. As he did so, they continued to walk along the pier, and he became animated in his narrative about Egypt.

"My, my, Mr. Davenport," Miss Whiting said. "And do you plan to traipse across the world alone or with a companion?"

"I admit that traveling alone has its benefits, but with a companion at my side, such as a wife, it would be much more pleasant to enjoy with someone I love."

"I wholeheartedly agree," Miss Whiting replied.

Beth remained quiet, and he wondered whether she imagined herself traveling outside the confines of English soil. Perhaps she found the idea to be frightening rather than engaging.

"And what of you, Miss Edwards? Do you ever ponder taking trips?" he asked, wondering what she thought.

"I have no means to travel around the world. My brother would surely not approve of it."

"But with a husband at your side, would he then approve?" Alexander knew his question led Beth toward an admission of the possibility.

"If I were married, Mr. Davenport, I would follow my husband's dreams and not the controlling wishes of a sibling." Her voice sounded terse, revealing her current sentiments regarding Francis's manipulation.

"Well said," Miss Whiting interjected. "Yet, it is important that two people have commonalities for a successful marriage. Don't you agree, Mr. Davenport?"

"Unquestionably," he answered.

"I have always been fascinated with India," Beth remarked.

"Definitely exotic," Miss Whiting agreed. "Tigers, elephants, spicy food, and all sorts of oddities far different from England."

Though Alexander loved the idea of Egypt, he would not mind a trip to India. It would make for an excellent location as a honeymoon. He smiled at the thought of it, but then reality returned. Such excursions cost money.

"You are pondering, Mr. Davenport," Miss Whiting said.

"Yes, daydreams rarely turn into reality," he admitted. "Aycliffe is my home and where my family and responsibilities reside." He smiled at Beth, making sure that her daydream would turn into reality. "However, there are certainly some dreams that do come to fruition if given the opportunity and time. Don't you agree, Miss Edwards?"

Her eyes sparkled at him in return. "Yes, we can only hope."

Realizing that his time had been long extended, Alexander gave his apologies to take leave.

"I must be going," he admitted woefully. "Responsibilities call at the office. It has, however, been a delightful chance meeting, and I do hope there will be more."

"Oh, I am sure there will," Miss Whiting replied.

"Well then, good day, ladies. Enjoy the rest of your afternoon."

He grinned at Beth and nodded his head, hoping that she could sense his sincere intentions. As he walked back toward town, the closer he came to the office and his father, the tightening constraints returned. Would he ever be free from it all? He wondered if Beth would elope with him on a whim, as he wanted to run away and start a life with her far from Aycliffe and the demands of family. On the other hand, he didn't wish to use her as a means to an end. It would be far more advantageous for all if his father would just relent and give him the freedom to live.

Chapter Twenty-Five

Like Sisters

As they returned to the estate after their walk on the pier, Annie eagerly asked about the outcome of Beth's private conversation.

"Did you enjoy Mr. Davenport's company? He appears to be an amiable gentleman, even if my uncle thought he possessed unwelcome motives."

"Yes, he is charming in demeanor, and I enjoy spending time with him," Beth admitted.

"Then we shall have to make sure we return to the pier on multiple occasions during your stay so you might cross paths again."

"It would be most enjoyable, but I fear that nothing will come of it," Beth sorrowfully admitted. As much as she enjoyed his company, she had to be honest with herself. Francis expected her to return home. "I am cautious not to let my affections run rampant when there is no hope that the two of us could be together."

"Why have you come to that conclusion?" Annie knit her brows together in disappointment.

"I sense that his father has other plans for him. Besides, in a few weeks, I shall be away to Dunwich and back home." Beth spoke in a nonchalant tone, hoping to hide her disenchantment and lack of faith.

"Well, I don't see why you cannot stay here in Aycliffe as long as you wish," Annie suggested. "Uncle tells me it will be months before I wed. You certainly can stay at Rosemont longer."

The idea was tempting. However, being near Lord Howard daily would be disconcerting. As cordial as his demeanor had been, Beth feared to stay too long in his presence. As hard as she tried to ascertain the caution that she harbored about him as a man, Beth couldn't quite put her finger on it. Perhaps the knowledge of what his father had done to her mother incited undue prejudice.

"I don't want to impose on your uncle. I'm sure having me underfoot would be a burden since he prefers to be alone." Beth avoided eye contact, afraid that Annie might discern her reasoning.

"He needs to get married again," Annie said. "I know for a fact that he is desperately lonely, but he hides behind the loss of his wife and son as if it were a shield."

"I get the impression he prefers to travel rather than keep close companionship, or maybe he finds enjoyable company when he travels." Beth grinned. "You never know. Perhaps he will meet some nice titled lady during his next excursion."

"You are right that possibilities await him," Annie answered.

They returned to the estate, enjoying afternoon tea and planning their time together. Each day that followed, Beth found herself amazed at how well she got along with Annie, bonding like sisters. Her stay at Rosemont Park as a companion had become a likewise amicable situation for herself. An older brother didn't provide Beth with the female companionship she needed as a young woman. Annie filled a void left by the passing of her mother.

Reading, needlepoint, and taking in the fresh air outdoors whenever possible were only a few of the activities they shared. Beth learned the art of archery, being surprised at Annie's ability to use a bow and shoot arrows with accuracy. She often missed the target altogether but had a good laugh at herself during each attempt.

Clifford, the butler, made sure they were well cared for and safe during the earl's absence. Annie, nevertheless, slipped by his watchful eye a few times and arranged clandestine walks on the pier that Beth could enjoy with Alexander.

Eventually, they invited Celia and Mrs. Wilson for tea, which brightened the parlor with friendly chat and faces. Celia's smile had returned, and Beth hoped that had put to rest any lingering affections for Edwin.

As they sat together sipping the hot brew and enjoying tiny finger cakes, Beth prodded Celia regarding her brother.

"Have you written to Francis, and if so, has he written to you?"

"I have, as a matter of fact," Celia responded. "And to my delight, I received a letter from him this very morning in the post."

That her brother had responded indicated that he held an unspoken fondness toward Celia. A slight smile spread across Beth's face. "Did he have anything of interest to say?"

Celia hesitated, and to her surprise, Mrs. Wilson answered. "Francis is busy back at his shop, taking care of business. Happy to be home, from what I gathered."

"Mother, did you read the letter?" Celia angrily narrowed her eyes. "I left it on my desk in my room. You are such a meddler," she snarled.

"It just happened to be sitting there, so I saw no harm in it," Mrs. Wilson defended her actions with a huff.

"Well, the next time he writes, I shall hide it from you," Celia stated in a firm tone.

Beth wondered if Mrs. Wilson worried about growing affections between the two, and the thought did not sit well. "Well, my brother must think highly of you, Celia, to take the time to write. I have never known him to be so attentive with a pen." She chuckled to make light of it and carefully noted Mrs. Wilson.

After some awkward silence between the three, Annie made an announcement. "Beth and I took an afternoon walk on the pier recently, and guess who we bumped into?"

Surprised that Annie broached the subject, Beth tried to steer it elsewhere. "You know, Annie has been teaching me how to shoot a bow. I am terrible at the new sport but find it most entertaining." Her comment fell on deaf ears.

"Who?" Celia asked. "Who did you see?"

By the excitement in her voice, she wondered if she thought of Edwin. "Alexander Davenport," Beth answered. "We just happened upon one another."

"That's odd," Mrs. Wilson commented in a severe tone. "Alexander? I assumed he would have been at the office with his father at that hour."

Beth shot an alarmed glance at Annie, who calmly replied, "Well, it was odd to see him in the afternoon. He mentioned that the day was so nice after the squall the day before that he felt like a breath of fresh air."

"Interesting," Celia mused aloud. "And what did Mr. Davenport have to say?"

"Nothing much," Beth answered nonchalantly. "Just idle talk for a few moments, and then he left."

"Yes, chitchat," Annie concurred, taking a sip of tea.

"The family is probably dealing with the embarrassment of Edwin's latest disaster," Mrs. Wilson quipped.

"That young man is a shame to the family."

"What disaster?" Celia spun her head around and glared at her mother.

"Why the break with his intended," Mrs. Wilson said. "I shouldn't gossip." She grabbed a small cake and stuffed it in her mouth to keep herself from saying another word.

"You mean Lady Ellen?" Celia squawked. Her complexion paled upon hearing the news.

Mrs. Wilson shook her head, unable to speak a word with her mouth full, taking her time to swallow the sweet cake.

"Perhaps things did not go well with Lady Ellen after the library incident," Annie remarked.

Upon hearing her comment, Mrs. Wilson swallowed hard. "Oh, you heard?"

"Yes, Uncle mentioned that he happened across Mr. Davenport with Lady Ellen in the library. Apparently, they were discovered in a compromising position."

Beth appreciated Annie's discretion in not implicating the three of them as having discovered the affair. In doing so, she courteously protected Celia's secret.

Finally, Mrs. Wilson swallowed. "His father is talking about sending him off to the military, hoping to change his ways."

"Really," Celia drawled. "I doubt he would do well in the militia."

"And I hear that Alexander will soon court Lord Dunley's daughter if his father has any say in it," Mrs. Wilson proclaimed. "Oh, there I go gossiping, and I said I wouldn't."

Upon hearing Mrs. Wilson's announcement, Beth experienced a sinking feeling deep within her chest, as if her heart had grown heavy with grief. Apparently, his father continued to insist that he pursue money rather than love, keeping him prisoner to demands and responsibilities.

"Oh fiddlesticks," Annie remarked. "Alexander Davenport doesn't want to pursue some lord's daughter. He wants to travel the world, and I hope he finds a sympathetic woman to travel with him."

"I have never heard of such a thing," Mrs. Wilson protested. "He has ambitions like his father."

"No, he doesn't," Beth remarked in a loud tone. "He wants to travel and break free from his responsibilities here in Aycliffe. I think it cruel that his father demands such things of him. Alexander should be free to pursue his dreams."

"You speak as if you know his private thoughts," Mrs. Wilson scowled.

"Well, he mentioned his thoughts to me when we were strolling your garden." After Beth expelled her remark, her hands shook, and her face flushed red as a ripe apple. Mrs. Wilson stared wide-eyed at her, and Celia grinned, knowing full well why she had spoken with such vehement emotion.

"You are in love with him," Celia concluded.

"I am not," Beth dismissed.

"Beth regards him highly," Annie said, "but as a friend. She has given me no indication of amorous feelings toward him."

"Well, I hope not," Mrs. Wilson replied. "The elder Mr. Davenport would never approve any match between the two of you."

"And why not?" Annie asked in a terse voice. "Beth is as fine as any other woman."

"Because his father wants him to marry money," Celia remarked. "Just like he wanted Edwin to marry money. Money, money, money. That's all the Davenports think about." Celia huffed in disgust.

"And why is that? Are they in need of money?" Beth pointedly asked.

"Now that is enough of the conversation," Mrs. Wilson said, scowling at everyone. "I don't wish to speak ill of the family or gossip any further."

For the next half hour, Beth endured the torturous minutes of tea and cake, disguising her anger and hurt. Whatever goodness her mother had once found in the Wilsons obviously had boundaries when it came to Beth and Francis. The fact that Mrs. Wilson never mentioned what happened between her mother and the older earl twenty years ago Beth deemed a disservice to her mother's memory. They had received the brunt of Aycliffe chatter since their arrival. Without a second thought at the outcome of such a topic, she accosted Mrs. Wilson with her words.

"Yes, gossip seems to have been the downfall of my mother's stay here in Aycliffe. Wagging tongues can do much harm."

Mrs. Wilson shot a surprised glare at Beth. "Whatever do you mean?"

"Lord Howard conveyed the incident between my mother and his father on the balcony the night of the ball. Apparently, he kissed her, which incited rumors to spread around town by those who witnessed the exchange."

"Good gracious," Celia yelped. "So that's what happened?"

"There isn't an ounce of truth to it," Mrs. Wilson balked. "Not one word of it."

"Are you calling my uncle a liar?" Annie set her teacup down with a clink, clearly distressed by Mrs. Wilson's dismissal.

"Not as such," Mrs. Wilson corrected herself. "The story is rather embellished and barely truth."

"Then what is the truth?" Beth pressed, narrowing her gaze. For the first time since her arrival, Beth harbored anger toward Mrs. Wilson.

"Celia, it is time that we take our leave," Mrs. Wilson suggested, rising to her feet. "It's been a long day, and I feel a headache coming on."

"You always have a headache coming on when you don't want to talk about something." Celia balked.

"Well then," Annie said. "I shall have Clifford see you to the door."

Beth, astonished at Mrs. Wilson's response, remained seated. Celia cocked her head and gave a slight pout, showing her disappointment over the abrupt departure. "Perhaps we will cross paths soon during one of my walks on the pier," Celia suggested.

"Yes, that would be nice," Beth mumbled reluctantly. After they left, Annie plopped herself on the settee.

"Good gracious, Mrs. Wilson's face turned sour as a pickle before her abrupt departure." Annie pulled her mouth to one side. "I took offense at her comment that my uncle lied to you."

"I have no reason to think he did," Beth admitted.

"He has never spoken to me about your mother, but I am sure whatever he conveyed to you must be the truth."

Beth took a sip of her tea that was now cold. Regardless of the temperature, it moistened her dry mouth.

"Shall I write another letter to Mr. Davenport for you?"

Annie stirred her pondering thoughts. It took a few moments for Beth to respond, wondering if she should continue to pursue the pleasure of his company when nothing would come of it. As much as her reason told her to forget the pursuit, her heart wanted something more. It might prove dangerous to allow her affections to grow. Being crossed in matters of love wasn't something she had ever experienced. She would just have to remind herself that they could remain friends if nothing came it.

"Yes, I think I could use a walk on the beach rather than the pier this time. Might you suggest we cross paths on the sandy shores?" Beth grinned mischievously.

"It would be my pleasure," Annie replied. "I shall suggest Sunday afternoon at one o'clock. If the weather holds, it should be a pleasant outing."

"Yes." Beth hoped the weather would hold for her sake, at least.

CHAPTER TWENTY-SIX

The Sands of Time

Prudence sulked as she glanced out the carriage window, watching the Howard estate disappear out of sight. The afternoon had turned into a rather unpleasant social gathering, except for the finger cakes that were sweet and creamed filled. She could have eaten five of them in a row if no one cared about her appearing like a glutton. Desserts had a magical effect on calming her nerves after indulging in the decadent sweets. Instead, as the carriage bounced down the trail back to town, jitters in the core of her stomach took hold.

She glanced at Celia, who pouted, fiddling with her reticule in her lap. For a moment, she wondered what in the world the girl carried inside the beaded handbag. Perhaps more letters that she had been hiding. The idea of her and Francis corresponding on the surface appeared innocent enough, and Prudence hoped that innocence would continue. It would be disastrous if either Celia or Francis had amorous feelings for one another. Her husband expressed the same concern, and the departure of Francis back to Dunwich doused those fears. Hopefully, it would continue as such.

Nevertheless, the sad fact remained that Celia had reached beyond the age she should find a husband. Of course, not any husband, but one with status and monetary funds to give her the lifestyle she deserved. There were a few times in the past months she detected a rather strange response from Celia whenever Edwin Davenport's name arose in conversation. Even though Celia vehemently deemed him a rogue of the worst sort, Prudence could not help but wonder if Celia had been one of his victims. Under no circumstances would they approve of such a match either if she held affections for him. Undoubtedly, his father would discourage it too.

As Prudence's brow furrowed, staring at Celia, she had no idea how or where to find her a husband. Nothing of promise came from the last social interaction at the Rosemont estate ball. The town did not hold a promising pool of bachelors either. Still, summer would soon arrive. New life would flood Aycliffe, perhaps bringing with it romantic possibilities. Prudence's weariness over caring for Celia's welfare had taken its toll for some reason, even though she loved the girl despite her outlandish personality.

"Why didn't you want to answer Beth's question?" Celia asked. "You embarrassed me in front of my friends with your rude behavior."

Knowing Celia eventually would say something about the exchange, Prudence remained calm. "What occurred over twenty years ago has no bearing on today's matters at hand."

"Did the earl lie to Beth or not?"

Prudence's lips tighten into a straight line. "It's a half truth, and nothing more needs explanation."

"I don't understand the secrecy. It breeds speculation of the worst sort. Even I have wondered about the lingering rumors and whispers about what occurred with Beth's mother."

"What speculation?" Perhaps she had underestimated the power of the tongue to keep silent even twenty years later. Prudence braced herself for whatever conjecture had teased Celia's mind.

"Well," Celia said, halting momentarily. "I have heard many stories, and I don't know which ones are true or not. You and Father seem to be the keepers of the secrets, and perhaps the Davenports as well."

A sigh of relief left Prudence's lungs when Celia could produce no specifics. It appeared that she had heard stories, but only one Prudence was intent on taking to the grave with her. Unfortunately, the town gossip was like a stubborn wildfire that was difficult to put out. For years it would die down, and Prudence would relax as if nothing had happened. Then something would spark its return, like the visitation of Catherine's children. Buried underneath the sands of time lay a secret hidden from everyone.

When they arrived home, Prudence watched Celia make her way up to her chambers. Turning in the opposite direction, she entered the parlor, surprised to see her husband. He sat by the window with his head buried in the London paper. Never had she seen any man in her lifetime so intent on reading each word of the printed page. She walked in and sat down in a nearby chair, attempting to make light of the situation.

"Has another brutal bare-knuckle fight caught your attention? You appear engrossed in the news."

Benjamin lowered the paper and peered over the top. As one brow rose slowly over his left eye, Prudence smiled at his reaction. "It's a sport, my dear. Merely sport."

"I would think kicking or hitting a ball sport, but not another person's face," she remarked.

"Have you come home from your afternoon tea to start an argument?" he asked, folding the paper with a crinkle, and placing it on his lap.

"Not at all, dear. But I am disturbed, I'm afraid."

"Disturbed about what? Was the tea not to your liking, or the finger cakes, perhaps?"

"Oh no, the finger cakes were deliciously sinful. It was the inquiring questions from Beth," Prudence admitted. For a brief second, she glanced at the parlor door, making sure no servants or Celia stood nearby to eavesdrop. Prudence lowered her voice to be careful. "I am afraid that Beth has continued inquiries about Catherine and insinuations in the guise of rumors."

"I have been afraid of that," he remarked. "Ever since I saw His Lordship take Beth aside for a private conversation."

"Yes, she remarked about the story he told her," Prudence said, shaking her head. "A pack of lies, to say the least."

"What sort of lies?"

"Well, he implicated his father, of all things, having wrongly stolen a kiss from Catherine the night of the ball. The incident, as he conveyed, caused her mother embarrassment when noticed by another couple, causing her to leave Aycliffe."

"Hmm," Benjamin pondered. "Well, the earl doesn't know the entire story either, does he? You can hardly blame him for his poor conjecture. Although I am convinced he buries his emotions behind his so-called mourning over the loss of his wife."

"Oh, I believe that he loved his wife, Benjamin. You don't think the man pines over Catherine?"

"Hardly," Benjamin concurred. "Underneath that outward facade of his impeccable character is a cold-stone, conniving heart like his father before him."

"You could be right," Prudence admitted. "Although, I have never imagined him a threat to Beth. Have you considered such a thing?"

"No, not in the least."

"Yes, but he's guilty as sin, as you and I both know." Prudence let out a frustrated puff of air from her lungs and touched her forehead. "Oh, Benjamin, shall we be able to keep the secret for much longer?"

"Now, don't you worry, my dear. Beth will return home, and that will be the end of it," Benjamin replied in an assured tone. "If the truth is never spoken, then who will know?"

"Yes, you are right. I worry for no reason." Prudence stood to her feet. "I think I shall lie down for a few minutes before dinner. Another headache seems to be on the horizon."

Benjamin viewed her with amusement, conceding to her excuse. As she walked out the parlor door and headed for the staircase, Prudence worried that the tenseness in her shoulders and neck would lead to a pounding skull, regardless.

Francis had engaged his mind and energy back into the business, overseeing the production of the watch that Mr. Davenport had commissioned. It would be a fine timepiece when done, and he hoped that more recommendations for his business would result.

During his absence, everything ran like clockwork, thanks to his foreman he had put in charge of the shop. His father had taught him to be fair and generous to those who toiled on his behalf, and he had a loyal staff to show for it. With contented workers, he knew that his business would continue to flourish.

As the days passed, he tried not to worry about Beth. She was, after all, in good company and well cared for during their time apart. He often found his mind pondering their stay at Aycliffe and the beauty of the ocean that he missed. The walks on the beach, the deep-sea fishing, and the social gatherings, for the most part, had left a pleasant memory.

Although the Wilsons had their quirks and Celia her questionable judgment, he felt a slight fondness for the family, regardless. A part of him missed Celia's bright face and exuberant personality when her wisdom hadn't clouded by Edwin Davenport's influence. Then there was Alexander, who he hoped kept his distance while Beth remained at Rosemont Park. He looked forward to Beth's return and life readjusting itself to normalcy.

One matter, nevertheless, loomed in his mind. He wanted to make changes at home. Soon after returning to Dunwich, it was clear that he needed a maid and cook to perform the female tasks required to run a house. He had no time to tend to the residence or attempt to cook, for that matter, being a bachelor with a business to run. After a few days of interviewing locals, he settled on an elderly woman to cook his meals by the name of Mrs. Little. To his delight, her delicious dinnertimes were a treat, much like Wilson's cook in Aycliffe. At least when Beth returned, he would have no need to tease her any longer about her poor skills in the kitchen with Mrs. Little to cook for them.

A young and energetic young girl by the name of Priscilla filled the position of a household maid. To Francis's surprise, she entered the station with a whirl-wind of purpose, cleaning, polishing, and rearranging things that hadn't been touched in some time. After the first week, the home sparkled and smelled fresher than it had since the passing of his mother.

With such enthusiasm in hand, Francis asked that she see to his mother's room. As siblings, they had barely touched the chamber their parents shared. It remained like a mausoleum of memories. After a year of mourning his mother's passing, Francis thought it time to redo the quarters and make it his private retreat. One day he would marry, and he intended to stay in the family residence. Beth, in turn, would wed and move into her household. He wrestled with no guilt over the decision and determined to pursue the endeavor during Beth's absence.

Priscilla stepped up to the challenge, stripping the beds, curtains, and rugs. At the same time, he thoughtfully planned for replacements and new furnishings. To curb Beth's disappointment, he planned to purchase new bedding and curtains for her room as well to cheer her upon return. As he engaged himself in the endeavor, Francis instructed Priscilla to get on her hands and knees and scrub, with a wire brush, the wooden floors. He intended to have them varnished before laying down new floor coverings.

After she had completed the tiresome task, Priscilla approached him to complain about loose floorboards she had discovered.

"They creak like a haunted house," she balked. "You best fix 'em before doing the varnish."

"Show me," Francis said, following her into the bedroom.

"Over there, where the bed sat." She wiggled her finger, pointing out the location.

"Well, no wonder they haven't been repaired," Francis replied. "If they were under the bed, there's been no foot traffic to reveal the problem." He laughed at the ridiculous scowl on Priscilla's face as if the loose plank had ruined her day. After a few steps, he walked across the area and heard the whining floorboard. Kneeling, he fiddled with the wood slat and discovered it hadn't been adequately secured.

"For heaven's sake," he said, pulling it up. "It just needs a few nails, and it will be fixed." As he examined the wooden plank, Francis's eyes drew to the hole in the floor. To his surprise, he discovered a bundle of envelopes, secured with a white ribbon.

"What's that?" Priscilla asked, peering over his shoulder.

"It appears to be correspondence." His hand trembled at the treasures as he brought them to the surface. After blowing the dust off the stack, Francis fingered the envelopes to see who sent them. Immediately, he smiled, noting the familiar name.

"Oh, here they are," he said, standing to his feet. "Letters from the Wilsons to my mother. Beth and I wondered what happened to them."

"Looks like your mam hid them for some reason. I betcha they got secrets," Priscilla said, reaching out as if to grab one.

Francis pulled back. "I doubt it, but these are not for your eyes, I'm afraid. They belong to the family." After putting the plank back in place, he anxiously wanted to read the contents. "I'll have the handyman nail the board before he varnishes." Francis glanced around the empty, clean room. "You've done well, Priscilla. Thank you for all your help."

"Hope your sis likes it when she gets back."

"I do too."

Francis gripped the package of letters in his hand and retreated to the parlor. After dinner, he would drink a glass of port and read the contents. Perhaps he would finally understand why his mother's relationship had been close to the Wilsons.

CHAPTER TWENTY-SEVEN

Temptations Abound

Alexander's frustration continued to grow. Between the demands of his father and his affections for Beth, he wrestled with reckless thoughts. His father boasted of the idea of courting Lord Dunley's daughter to the Wilsons. Alexander feared the tittle-tattle had reached Beth's ears, extinguishing any regards she held for him. Naturally, the probability that anyone would approve of their match would be an uphill battle they could not win. It only brought Alexander to ponder other possibilities to break free from expectations.

To his delight, he had received another clandestine invitation to cross paths with Beth and Annie on the sandy shoreline Sunday afternoon. By excusing himself after the customary after-church luncheon with the family, it raised no suspicions. Alexander often enjoyed a shoreline stroll or swim midday.

He arrived earlier than requested and stood, enjoying the view a few minutes before their arrival. The day had dawned pleasantly in the morning, but he noted ominous clouds on the horizon heading toward Aycliffe. In the past half hour, a gusty breeze swept toward shore, confirming the sun would soon be shrouded. Regardless, he would not allow the threat of an approaching storm to dampen his enthusiasm.

Within the next few minutes, his eyes caught sight of Beth in the distance. To his amazement, she approached alone. Miss Whiting did not accompany her. Astonished that Beth had taken the risk of crossing paths by herself, gave Alexander hope that her affections had perhaps won over propriety. Such evidence brought a smile to his face.

"Why Mr. Davenport," she said, twirling her parasol around in circles. "What a coincidence to happen across your path today."

Beth wore a burgundy day gown trimmed in white lace. Her bonnet was a simple head covering with color-matching ribbons that fastened underneath her chin. Alexander couldn't help but smile, enjoying the simplicity of her loveliness. The quality had been attractive, unlike so many other women that his father wanted him to court. Beth had no airs about her whatsoever, causing his affections to grow each moment they spent together. She was altogether a sensible lady, both beautiful and with a gentle character.

"Yes, fortuitous indeed. I always walk on the beach after Sunday lunch with my family. We have a regular ritual of the church, food, and afternoon relaxation."

"Sounds delightful," Beth said.

"Will Miss Whiting be along in a moment?"

"Well, Miss Whiting decide to forgo a walk on the beach this afternoon, complaining of being out of sorts. I gave her leave to rest instead."

"I hope that it is nothing serious," Alexander remarked. He knew full well that Miss Whiting played a game of matchmaking.

"Not in the least. No doubt she will miraculously recover upon my return home. I am, however, restrained in that the estate's carriage and driver wait for me to return at the end of my excursion."

"Well, if you will give me your arm, let us commence with a leisurely stroll," Alexander said, extending the invitation. "Unless you feel it unadvisable to display closeness while unescorted by a chaperone."

"I am of age and can make my decision." She wrapped her arm around his. "It doesn't appear that too many people are out and about this afternoon. The horizon looks threatening."

"Yes, I noted, but it shall not intimidate us." Alexander led Beth down the beach, enjoying the sensation of her touch. Again, her presence calmed him inwardly. "I do so enjoy your company, Miss Edwards."

"Call me, Beth, please. Let us not be so formal with one another while alone." She paused for a moment and then continued. "I feel that we are close friends now."

Friends. A term that Alexander feared to hear. It caused him to withdraw as his heart yearned for more. Perhaps Beth feared to allow her emotions freedom because soon she would return to her brother. Thinking of how Francis controlled her life caused a scowl to etch across his face. Before he realized his outward reaction, Beth halted.

"Oh dear, I've wounded you, haven't I?" Beth faced him and dropped her arm from around his.

"No, you haven't wounded me," he answered truthfully. "Your friendship means very much to me. But. . ." He couldn't bring himself to confess his growing affections for fear they would not be reciprocated.

"But you wish that I felt more than friendship," Beth remarked in return, saying the words for him.

He lowered his headed and nodded. "I am not ashamed to admit, Beth, that I have grown awfully fond of you."

A smile spread across her face. "And I, you," she

admitted with a blush in her cheek. "I am afraid to open my heart entirely since it appears everyone is intent on planning our lives for us."

"Yes, my father and your brother," Alexander remarked. "Come," he said, offering his arm again. "Let's continue our walk before the storm clouds off-shore drench us. For now, we can at least enjoy each other's company regardless of the opposition we face."

She wrapped her arm around his, and he pulled her to his side. A few more yards down the sandy beach wouldn't hurt, even though the sun had dulled by the approaching bank of clouds. Alexander saw the cave up ahead. The tide was high enough that the waves had reached the entrance.

"Well, it appears we cannot reach the cave since the water is blocking the entrance," he nonchalantly remarked.

"Oh yes, the cave," Beth remarked on a droll tone.

"Have you seen the inside?"

"Yes, Francis and I wanted to explore it when we first arrived, but others were there before us."

"Others?"

Beth grew silent, and he sensed an uncomfortable-ness about her stature. Perhaps they had happened across two lovers, which wouldn't have been unheard of. The location had a reputation that his brother had often bragged about when they were alone. However, he never bragged about the company he kept.

"Oh, I see what you mean," Alexander remarked. "I know villagers use it as a secret hiding place."

"You do?" Beth halted in her step and faced him. "You mean you know about Celia and Edwin?"

Nothing could quite prepare Alexander for the announcement that Beth had made. Whether or not it was intentional, it was a surprising revelation. "Well, I know that Edwin boasts of his conquests to me at this location. As far as Celia, I'm afraid I haven't been privy to that bit of information."

Beth brought her gloved hand to her mouth. "Oh dear, I have spoken a dreadful secret. Please, say nothing! I did not mean to gossip as I chatted without forethought."

"Well, I'm not so surprised as to think Celia hasn't had her eye on Edwin for some time. I have noticed her attempting to hide her amorous gazes."

"I can assure you that her feelings are much changed after coming to terms with your brother's roguish ways, if you will forgive my use of words."

"Roguish is too kind, Beth. I could term him with other words that a lady should never hear." He laughed. "But that is my younger brother."

"You, on the other hand, are a gentleman," Beth said, looking up at him with an amorous gaze.

"I am a man," he honestly remarked. "I still have desires. The difference between my brother and me is that he throws all self-constraint to the wind while I have the moral sense not to act upon temptations."

He looked longingly at Beth, while his body flooded with unspoken needs. How he wanted her by his side each moment of the day. She would calm his soul, like the caressing winds and rolling waves of the ocean. The blueness of her eyes would compel him to drown in the pleasures of the flesh. As he thought about the bliss it would bring, unconsciously he brought up his hand and grazed his fingertips over the smoothness of her pink cheek. His thumb ran across her lips, which caused Beth's eyes to close. Should he dare to steal a kiss? Alexander glanced around at the empty beach and felt the sprinkle of a single raindrop hit his face. He could not lose the moment.

"My dearest, Beth," he said, bringing his lips closer to hers. "I do so love you." He touched her tenderly, and she flinched at his show of affection. As he pressed his lips closer to hers, she melted into his arms. With a firm embrace and the sweetness of her mouth, Alexander prayed the moment would never end. If it were not for the continuing pelting of chilly rain that had dropped from the skies above in a torrential downpour, he could have stayed there forever.

When he released her, Beth looked up at him with a satisfied gaze. "I believe, Mr. Davenport, that we are about to get wet."

"It appears so, Miss Edwards. Shall we sprint back to your carriage?"

Afraid that by the time they reached their destination the rain would drench her, Alexander removed his frock coat and wrapped it around her shoulders. At least she had a parasol to hide beneath, but it appeared the rain saturated and weakened the fabric. In all honestly, he didn't care if he got soaked to the bone. He had kissed Beth and enjoyed the glorious moment.

Annie planned to let Beth have a few moments of privacy with Alexander. After convincing her companion that it would be all right to go by herself, Annie delighted in her matchmaking talents. As far as she was concerned, there existed no reason the two could not overcome obstacles and be together. Of course, she needed to tell Clifford a slight white lie about Beth borrowing the carriage to visit the Wilsons, and he, unassuming as ever, believed the explanation.

While alone, Annie spent the time enjoying the

warm afternoon and sun on the balcony. As she sat there holding a book in her lap and sitting in a comfortable wicker chair, her mind wandered. Her heart pondered her uncle's trip to Scotland and the outcome. Hopefully, he found the duke's son to be an agreeable young man, for she genuinely wanted the opportunity to fall in love. After all, her mother's parents had arranged her marriage, and everything turned out well. Even her uncle's marriage to her Aunt Margaret seemed a success. Annie had been groomed to expect an arrangement of convenience and thereby refused to fear the future. She trusted her uncle explicitly.

Annie leaned her head back and enjoyed the sun warming her cheeks. A minute later, they grew cold as clouds from overhead sheltered her face from the rays. She opened her eyes and noticed the growing gloom sweeping in from the ocean.

"You should come indoors before you get wet." Her uncle's voice came from the balcony glass double doors.

Her head spun around to find him standing there with a grin on his face. "Uncle! You have returned!"

"Indeed, I have," he announced.

"But it's only been three weeks. I thought you would be away for a month." She stood to her feet and walked toward him.

"Things went well, so I returned early." He glanced around. "I don't see Miss Edwards anywhere. Is she up in her room?"

"Miss Edwards?"

"Yes, the young lady who I asked to be your companion," he remarked. "Have things not gone well?"

"Well?" Annie stumbled over her words as her nerves pricked with guilt. "Yes, they have gone very well, indeed. Beth is like a sister to me."

"I'm glad to hear it. So where is she?"

"Where is she?"

"Stop repeating me, Annie," he said, furrowing his brow in irritation. "Where is she?"

Annie halted momentarily, staring at her uncle. She didn't want to lie and considered telling him that she had gone to the Wilsons. It was one thing to say a mistruth to Clifford, but her uncle was another matter. She did not want him to be cross with her. Of course, that didn't mean she had to tell him the entire truth. Perhaps a tiny fib would do.

"Well, Beth wanted to take a walk on the beach, and I didn't feel like going. I allowed her to take the carriage and have a few hours to herself."

"Unchaperoned?"

"She's of age, Uncle, and able to care for herself. I'm sure she's perfectly safe." As she spoke the words, a sudden deluge of rain fell from the sky. Her uncle grabbed her by the arm and pulled in her indoors.

"And no doubt it has caught her in the rain. Honestly, Annie, what a foolish thing to do."

"Well, she may have company," Annie admitted, immediately regretting her confession. Perhaps her uncle wouldn't worry so much if he knew someone would protect Beth.

"Please don't tell me she has gone to meet Alexander Davenport," he growled.

"If she has, I'm sure it's by coincidence." Annie grimaced, trying to save the situation. Her uncle turned on his heel in heated anger. "Where are you going?" she called after him.

"To check on her welfare. Where do you think?" he yelled with a tone of frustration.

Annie's stomach knotted at the thought of what her uncle might find. Hopefully, Beth had already left Alexander and was on her way back to Rosemont.

"I've done a foolish thing," she scolded herself aloud. Hopefully, she hadn't ruined everything for Beth and her handsome Mr. Davenport.

CHAPTER TWENTY-EIGHT

Appearance of Impropriety

Brandon ordered a groom to saddle a horse, as the coach that had brought him back to Rosemont had departed minutes earlier. He mounted the steed and sped off toward town. Tired from the long trip from Scotland, the last thing that Brandon wanted to do was travel through the pouring rain to find Beth. When he left weeks ago, he felt assured the two young ladies would be safe. Why in the world had Clifford allowed her to leave the estate alone? Upon his return, he would give him an earful for not watching the young woman more carefully. Annie, too, would receive a stern reprimand.

As he approached the pier, he recognized his waiting carriage. The driver stood anxiously by the horses, apparently waiting for Beth's return. The earl dismounted and scanned the surroundings. Anyone on the pier had scurried back in town to find shelter from the rain. As his eyes shifted to the sandy shoreline, Brandon caught sight of two people running down the beach hand in hand. As he suspected, Alexander and Beth were side-by-side. Whether they had met by chance or arrangement, he wasn't sure. All the same, Alexander had used the opportunity to his advantage without regard to how it would appear. His frock coat had been taken off and wrapped around Beth's shoulders.

Perhaps he had done so to protect her from the weather. Though chivalrous on his part, the act spoke of intimacy. A fit of intense anger rose in his gut, and he burst forth like a howling gale.

"Let go of her hand," he demanded. They halted before him, heaving out of breath. Immediately Alexander obliged but remained steadfast next to Beth, taking a protective stance, not yielding to intimidation. The smile he noted on their faces, speedily disappeared as he stood before the two.

"Your Lordship," Beth gasped. "What are you doing here?"

The poor lass shivered, drenched from head to toe. A parasol in her hand had broken by the gusty wind and heavy rain.

"I think, young lady, you should get in the carriage immediately before you catch your death of cold," he ordered, softening his tone for her sake. "And you, Mr. Davenport, should return to your home posthaste. I shall care for Miss Edwards from this point forward." Alexander opened his mouth to speak, but Beth interjected.

"Perhaps I should explain," she offered. "I came here for a walk on the beach, and by chance, Mr. Davenport and I crossed paths."

"And you expect me to believe this encounter was by chance?" he retorted, irritated by the rain splattering his face. "Get into the carriage. I shall not ask again." Beth glanced at Alexander, casting a sorrowful gaze.

"Do as His Lordship bids, Miss Edwards, for I fear you will catch cold."

"You are far more drenched than I," she spoke kindly, taking off his coat and handing it to him. "Thank you for the protection of your garment and the engaging conversation."

Beth's countenance paled, leaving Alexander's side, which confirmed to Brandon that affections had grown between the two. The uncanny urge to protect her reputation incited him to take her by the arm and lead to the carriage. Why he felt so protective had eluded him entirely. Perhaps a pang of guilt from the past fueled his rage. In his younger days, he wouldn't have cared whose character he soiled.

"Good day, Mr. Davenport," he bid in a stone-cold grimace. "From this day forward, you are no longer welcome at Rosemont Park."

Beth scowled at him and jerked away from his hand. Brandon tethered his horse to the back of the carriage and instructed the driver to return to Rosemont. After climbing inside, the carriage lurched forward, and so did Beth's displeasure.

"Mr. Davenport does not deserve your cold disregard," she scolded. "We only crossed paths and walked together on the beach. Is that so terrible?"

"As an unchaperoned young lady, I would say it is reckless on your part to venture out on your own," Brandon preached like a domineering father figure. "While you live under my roof, I am responsible for your welfare." His eyes narrowed at her as she pursed her lips in a straight line of annoyance. "As far as Mr. Davenport is concerned, he should have nodded to you in greeting and then continued on his way. If the man truly cared about you, he would have had the sense to protect your reputation."

Beth puffed an exasperated breath and crossed her arms like a spoiled child. The act reminded him of Catherine, and Brandon wondered if she had picked up the habit from her mother. A memory flitted through his mind, which caused a slight grin to curl his lips.

"Apparently, you find some humor in this situation,"

Beth remarked angrily.

"You remind me of your mother. Your mannerisms are similar in many ways," he replied, reverting to a severe demeanor. "I do not wish you to suffer the same fate as her."

"Well, I blame your father for ruining her reputation. I'm sure she would never encourage such behavior on his part by acting unladylike."

Beth's poking at his conscience caused him to rail in return. "And what do you know of your mother as a young woman or how she behaved? Absolutely nothing."

"I will not sit here and listen to you sully her character. Since you have returned to Rosemont, perhaps I should return to Dunwich."

He didn't want her to leave because she reminded him so much of Catherine—youthful, innocent, and naïve. Perhaps that is why he needed to protect her from Alexander since no one had protected Catherine from him. Beth could easily fall for the wiles of a man as her mother so long ago. An ache of culpability ran through his heart.

"You are welcome to stay at Rosemont. Annie will not marry until the year's end, and I'm sure she would be heartbroken should you suddenly depart on a whim."

The carriage pulled in front of Rosemont and halted. When the driver opened the door, Beth sprinted inside. Clifford appeared, looking guilty for being derelict in duty. Brandon watched her climb the staircase and heard the door to her room slam so hard the sound reverberated through the halls.

Annie ran into the foyer. "Have you found her?"

"Yes, she's up in her room. You should tend to her. Make sure she gets out of her wet clothes and takes a hot bath."

"Clifford, send a ladies maid to attend to Beth. Afterward, meet me in my study for a word."

The footman took his wet hat and coat, and Brandon strode to the study. Grabbing a decanter of brandy, he poured a full glass and gulped it at once. The alcohol brought swift relief. Thankfully, a maid lit a fire, and he stood by the hearth, warming himself.

"Damn it," he growled under his breath, scowling at the flames.

"You wish to speak to me?" Clifford stood in the threshold.

The poor man had been a good servant throughout the years. Nevertheless, a stern reprimand was due.

"Yes, sit down, Clifford. I think you know what we need to talk about."

"Indeed I do."

Brandon walked over to the study door and shut it, determined to be firm but forgiving.

Shivers ran down Beth's spine. She couldn't discern whether it was from being cold or angry. Her fingers trembled, unfastening the buttons of her dress. The time spent with Alexander had been glorious. Even though she never considered they would kiss, the fact that he expressed such amorous emotion, taking her in his arms, melted her fears. She wanted to lose her heart no matter what obstacles they faced.

They clasped hands and laughed aloud, running back toward the pier. The rain pelted their bodies, drenching and breaking her parasol, but Beth did not care. It was the most freeing moment of her life until she saw Lord Howard, standing like a dark, menacing obstacle by the pier. She could not believe her eyes. When he opened his mouth, he took no hesitation in dispelling his disgust at what he discovered.

A knock came at the door, and she froze in distress, fearing the earl had returned.

"Beth, it's Annie. Can I come in?"

"Yes," she muttered. The door flew open, and Annie entered with her lady's maid, Agnes.

"Let us help you get out of those wet clothes," Annie said.

"I can do it," Beth protested.

"Then I'll draw a hot bath, Miss Edwards," Agnes offered, scurrying off.

"Oh, Beth, I'm so sorry," Annie wailed. "Who would have thought Uncle would return so soon? Was he very cross with you?"

"Yes, and unreasonably annoyed at Alexander. He reprimanded us both so severely that it would have brought me to tears if I hadn't been so livid at him for ruining everything."

"Did you have a pleasant time?" Annie asked while helping Beth to unfasten her corset.

"Yes, it was wonderful." Beth lowered her voice. "We kissed."

"Oh my." Annie's eyes sparkled in delight. "What was it like?"

"Heavenly." Beth sighed, remembering the blissful event. "He did not take advantage of me in any other fashion. Of course, I may have been saved from the downpour of rain at the most inopportune moment," she chuckled.

"Thoughtless rain," Annie pronounced.

"Your uncle mistreated him, telling him he was no longer welcome at Rosemont Park. I think that it is cruel and unnecessary."

"I will speak to him about it. No matter, Beth. If you love Alexander, follow your heart." Annie encouraged her, giving her a big hug.

"Your bath is ready, Miss Edwards," Agnes announced.

"Well, I will leave you alone to soak and get warm. Come see me when you are dressed and relaxed. I will be hiding from Uncle in my room lest he gives me another rebuke."

"I hope I did not get you in trouble," Beth said.

"You need not worry. I will own up to my complicity in the matter." Beth watched Annie lower her head as if she fully expected a harsh scolding. She wondered if Lord Howard had arranged her marriage or not.

"Will you need me any further?" Agnes asked.

"No, thank you. You may go."

Beth slipped under the comforting warm water and lay her head on the edge of the claw-foot tub. She wondered if Alexander worried that her affections had altered and decided to pen him a note to assure him otherwise. Francis would no doubt be furious at her for allowing Alexander to show such emotion in a public place. No one was near, so what did it matter? She was not her mother being encroached upon by an unwelcome advance. No, she was woman who wanted to experience love.

Sinking down into the water, Beth's warm thoughts turned to concern. Yes, Alexander cared for her, but did he love enough? It would take courage to disobey his father, who would never approve. If that wasn't bad enough, Francis expected her to return to Dunwich.

"It's impossible," she groaned, slipping her head underneath the water. Everything and everyone wanted to drown their dreams.

An hour later, Beth and Annie were summoned by

Clifford, who looked rather sheepish. They arrived together in the parlor where Annie's uncle stood pensively, looking out the window into the garden. It continued to rain and appeared that the rest of the day would remain as gloomy as Beth felt at that moment. She knew full well they were about to receive the brunt of his discontent. After thinking about it, scolding them together would be a better course of action.

Annie cleared the lump in her throat, and Lord Howard turned around. He faced them and nodded toward the settee. "Have a seat, ladies."

They obeyed, and he remained standing, hovering over them like a father goose. For someone with no children, Beth thought he played the role well. Her body stiffened in anticipation of receiving his displeasure. After all, he wasn't her father or any close relation that he should scold her for misbehaving like a ten-year-old. She didn't misbehave, and she crossed her arms again, showing her indifference.

"Whose idea was it?"

"Mine," Annie said.

"No, it was mine," Beth replied, defending her friend.

"Hmm, it appears you are both going to protect the other."

"Uncle, you are unfair," Annie balked.

"Because I have your best interest at heart?"

"Perhaps you do for Annie, Your Lordship, but I'm capable of taking care of myself."

"I made a promise to your brother to protect you while staying at Rosemont."

"My brother is overprotective of me. I am of age and can make my decisions," Beth asserted.

"And what decision would that be? To give your affection to a man whose father will not allow him to marry you? You could ruin your reputation, like. . ." His words trailed off and pulled his eyes away.

"Like my mother?"

"I mean no disrespect to your mother," he said with distraught lines on his face.

"Can we change the subject?" Annie interjected. "How was your trip to Scotland? You have said nothing to me about an engagement."

The earl shifted his gaze to his niece and hesitated. "After recent events, I wonder if you are mature enough to wed. Perhaps I am mistaken. Your judgment is not as it should be."

"Perhaps I should leave you alone to discuss matters," Beth offered, standing to her feet. "Please excuse me."

Surprisingly, Lord Howard made no objection for a moment of privacy, and Beth exited the parlor. As she was about to return upstairs, Clifford approached, holding an envelope.

"This just arrived for you, Miss Edwards," he said, handing it to her. She recognized her brother's handwriting.

"Thank you, Clifford." The butler nodded and turned to leave, but Beth reached out and touched his arm. "I hope His Lordship did not scold you for my disappearance. If he has, I am sorry to have put you in such a position."

"Thank you, Miss Edwards. It is not the first reprimand I have received from the family in my thirty years of service. I'm adept at handling them by not taking them to heart."

"I'm glad."

Beth retreated to her bedroom and sat down on the window seat, glancing outdoors at the pouring rain. Surprised that Francis had written to her, she opened the letter with anticipation and read its contents.

"*Come home at once. You are not safe at Rosemont Park. Everyone in Aycliffe has lied to us. I will reveal all when you return. Francis.*"

CHAPTER TWENTY-NINE

Disenchantment for All

The morning after, Beth sat at the breakfast table, occasionally glancing at Lord Howard. She had slept very little the night before after reading Francis's letter. The words disturbed her deeply, making her wary of everyone and everything. Francis never lied to her, and if he thought she might not be safe, perhaps she should take heed. The question loomed—what or who was the threat?

Annie remained silent, fiddling with the eggs on her plate and barely eating. Her actions convinced Beth that something did not go well with the earl's trip to Scotland, but she feared to ask in front of her uncle. Since he had returned home, now would be an excellent time to suggest that she return to Dunwich. The notion saddened her because returning meant that she would have to leave Alexander. If she left, nothing would come of them. He would forget her, be forced to marry some aristocratic daughter, and live the remainder of his life miserably. His dreams of traveling the world would come to naught, but his father would rest assured that they would be part of a titled family with wealth.

"Now that I have returned, Miss Edwards, would you consider extending your stay here at Rosemont Park?" The earl raised his head and looked at her directly, pulling her from her heartbreaking contemplations.

"I am not sure. Francis has written and wishes me to return posthaste."

"Why?" he asked, frowning.

Beth didn't wish to divulge his words as vague and cryptic as they were. "He misses me, frankly."

"And will you return? You are a mature, determined young lady who can decide to either stay or go. It's a quality you have reminded me of often."

"Oh, do stay," Annie begged, reaching out and touching Beth's hand. "You know how much I enjoy your company."

"But what of your pending engagement? You shall not need me much longer," Beth asked, probing for the outcome of the trip.

"I have had second thoughts about whether Annie is mature enough to wed. Candidly, I've been selfish in hurrying her to the altar so I may be free to pursue my guilty pleasures."

"I'm sorry to hear of it, Your Lordship. But you may be wrong about your niece. She is ready to be a wife."

"She will need to convince me, I'm afraid. Nevertheless, the Duke of Montrose, his wife, and son will visit Rosemont Park in a few days. I had extended the invitation, and it's too late to rescind it now. No doubt they are traveling as we speak."

"Oh, I see," Beth said, glancing at Annie.

"I am looking forward to meeting him. You would be such moral support if you stayed," Annie pleaded.

"I will hold a dinner party and intend on inviting the Davenports so they may make fools of themselves." Lord Howard smirked as if he looked forward to it. "No doubt the elder Mr. Davenport will attempt to convince the duke to invest in ailing Aycliffe, as if he would give a damn about a poor seaside resort."

"And what about the elder son, shall he attend too?" Annie said, having the audacity to ask her uncle.

Beth cringed at Annie's boldness, bracing herself for his answer.

"In no case shall Edwin or the sister attend. Richard is far too young for a formal dinner party. I shall neither invite the Wilsons, as they have no social standing to speak of."

"You didn't answer my question, Uncle. It would be pleasant for Beth to have someone to talk to."

"I'm sure it would." The earl glimpsed at her with a narrowed gaze. "Do you want me to invite your Mr. Davenport?"

"If you intend on being rude and discourteous to him, I do not. However, if you will be civil, then yes, I would enjoy his company."

"My word, Miss Edwards, you have no qualms about putting me in my place, do you?" He eyed her with a raised brow.

"Only with the deepest respect I do so, Your Lordship," Beth replied contritely.

"Very well then. I shall invite Alexander. I will undoubtedly enjoy watching his father squirm at the revelation that you have grown affectionate toward one another. He might give me a bit of sport for the evening."

"Really, Uncle, you can be most wicked at times," Annie insisted. "Shall you tease me in the presence of Percival Montrose?"

"Percival?" Beth giggled.

"I know," Annie groaned. "The name is atrocious. I hope he looks better than the sound of his name."

"You need not worry about his looks, although he has a club foot," the earl joked.

"Stop teasing me," Annie railed at him.

Surprised that Lord Howard had relented and would invite Alexander, Beth found herself in a quandary.

"Well, Miss Edwards, I'm assuming then you will stay at Rosemont a while longer," he commented with certainty.

It did not take long for Beth to follow her heart rather than her brother's demands. "Yes, I suppose I will."

Francis would have to wait for her return. Whatever he needed to tell her about the lies they had been told could stay buried as she was in no hurry to hear ill news. Undoubtedly, it had something to do with her mother, which made her wonder what deceit the Wilsons had perpetrated. Then again, perhaps the earl had lied to her about the past too. Whatever the matter, being with Alexander took priority.

The duke, duchess, and their son arrived two days later. Introductions exchanged, and Beth had been presented as Annie's companion. The aristocrats paid little attention to her attendance, making her feel awkward and unworthy. For Annie's sake, she remained nearby, curiously watching the interactions transpire with Percival and his parents. Beth thought the young lord did not appear impressed by Annie. He acted aloof and strained in behavior as if an arranged marriage had not been his preference. Regardless of the telltale indications, he remained courteous.

Annie dispelled her frustrations privately before the dinner party. "He is rather peculiar, if you get my drift.

I don't think he likes me at all," she spat in an exasperated tone.

"Do you like him?"

"Not particularly," Annie admitted. "He's pleasant to the eyes, but restrained in personality."

"Perhaps when you are alone, he will be more amicable in nature. He might be uncomfortable expressing his true opinion of you in front of your uncle and his parents."

"You might be right, but I am having doubts, to say the least." Annie lowered her head in her hands. "Oh, I was so looking forward to a spark of romance like you and Alexander share. Shall my marriage be nothing more than an arrangement of monetary gain? If he doesn't love me, then he shall take a mistress, and it will relegate me to giving him heirs and nothing more."

Beth placed her arm around Annie's shoulder and drew her into a hug. "I'm so sorry, Annie. I must admit that I don't understand the ways of aristocratic households and arranged marriages. It seems, though, even the upper-class professionals have their way of influencing their sons and daughters as to whom they should marry too. It's as if they put aside love for the sake of personal gain."

Annie's earlier expressed confidence in the arrangement had faded into a distant hope. After having a good cry over her disenchantment, Beth encouraged Annie to dry her tears. The dinner hour approached as well as the arrival of guests.

"We need to get ready for this evening," Beth encouraged. "Wear your prettiest evening gown tonight, and perhaps you will catch his heart."

"It remains to be seen if he will catch mine," Annie replied. "I am not sure that I wish for it. Since Uncle thinks I'm immature, I might act like it tonight to get out of the arrangement."

"You wouldn't," Beth said, astonished at Annie's suggestion.

Annie flashed a mischievous grin. "It would surprise you what I am capable of doing. I believe I get the devious streak from my uncle."

As expected, the Davenports accepted the invitation, and Beth excitedly waited to see Alexander. Lord Howard introduced the mayor of Aycliffe, his wife, and Alexander. To her surprise, His Lordship added a compliment that Alexander displayed a keen business sense among his peers. Beth could not help but smile at the sight of him, and he acknowledged her likewise. She listened as he expressed his gratefulness for the invitation.

"Thank you, Your Lordship, for the kind, albeit surprising, invitation."

"You may thank my niece and her companion, Miss Edwards, for helping me to admit my earlier rash and discourteous words."

Alexander's father watched the interaction curiously, no doubt not understanding the exchange. It was short-lived as he soon spoke to the duke about the benefits of the sea air and Aycliffe. Percival had wandered over toward Annie, attempting to make small talk, while Beth took advantage of Alexander's presence.

"Might I ask how you changed his mind?" he inquired.

"Annie encouraged him to invite you. I credit her for the change in heart, although I did express the importance of him being civil to you upon arrival. It appears he has taken my advice."

"I admit that after he spirited you away the other day, I felt dreadful. Perhaps I should not have compromised your reputation."

"Please, Alexander, do not worry about it. I am fine and am thankful for whatever time we share. They are precious stolen moments."

"Indeed, they are."

"Mr. Davenport, may I introduce you to Lord Montrose," Annie said, walking over and joining them. "Alexander Davenport is a fine gentleman in his own right," Annie boasted. "He has ambitions to travel the world."

"I find travel stimulating," Percival remarked. "Father has allowed me to go abroad on a few ventures."

"Might I inquire where?" Alexander asked, looking intrigued.

"Egypt, most recently. I'm a bit of an archaeology enthusiast and returned with a few fine artifacts for my collection."

"How very fascinating," Annie said.

Beth sensed Alexander's heightened interest, and the two men started an in-depth conversation about the faraway country. It felt as if she and Annie had all but been forgotten. The two men walked away and entered an intense discussion. Alexander appeared animated as if he had drunk water after trekking through a desert of disappointment.

"Perhaps they should marry," Annie smirked. "It appears Alexander has more in common with Percival than I do."

"I don't mind. Alexander talks so much about his dreams of visiting Egypt. I do hope one day that they will come true. He deserves happiness."

"And so do you," Annie remarked.

The butler appeared in the doorway, announcing dinner, bringing the attention of the men back to the ladies. Alexander offered Beth his arm, and Percival escorted Annie. Her uncle appeared pleased that they were interacting. The Davenports had remained attached to the duke and his wife. By the look on His Lordship's face, Beth feared the remainder of the evening would turn into an uncomfortable occasion. Nevertheless, since his relationship with the elder Mr. Davenport did not concern Beth, she determined to enjoy her time with Alexander. Concurrently, she would observe the interaction between Percival and Annie to see if she pursued her mischievous act or attempted to gain his affections instead.

CHAPTER THIRTY

The Bear is Stirred

Alexander sat next to Beth during dinner, while his father and mother took seats across from the duke and duchess. The earl positioned himself at the head of the table. Annie took a chair next to her intended.

He watched in interest the interaction between Lord Montrose and Miss Whiting, which appeared strained on the surface. It only confirmed to him, as he glanced at his father in disgust, that he would not fall prey to being told who he must marry. He loved Beth, and the kiss enjoyed on the beach during that rainy afternoon confirmed his amorous sentiments.

The past few days apart, though, had brought turmoil and unrest at home. Alexander brooded about how he could break free from the responsibilities heaped upon him by his father. From desertion of his family to the military, ideas floated in his head one from another. He considered again asking Beth to marry him and run away but denied the temptation, knowing it was not in her best interest.

He initiated inquiries to firms in London about possible employment. Since Dunwich was only an hour by carriage from the bustling city, it would be possible to see Beth and maintain their relationship. During that period, perhaps Francis would relent after seeing his devotion to his sister and not object to their engagement. He could not bear the idea of her leaving and returning home with no hope of a future together.

"Have you heard from your brother?" he asked Beth, curious to know if they kept in touch.

"Yes, as a matter of fact. I received a letter from Francis a few days ago, demanding my return home as soon as possible."

"Why for heaven's sake?" The thought disturbed him.

"I am unclear as to his reason except that he has news to share with me," Beth said in a low tone.

"What news?"

She turned and looked at Alexander with a befuddled expression. "I'm not sure, Alexander, except to say I have disobeyed his edict so I might see you again."

"Then I am flattered," Alexander confessed.

"Mr. Davenport," the duke interrupted. "My son tells me you are curious to visit Egypt."

Aghast that attention had turned to him, Alexander dabbed his lips with a napkin. "Yes, Your Grace, I have been curious about Egypt for some time. While in university, I studied Egyptology, and it frankly got in my blood." He glanced at his father, ignoring the scowl on his face. The man never cared about his interests in life.

"I also hear you have an impressive deal of commercial sense and have a degree in business. Is that correct?"

Embarrassed, Alexander downplayed any proficiency. "As far as my aptitude, yes, I find business an industrious pursuit of my talents."

"My son is interested in building a business of exporting goods from Egypt to England. We should like to speak with you about it later if you find the conversation of interest."

Surprised at the invitation, Alexander avoided glancing at his father. Instead, his eyes shifted to the earl, who nodded at him approvingly. "Indeed, of great interest. It would be a pleasure to discuss it further."

"Alexander, that sounds wonderful," Beth whispered. "If you went into business with them, then they would surely send you to Egypt to procure goods for import."

"Yes, it sounds intriguing," he remarked. "But I shall not do it without a wife at my side." He looked at Beth directly, hoping that she understood his meaning.

"Then you will need an adventurous woman as a companion, Mr. Davenport."

"Are you adventurous, Miss Edwards?"

"I might be persuaded."

Alexander wanted to drop on his knee and ask her to marry him in front of everyone but pulled himself back to his good senses. Many obstacles remained, and the duke had only made a passing suggestion.

Dinner concluded, and the ladies retired to the parlor for tea. At the same time, the gentlemen ceremoniously remained behind for after-dinner drinks and conversation.

"Mr. Davenport, let us pursue the conversation we struck up at the dinner table," the duke remarked, looking at Alexander and puffing on a cigar.

"Yes, please do," he encouraged.

"I'm interested in hearing of this business venture," Lord Howard announced. "How about you, Mr. Davenport?"

The earl bore a challenging stare directly at his father. Alexander deduced that he intended to rile the bear for sport. His father obviously grumbled silently, apparently attempting to choose his words carefully.

"New business ventures are always of interest," he

replied with a tense jaw. "However, my son has plans here in Aycliffe."

"Plans can change," Lord Howard suggested. "What is the venture you are considering?"

For the next half hour, the duke and his son laid before Alexander an intensive proposal regarding importing goods and some artifacts from Egypt to England. Apparently, a surging interest in Egyptology had swept across the Empire and the Continent. Montrose and his son were interested in pursuing the acquisition of goods, concluding it a prime time to open a venture. Of course, that meant they needed an agent to travel to Cairo, set up an office, and hire buyers to search for goods to import.

"Do you find that position of interest, Mr. Davenport? I should like to discuss the opportunity more in-depth with you privately tomorrow," the duke pressed. "If we come to an amicable agreement, my son and I will pay for your travels and provide a comfortable salary with an opportunity for partnership as the company grows."

"I find it of significant interest." Alexander hardly believed the opportunity presented, and he felt his heart thump in anticipation.

"Perhaps my son and I should discuss it further before he makes any commitments," his father interjected. "Such a decision should not be made hastily."

Lord Howard would not let the remark go unchallenged. "The man is in his prime, Davenport, and an intelligent adult. He can make his own assessments." He glanced down at Alexander's ankles. "I do not see any shackles keeping him here in Aycliffe. A father should allow his sons to make their way in the world, don't you agree?"

Alexander's father turned red in the face, noticeably

embarrassed by the reprimand. Concerned that he would spout angrily in return, Alexander interjected.

"I can indeed make my choices but shall also give my father respect by conferring with him before I do so." He looked at the duke. "Tomorrow then. It shall please me to continue the conversation in more detail."

"Well, that is settled. I suppose that we should join the ladies," Lord Howard remarked, standing to his feet.

They departed and reunited with the women in the parlor. Alexander came to Beth's side, which even his mother noted with a frown. She had appeared to enjoy the duchess's company during dinner. Thankfully, his father stopped pestering the two about the resort. Undoubtedly, their estate in Scotland boasted of far more amenities than the sleepy village in which his family resided.

"Did you have an enjoyable conversation?" Beth asked.

"Yes, and I received an invitation to return tomorrow to discuss the opportunity further with the duke and his son."

"I am glad to hear of it," Beth replied, looking genuinely excited for him.

"Do you plan on returning to Dunwich soon?" Alexander's father said, coming over to interrupt their conversion. "I'm assuming now that the earl has returned, Miss Whiting no longer needs companionship."

"I am not sure," Beth admitted. "Lord Howard has asked me to stay on a little while longer."

"I see," he said, glancing at Alexander. "Well, perhaps your brother will come to fetch you if you linger too long."

Alexander kept silent as his father made his point and then wandered back to the others.

"He doesn't like me," Beth remarked in a low tone.

"It's not you, Beth. He doesn't like that I have affections for someone who lacks the monetary value he seeks."

"What will you do?"

"Make my own choices," Alexander assured her. "I know what I want in life, and no one will dissuade me from my goals." He smiled warmly at Beth and gave her a quick wink. "Besides, having you at my side gives me the courage to break free."

The evening ended, and Alexander said his good-byes to Beth. As expected, it didn't take long for his father to vocalize his displeasure about the evening as the carriage brought them home.

"Tomorrow I thoroughly expect you to humor the duke. You should not seriously consider such a proposal," he remarked.

"What proposal?" his mother asked.

"The duke wishes to speak with our son about taking a position in a new business adventure and traveling to Egypt, of all places."

"For what?"

"Egyptian trinkets," he spat. "The thought of it disgusts me. What kind of career would that be? An export man when you could be the mayor of Aycliffe and run this town like our ancestors and me."

"It's what you want, but not what I want out of life," Alexander asserted. "I am my own man, Father, and I have catered to your edicts too long."

"Alexander, you should not speak to your father with such disrespect," his mother scolded. "He has your best interests at heart."

"He has his interests at heart," Alexander spewed in anger.

"And Miss Edwards. It's clear to me you have

allowed your affections to run rampant. She is a nobody like her mother. No dowry, title, or place in society."

"You know damn well I don't care about those things."

"What is this I hear?" his mother squawked. "You are in love with Miss Edwards?"

"I am in love with her, and I intend to ask for her hand in marriage," Alexander announced.

"Over my dead body," his father bellowed.

"You still have Edwin to control," Alexander reminded. "See if you cannot patch up this matter with Lady Ellen. You can assert your energy over him rather than me."

"How dare you," his father growled, narrowing his eyes at him.

Alexander shook his head. There would be no convincing his father to release him from his shackles. Regardless of the resistance, he would break free.

"I intend to have the conversation with the duke tomorrow. If I conclude it is a reasonable offer that can provide me an income to support a wife and family, I intend to pursue the opportunity."

"And I suppose you will marry this Edwards girl. Do you think she will want you traipsing off to Egypt?"

"It would be terrible for you to do so, Alexander," his mother moaned. "Marrying her and then leaving her behind in England."

"There is no reason I cannot take a wife with me."

"What, to that godforsaken desert landscape! No doubt it is dirty, reeks with poverty, and is filled with frogs, locusts, and flies."

Alexander bellowed a laugh. "Mother, the plagues brought on the Egyptians by God are over."

"Well, I just cannot imagine such a location," she groaned.

"How little you know me. Since I was a boy, I dreamed of traveling the world. That is all I have ever wanted. You have attempted to mold me into what you have wanted, and by God, it's time your demands cease."

"We will see about that," his father grumbled.

"We will." Alexander refused to allow him to get the last word in on the subject.

CHAPTER THIRTY-ONE

The Past Revealed

Even though Francis had written to Beth and told her to come home, he somehow knew that she would ignore his demands. He should have been more specific about the reasons why instead of alluding to lies. As the carriage descended the hill into Aycliffe, Francis concluded that perhaps it was better this way. What he had learned over many glasses of port and reading letters that his mother had kept hidden away for years rocked the foundation of their family. Perhaps she had hoped to bury the secrets in the floorboards of her room where they would remain concealed forever. Her mistake had been saving the correspondence as keepsakes to read when her heart experienced pain and regret.

The coach arrived at the Wilson's residence in the late afternoon. He would make no apologies for showing up on their doorstep uninvited and unannounced. What he had to say to them should be conveyed person to person. Francis wanted to see their actions, hear their explanations, and challenge them to tell the entire story once and for all. The thought of having Beth at his side during his interrogation was out of the question. He would ease her into the shocking reality in person, behind closed doors, so she could handle the weight of it all.

The door opened, and Wilford's eyes widened at the sight of him. "Good afternoon, Wilford. I have come to call upon Mr. and Mrs. Wilson. Are they home?" It took the servant a moment to answer.

"Mr. Edwards. This is indeed a surprise. You have returned from Dunwich, but I do not believe the Wilsons were expecting you."

"No, they were not."

Wilford barred his entrance, gawking at him.

"Who is it, Wilford?" Mrs. Wilson came into the foyer and halted upon seeing Francis.

"Good gracious, Mr. Edwards. You startled me standing there. What are you doing back in Aycliffe?"

"May I come in?"

"Of course, come in. Wilford, stop being rude and let Mr. Edwards through the door."

Francis stepped inside and glanced around. "Is Mr. Wilson here?"

"He will be shortly," Prudence replied.

"And Celia?"

"She is with Susan, a friend of hers, and I don't expect her back until dinner," she answered.

"Good then, as I do not wish her to hear what I have to say," he sternly conveyed.

"Whatever do you mean?"

As soon as Francis finished speaking, Mr. Wilson arrived home. Surprised as his wife, he froze when he saw Francis. "Good Lord, young man. What are you doing here? Is everything all right with Beth?"

"Yes. As far as I know, she is fine. I've come to speak with you."

"All this way? It must be important," he remarked. Mr. Wilson gave his hat and cane to Wilford, who took them and closed the door.

"Come into the parlor. Can we get you a cup of tea,

or would you like a sip of brandy?"

"Nothing for me," Francis said, although he would have cared for a drink of alcohol to calm him. He needed to speak rationally and not allow his emotions to get the better of him. If he took an aggressive stance with the Wilsons, it could make them defensive. It was vital that they talk and not bury the past.

"Well, sit down then. So, what brings you here? Have you come to fetch Beth home?"

"Yes, do tell us. You have my curiosity," Prudence said with a slight nervous quiver in her tone.

Francis slipped his hand into his inner pocket and took out a compact bundle of letters. They were not all of them, but they were the important ones that revealed the past. He held them up in his hand. "I have come to talk about these."

"They look like letters," Benjamin acknowledged, acting unimpressed.

"Yes. You wrote them, Mrs. Wilson."

"Me?" She glanced nervously at her husband.

"Yes, you. When I returned home, I decided to clean and decorate the quarters that my parents used in anticipation of taking the room myself. To my surprise, I discovered this correspondence, along with many others, hidden underneath a loose floorboard."

"How odd." Benjamin acted oblivious to their content.

Francis laid the letters down on the table between them. "So had both of you decided that you would never tell us we had a half sister?" The blood in Prudence's face drained, and Benjamin lowered his head.

"Your mother should have destroyed those letters," he solemnly remarked. "She promised to do so."

"Clearly, she didn't and held on to them for sentimental reasons," Francis countered in a strained tone.

"Oh, dear God," Prudence said, grabbing a few of them to read the contents.

"When were they written?" Benjamin asked his wife.

"These are after she left Aycliffe," Prudence answered.

"Why don't you read it aloud?" Francis wondered if she had the courage.

"Don't," Benjamin sternly replied. He took the letters from Prudence's shaking hands, folded them up, and shoved them in Francis's direction. "Put these away before Celia sees them."

"So she doesn't know?"

"No, she doesn't know. We raised her as our child for your mother's sake. She is none the wiser that we are not her parents."

"There is one thing missing in the letters I haven't found. Who is the father? You never mention his name."

"Why would we write his name?" Prudence spat. "It was despicable what he did to your mother."

"Was she raped?" Francis asked, scowling at the terrible possibility.

"No, not raped. Duped by the feigned affections of a rogue," Benjamin admitted. "It was a terrible thing."

"Lord Howard's father, I assume, as we have been told," Francis said with an air of certainty.

Benjamin and Prudence glanced at one another. For a moment, they were silent, and then Benjamin nodded his head as if to give permission the truth be told.

"No, it was Brandon Howard, the current earl," Prudence confessed, her voice shaking at the revelation.

"What?" Francis could not believe his ears. "And you saw nothing amiss, letting Beth go to Rosemont Park for a month?"

"Well, why should we?" Benjamin defended. "The earl is in Scotland. She's staying there with Miss

Whiting. I'm sure she is safe."

"I want to hear the story from beginning to end, and don't leave one detail out," Francis demanded, clenching his jaw.

For the next hour, a story beyond belief unfolded in Francis's hearing. The young lord of Rosemont Park had implicated his father in the incident of scandal when it had been him all along. The story had gone far beyond an innocent kiss on the balcony the night of the ball. Instead, his mother had foolishly fallen for Brandon Howard's flatteries and given herself to him in a moment of weakness and feigned promise of a future together.

When the Davenports discovered that Catherine was pregnant, they concocted a scheme to save her reputation. Because the Wilsons were childless, an elaborate ruse had been perpetrated by all involved. They had sent his mother to the country to have the baby, disappearing from Aycliffe. The Davenports convinced a distant family member in a neighboring town to take her in. During that time, Mrs. Wilson played the expectant mother. In order not to raise suspicion, she remained at home, only occasionally surfacing in public with a rounded pillow under her gown. When his mother delivered the babe, the transfer occurred, and no one was the wiser.

"And Lord Howard never acknowledged his complicity in the matter?" Francis asked, confused as to his lack of involvement.

"Catherine told him she was with child, but he refused to concede any responsibility. His stony heart shunned and pushed her aside. Besides, His Lordship was engaged to Lady Margaret, and he was heir to Rosemont Park," Mrs. Wilson explained. "What else could he do?"

"And the rumors about town regarding Mother?" Francis asked.

"Well, there was much speculation about her abrupt departure. The gossips began circulating stories, but we attempted to put out the fires, explaining that Catherine was homesick and returned to Dunwich."

Francis shook his head. "I am astounded. You have woven a web of deceit that has lasted twenty-four years."

"Lord Howard has no idea that Celia is his child even to this day," Benjamin soberly conveyed. "We saw no purpose in telling him. In fact, Catherine begged us to bury the secret, and we agreed."

"And he has never asked the Davenports?"

"No, not one inquiry," Benjamin replied.

Francis brought his hand to his head, thinking it would surely burst with the knowledge of what happened. "Instead, he implicated his father caught in a scandalous kiss with my mother. That is the ruse he told Beth."

"Well, his father was no different and took many mistresses in his lifetime. What the earl conveyed is believable."

"He is the most despicable of men, yet you all seem to revere him." Francis could not comprehend their previous accolades.

"Only to protect your mother's memory and Celia of course. Had we been open about our disdain for him, you would have asked the reason why," Prudence explained.

"Why didn't Mother keep Celia?" Francis pressed.

"Think about it, Francis. She was an unmarried woman. It would have ruined her prospects of ever marrying. She would have lived in poverty and dealt with rejection. Alone and with no family to support her, it would have been a disastrous outcome. We loved her dearly as a friend. Since Benjamin and I were childless, we more than willingly took Celia as our own." Mrs. Wilson broke down into tears.

"You could have explained everything to us when Beth and I came to visit. Why didn't you?"

"To preserve the memory of your mother, of course," Benjamin rationally expounded. "When Catherine wrote to us about meeting your father and that she had accepted his proposal, we were beside ourselves with joy. Everything turned out as it should have. She lived a content life and had two beautiful children."

Mrs. Wilson sniffled, patting her eyes with a handkerchief.

"You should tell Celia," Francis remarked. "She has the right to know."

"Have you spoken to Beth?" Mr. Wilson asked, avoiding his suggestion.

"Not yet, but I fully intend to go to Rosemont Park and take her out of the household immediately."

"The two of you can stay here with us as long as necessary until you return to Dunwich," Mrs. Wilson offered.

"I appreciate the hospitality under the circumstances." The anger he felt earlier subsided since all had been revealed. He could place no blame upon the Wilsons or Davenports for shielding his mother and helping her so long ago. As he thought of his young and naive mother, he could not blame her for falling for the wiles of a titled and handsome man. He wondered whether Edwin had known the truth and saw in Celia the same weakness to exploit. It could be very possible.

"Will you tell Celia? She deserves the truth," Francis insisted once again.

"Mrs. Wilson and I will discuss it," Benjamin replied.

"You must understand, Francis, that we have loved Celia like our own daughter. She has brightened our lives and challenged our patience," he grinned. "We need to handle the matter delicately."

"Understandable," Francis agreed. "With the truth out, will you tell Lord Howard who she is?"

"Under no circumstances shall we reveal she is his child. There is no telling what he would do to cover up the matter. He cared nothing of her conception, and I fear his rejection of her now would only break her heart." Mrs. Wilson conveyed a convincing argument.

"Well, I shall not forgo the opportunity to give him a piece of my mind when it arises, but I will keep the identity of the child a secret if you wish."

"Thank you," Benjamin replied.

"Have you seen Beth recently? Is she all right?" Regardless of whether or not the earl was in Scotland, he still felt anxious about her being at Rosemont Park.

"Yes, Celia and I had tea with her and Beth earlier this week. She is doing well," Mrs. Wilson offered.

"Has Alexander stayed away from her?"

"I was told that they crossed paths while taking a stroll on the pier one afternoon. Nothing came of it, and Beth insisted that they are just friends."

Mr. Wilson interjected. "Well, that is not what I heard from Mr. Davenport today. He was railing like a wild boar after having dined with the earl last night and the Duke and Duchess of Montrose."

"He's back from Scotland? Why didn't you say so?" A shock of fear ran through Francis at hearing the news.

"I just found out this afternoon. Apparently, Alexander is being tempted to work for the duke's son on some import and export scheme. He indicated to his father as well that he may very well take the position and ask Beth to marry him. Alexander supposedly went there today for another conference to solidify the matter."

"Then I must be off posthaste and retrieve my sister," Francis said, jumping to his feet. "May I borrow your carriage, Mr. Wilson?"

"Yes, of course. I'll tell Wilford to have it brought around."

"Oh, do be careful," Mrs. Wilson cried, wringing her hands. "Will you confront the earl about your mother?"

"I'm not sure. All I care about now is to fetch Beth and have her here safely by my side. The rest I will deal with as the opportunity arises."

Francis could think of nothing more urgent than to retrieve Beth from Rosemont Park. If the earl had seduced his mother, he could very well attempt to do the same to his sister. The thought sent a jolt of alarm through his body.

CHAPTER THIRTY-TWO

The Proposals

The day had been an interesting one. Annie and Percival spent the morning together, apparently becoming more congenial with one another. Since Beth hadn't seen her revert to any childish behavior, she concluded that Annie did, in fact, find him a worthy suitor. She was glad to see it.

Midafternoon Alexander arrived and spent over two hours behind closed doors in the earl's study with the duke and his son. Beth hoped that the meeting would prove fruitful. It would be a dream come true for Alexander to pursue. On the other hand, Beth questioned whether she would have the courage to follow Alexander to a faraway land. Francis would never agree, but then again, she did not need her brother's permission to wed. Regardless, such a choice would take bravery, although she admitted it would be exciting.

As Annie spent time alone in the parlor, they chatted about their choices.

"Do you like him now?" Beth asked.

"You mean Percival?"

"Of course, Percival. Perchance when you are wed, you can call him Percy instead. That sounds a tad better."

"Spending more time with him has softened my

opinion. You were correct in your assumption that he maintained a reserved attitude because of the circumstances."

"Do you find the duke and duchess to be amenable? Are they expressing outward approval as well?"

"I believe so," Annie remarked, lowering her voice. "The duchess has been encouraging, which is an excellent sign. One's mother-in-law should always be tolerable, to say the least."

"I never considered that," Beth admitted. "You are marrying into a family, so yes, that would be important."

Beth pondered the Davenports. Instinctively she knew Alexander's father would not be welcoming. She was unsure what Mrs. Davenport thought. Then there was Edwin, Lydia, and Richard. Of course, it wouldn't matter at all if she got along with any of them if Alexander moved away. Here she was, planning her future in her head when she didn't even know if they had a future.

"I wouldn't be surprised if he asks for your hand in marriage very soon," Annie remarked.

"Who?"

"Alexander, of course."

When she spoke his name, Beth heard the door to the earl's study open and male voices coming toward the parlor. Her stomach fluttered. Alexander entered and smiled when he caught the eye of Beth. She dared not ask how the meeting went lest she embarrassed him. Percival approached Annie.

"Shall we take a walk in the gardens?" he suggested, offering her arm.

"Yes, I would like that very much." Annie looked at Alexander. "Mr. Davenport, why don't you escort Miss Edwards and join us? I'm sure she could use a breath of fresh air."

"Do you mind, Miss Edwards, if we take a walk together in the gardens?" Alexander looked at her with hopeful eyes. Beth obliged by rising to her feet and taking his arm.

The couples exited the double glass doors that led to the veranda and walked to the pristine gardens of the estate. Rosemont Park boasted the finest in flowers, trees, and shrubbery, with small ponds of water and a lovely fountain that Beth enjoyed. Annie and Percival appeared to want time alone as the distance between them widened substantially. Finally out of their hearing, Beth asked, "How did your meeting go?"

"Very well. I have decided to accept the offer."

"Oh, Alexander, how wonderful!" Beth felt as if she held a two-sided sword that would slice through her heart in the next few minutes. Soon he would announce his departure and travel abroad. Would he leave without her? "But what about your father? Surely he will object."

"He will object, but this is my life and my choice." He halted his step. "Beth," he said almost in a whisper. He grabbed both of her hands and gripped them. After inhaling a few anxious breaths, he lifted his eyes until they met hers. "I have accepted their offer, but I do not want to leave you. I will go only on one condition."

"What condition?" Her heart thumped in her chest, hoping he would ask her the question she longed to hear.

"That you accompany me as my wife. Will you marry me? I cannot think of leaving Aycliffe without you by my side. Tell me you won't be afraid." He squeezed her hands in assurance.

"I will care for you, protect you, and let you ride a camel," he grinned. "You have given me the courage to stand up to my father. None of this would have been possible without your encouragement and support."

She knew that Alexander would give her courage too. Unafraid to follow him to the ends of the earth, she gushed her answer. "Oh, Alexander, yes, I will marry you." Not an ounce of hesitation restrained Beth from putting her arms around him. They kissed, and she did not care who witnessed the seal of their engagement. As they enjoyed each other, she heard Francis's voice calling her name. Why had he invaded her mind of all times? His controlling personality haunted her with guilt because she knew he would not consent to the arrangement.

"Beth!"

She released Alexander's lips and spun around. The voice had not been in her head. It was Francis, standing three feet away from her and Alexander, scowling at her like a naughty child caught with a sweet treat she shouldn't be eating.

"Francis! What are you doing here?" Her face burned with embarrassment.

"Mr. Edwards, this is a surprise," Alexander remarked, straight-faced.

"Come with me," Francis ordered. "I am taking you back to the Wilsons and then back to Dunwich. We are through with Aycliffe."

"But Francis, I cannot leave," Beth protested.

"You must leave. It's for your safety," he insisted.

"I assure you, Mr. Edwards, that I am no threat to your sister, regardless of your opinion of me," Alexander insisted.

"It's not you who I am concerned about," Francis said. "It's Lord Howard."

"I do not understand what you are saying," Beth protested. Francis leaned in toward Beth's ear and whispered.

"He was the one who seduced our mother. I discovered Mother's letters and will explain all once we are away from here." Francis pulled back and tilted his head as if to see if she could understand the urgency to take leave.

"Oh, dear God!" She brought both hands to her mouth.

"What is it?" Alexander said, frowning over Beth's reaction.

"We must go, Alexander. Please, come with us."

"If you insist," he said with a befuddled look upon his face.

Annie approached. "Francis, what are you doing here?"

"I have come to fetch Beth home," he said.

"But why?"

"Personal affairs, I'm afraid, call us back to Dunwich."

Beth gave Annie a quick hug. "I'm so sorry. Will you have Agnes pack my things and have them delivered to the Wilsons as soon as possible?"

"Why yes, of course," Annie said, scowling at them. "But I don't understand the urgency for you to run off like this."

"It is best that you do not," Beth said. "I love you like a sister, my dearest Annie. Be happy." She nodded at Percival. "Be good to her."

Appearing as confused as Annie, Beth returned to the parlor with Francis and Alexander. She came to an abrupt halt upon seeing His Lordship alone.

"I see you found your sister," the earl remarked. "Are you still intent on taking her from Rosemont Park?"

"I am, sir. If you will excuse us, the Wilsons are expecting us both this evening," Francis said in a stern voice.

"Miss Edwards, I am sad to see you depart so quickly," he said, approaching Beth and standing in front of her.

He reached out to take Beth's hand, but she pulled back. The thought of his touch sent a shiver through her spine. Could it be true? Had he done what Francis said?

"I must take my leave," she said, quickening her step. "Thank you for your hospitality." Francis led the way to the foyer, and Alexander stood by her side. He appeared as confused as everyone. His beautiful proposal minutes earlier had faded into a distant memory as her heart pounded over the sudden change in circumstance.

"Do you mind, Mr. Edwards, if I accompany you to the Wilsons?" Alexander asked, standing by the carriage door.

"Please let him come, Francis. I beg you," Beth cried.

"All right, if you insist."

The three of them climbed in the carriage, and Beth saw Annie standing by the doorway with a sad countenance. She waved as the coach pulled away from Rosemont Park. A tear ran down her cheek. Francis sat across from her and Alexander, and she entreated him, "Tell me. What did you find out?"

Francis slowly revealed the sordid details that sounded as if they came from a novel. Tales of seduction, rejection, secrecy, deception, and the birth of a baby given to another couple. She interrupted Francis and glared at Alexander.

"Did you know any of this?"

"I swear to God, Beth, I knew nothing about this matter or my parent's complicity in it all," he assured her, reaching out and squeezing her hand. "Believe me."

"Beth, I'm not finished," Francis said.

"The baby. What happened to the baby?" Beth asked.

Francis shifted in his seat, lowered his head, and shook it. "Celia." His voice quavered. "Celia Wilson is our half sister."

Beth gasped aloud. The shock caused the familiar tightening in her chest. Her breathing became short and labored, but she sputtered a response.

"I—I cannot believe Celia is our sister," she panted. "Does she know who her father and mother really are?"

"No, she doesn't. In fact, Lord Howard doesn't even know Celia is his child."

Beth placed both hands on the side of her head. "Don't tell me any more, Francis. I cannot bear another word of it right now."

The carriage pulled into Aycliffe and turned down the avenue where the Wilsons resided. Thankfully, Beth could control her physical response, averting an episode where she could not breathe.

"If Celia is home, do not speak to her about it. Mr. and Mrs. Wilson will tell her, but I'm unsure if they have."

Francis looked at Alexander. "If you do not mind, I think Beth and I need our privacy now."

"I fully understand," Alexander concurred.

The carriage door opened, and Beth grabbed Alexander's hand. "My answer has not changed," she assured him. "I will send for you tomorrow."

"Until then," he said, smiling warmly at her.

She knew that he hesitated to touch her in front of Francis, but Beth needed his comfort. After giving him a quick embrace, she followed Francis indoors to face their deceivers.

"I see things have progressed between you and Mr. Davenport," Francis remarked in a flat tone.

"Yes, they have. Alexander has asked me to marry him, and I have accepted." Beth looked at Francis, glaring at him as if to warn him that an objection at this moment would be ill timed.

"We will talk of it later," he said, understanding her reasoning.

The door to the Wilson's residence opened, and the tearstained face of Celia greeted Beth and Francis.

CHAPTER THIRTY-THREE

Revelations

The day had gone by like any other. Celia had achieved nothing of consequence. Breakfast in the morning, a few minutes of embroidery, one song on the piano, and a leisurely walk before lunch. Since Beth and Francis had left, Celia had little to fill her time. It made for dangerous pondering regarding Edwin and who he would choose next in his lengthy line of conquests. Nevertheless, the time apart had mended her broken heart, opening her eyes to how foolish she had been nearly giving him her virtue

She had received no correspondence from Francis, although she wrote to him a few days ago. By now he should have received the letter, but it didn't appear that he was too keen on answering. He had probably settled back into his business. Watchmaking had to be more important than picking up a pen. Whatever the reason, it had become another disappointment in her life because she enjoyed his company.

When the thought of the afternoon with nothing to do loomed before Celia, she asked to take leave to visit her friend Susan. Two bored young ladies together would be better than one. Perhaps they could take a walk on the beach and ponder the summer when single young men would visit for a holiday.

Like many other pursuits, the afternoon had sped

past, and Celia returned before the dinner hour. She intended to read afterward as she had purchased a new novel laced with romance that her parents would no doubt disapprove of. That is why she had hidden it in the bottom of her dresser drawer to open late at night while snug under her covers. Reading by candlelight always added a bit of romanticism to the story. At least she could daydream about love in the privacy of her room, even if she had no one to love during the reality of her days.

What she did not expect upon her return home was that her father and mother would ask to speak with her straightaway about something of utmost importance. She sat in the chair across from her parents, who appeared nervous. Her mother wrung her hands together, while her father shifted in his seat as if he sat on a thorn.

"What's wrong?" she asked, looking at her mother's pale countenance. "Has something happened? Did someone die?"

"No one has died," her father answered, "but your mother and I have something that you need to know."

"Mother is ill," Celia concluded. "It's those head-aches that plague you, isn't it, Mama? The doctor thinks something is terribly wrong with you," Celia exclaimed in fear. Maybe her mother's headaches were not always an excuse not to talk but an awful physical condition.

"No, Celia, it has nothing to do with my health. Now sit quietly and listen to what your father must tell you," she said.

He scowled. "I thought you would tell her," he rattled in a low tone.

"You will be much calmer in the delivery than I," Prudence insisted. "Now, go ahead. I'm right here to support you."

"Oh, for heaven's sake. What is it?"

"Well, you see. . ." His words trailed off. "Um, it seems. . . there is something. . ."

"What?" Celia shouted in agitation.

Her mother huffed an exasperated sigh and spoke since her father couldn't formulate the words. In a slow and steady voice, she recited. "You are not our natural daughter, my dear Celia. You are the daughter of Catherine Ashby."

Words indeed had unseen power. At that moment, Celia forgot how to breathe. Her hearing must have deteriorated, so she brought both hands to her ears as if she had gone daft in the head. Her parents witnessed the reaction, and her father leaned forward, ready to catch her should she swoon on the floor.

"I'm the daughter of who?" Celia questioned, needing the announcement spoken again to confirm what she had heard.

Her father finally spoke an intelligent sentence. "You are Beth's and Francis's half sister and the daughter of Catherine Ashby."

"What on earth are you talking about?" Celia squawked. "Surely, this is some type of jest you play on me for an afternoon sport."

"It is not," her father reiterated. "Catherine Ashby had a brief affair and became pregnant. Your mother and I could not have children, and Catherine could not take care of you. We brought you into our home, and you became our daughter. We have loved you like our own."

"Yes, dearest, like our own flesh and blood," her mother reiterated.

A numbness flowed through Celia's extremities. Thoughts in her brain raced like buzzing bees. An urge to sprint to the door and run away overtook her senses, but her body remained seated as if heavy weights prevented her from moving. Without forethought, an unanswered question spouted from between her lips.

"Who is the father?"

"The current earl, Lord Howard," her mother said. "But he does not know that you are his daughter."

"Good God," Celia groaned. "You mean to tell me I am the illegitimate daughter of an earl?" A single tear rolled down her face.

"Yes, I'm afraid so," her father confirmed. "Catherine told him she was pregnant, but he denied responsibility."

Denied responsibility. Had Catherine been seduced, like Edwin had nearly seduced her?

"Do Beth and Francis know?"

"Francis has come to the knowledge of it recently, having found letters we wrote to his mother. We corresponded these twenty years past, sharing with her your growth into a young woman. She was proud of what you had become and grateful that we gave you a suitable home."

Celia didn't quite know what to make of the news. A sudden lack of self-worth washed over her, possessing the knowledge that she was the product of scandal. The innuendos and rumors that had floated about town for years suddenly made sense.

"Everybody must know I am a bastard child," she wailed. "How could they not with the rumors people speak of?" No wonder Edwin's father would not permit their marriage. Obviously, she was nothing in their sight.

"I assure you, Celia, no one knows. Mr. and Mrs. Davenport arranged for Catherine to go away. While she was away, I told all our friends I was pregnant and feigned the event by stuffing pillows under my dresses when out in public. When you were born, you came to us immediately, and Catherine returned to Dunwich. No one has been the wiser."

"Why does the earl not know that I am his child?"

"After the cruel way that he discarded Catherine, she didn't believe he needed to know, and we wholeheartedly agreed."

"It is appalling," Celia cried, as her emotions overflowed with grief. "All these years, you lied to me, making me think you were my parents. You buried this secret from me, Francis, and Beth. How could you do such a thing?"

"We thought it for the best, dear," her mother blubbered, crying and distraught.

Celia couldn't sit still another moment and jumped to her feet. At first, she wobbled like a weakling with a quick bout of dizziness. Her father reached out to steady her, but Celia pushed him away. Eventually, she gathered her wits about her. Tears streamed down her face unabated, and she had no power to stop them. The painful revelation had opened the floodgates.

"I cannot sit here any longer and listen to another word," she announced. Celia sprinted out the parlor door and to the front entrance. Intent on running until she could run no more, she flung the door open. To her surprise, there stood Francis and Beth, blocking her departure. She froze and stared at them in disbelief. They were her sister and brother, having shared the same mother. The inconceivable idea caused her to tremble.

"Celia." Francis reached out and grabbed her arm to steady her bobbing stance in the threshold.

"They told me," she blubbered. "They told me I'm nothing more than a bastard child. Isn't it dreadful?"

The tearful face of Celia broke his heart. Francis's thoughts about her had run the gambit from being amicable, immoral, adorable, even to ponder the possibility of a future with her. Now, as she stood there before him, he had to accept they were related. His mother was her mother, and the oddity of it all almost brought him to tears. A momentary urge to hug her came over him, but Beth took it upon herself to take the sisterly role of comforting Celia.

"Oh, Celia, it is not dreadful. We have gained a sister and a most wonderful sister at that."

Celia embraced Beth in return, sobbing in the crook of her shoulder like a child. Francis couldn't help but smile as a different sentiment of affection rose in his heart.

"Well, having one sister has been trying indeed, but now it appears I have two to deal with," he remarked in a jovial tone.

His comment caused Celia to chuckle, and she pulled back.

He handed her a handkerchief from his pocket. "Dry your tears and let's go inside. We have much to talk about."

Celia took the offer and did so while they wandered into the parlor together. When he glanced at the Wilsons, they appeared distraught as if they had lost a loved one to death. Francis realized that telling Celia the truth had taken a toll upon them and would for eternity change their relationship for better or worse. As the five of them stood within a few feet of each other, Celia had taken hold of her emotions.

"I'm sorry for being so upset," she said, looking at

the Wilsons. "This is so strange. I don't know whether to call you Benjamin and Prudence or Mother and Father."

"We understand, dear," Mrs. Wilson remarked. "But in our hearts, you are our daughter and always will be."

"Indeed," Mr. Wilson remarked. "Address us as you wish, Celia, but be assured we have loved you as our own."

"But you are not, and I must come to terms with whom Catherine Ashby was and the awful fact that Lord Howard is my father. Dear God, what a conundrum."

"Agreed, it is one," Francis announced.

"Well, dinner is ready, does anyone think they can eat or would you like a tray brought to your rooms?" Prudence asked.

"I'm famished," Francis admitted. "Beth, how about you?"

"Yes. Come sit by me, Celia," she suggested.

"All right. But I haven't much of an appetite."

Francis looked forward to the meal and hoped that in the next hour everyone's emotions would settle amicably. Overwhelmed by the sudden change in circumstance, another matter weighed on his shoulders. Beth had accepted Alexander's proposal of marriage. He somewhat expected that during his absence the man would take advantage of the situation one way or the other.

Surprisingly, he fostered no anger when he should have given Alexander a tongue lashing for his forwardness. As much as he wanted to maintain control of Beth's life, he reluctantly realized that insisting she break the engagement would only tear them apart. After dinner, they would discuss the matter in private. For the moment, he would turn his attention on Celia.

CHAPTER THIRTY-FOUR

Breaking the Shackles

The afternoon had turned into a whirlwind of events. They had offered Alexander the opportunity to act as an agent for Lord Montrose in his new business venture. They would pay his passage to Egypt, and upon his arrival, he would open an office in Cairo. The city was on the cusp of being the most important center of trade in the region, and Montrose wanted an early foothold. As an agent, Alexander would hire buyers to procure a variety of goods from Egypt for importing to England. Everything from trinkets to cotton, and for those who could afford the finest, artifacts for their collections. English cotton mills were looking beyond the Americas to Egypt and India for their cotton, not wishing to partake in slave labor. Business owners were hungry for supplies elsewhere.

Alexander's daydreams had turned to reality, and the opportunity to travel abroad sat before him like a bar of sweet chocolate. As he sat in Lord Howard's study, listening to their proposal, he knew that he would not make the trip alone. He wanted Beth at his side to enjoy the fascination of Egyptian culture and be his wife. Foreigners from England and Europe were flocking to Egypt by the thousands, who were engaged in trade, banking, and finance. Alexander knew that while he worked, Beth would not be alone. Wives and families from English homes resided in Cairo, and they would intermingle in those social circles. All he needed was for Beth to accept his proposal, and his life path would change. Albeit, a few obstacles remained, such as speaking with his parents.

Regardless, the afternoon had turned into a somewhat convoluted surprise when Francis arrived to spirit Beth away from Rosemont Park as if she were in danger for her life. When he shared the reason on the way to the Wilsons, Alexander could not believe the news. Celia was Catherine Ashby's daughter, and for the life of him, he could not understand how that secret had hid from everyone. His parents and the Wilsons were masters of deceit, and no one had been the wiser.

After a brisk walk home from the Wilsons, he entered the house shortly before dinner. He wondered how Beth and Francis were faring, while he would soon face a problematic revelation to his family. It took a few minutes to ponder what avenue he would use to announce his plans. A new position, the engagement, the impending wedding, and the trip abroad would all come as a vast surprise. If he discussed it privately with his father, it would turn into a shouting match. However, announcing it at the dinner table with Edwin, Lydia, Richard, and his mother nearby might soften his father's response. Everyone's reaction would be fascinating.

"You are late," his mother said, as he entered the parlor. "We were about to start dinner without you. Where have you been?"

"At Rosemont Park for a meeting," he replied.

"Well, go change for dinner and be quick about it, or Father shall be irritable for the rest of the night."

"He's always irritable," Alexander remarked. Since his parents dressed for the evening meal, Alexander returned to his room. After a quick splash of water on his face, combing his hair, and dressing, he trotted back downstairs. The family sat at the dining table, waiting for his arrival. Benson, their butler, stood supervising the footman as they were served.

"I apologize for my lateness," he said, glancing at his father. Rather than anxiousness, a peace settled Alexander's heart that had not been there for some time. Nevertheless, he braced himself for the objections and lectures that would soon be forthcoming. Instead of spoiling dinner, he waited to speak toward the end of the meal. Surprisingly, his father asked him nothing about his meeting with Lord Montrose, perhaps delaying it for a private discussion after supper. When the moment presented itself, Alexander got their attention.

"I am glad that we are all together because I have an announcement to make that will affect the family." Alexander dabbed his lips with a napkin and then set it down.

A steady stare from his father met his gaze, while his mother looked somewhat surprised.

"Announcement about what?" she asked.

"Do tell us," his father remarked in a snarly tone.

"I have accepted a position with Lord Montrose and will travel to Cairo, Egypt, in four weeks to set up an office there. He has engaged me as his agent for his newly established import business."

His little brother's eyes grew wide with excitement. "Stellar news, Alexander. What an opportunity," Richard gushed.

Alexander knew that he would find it agreeable since Richard always had his nose in a book. Geography had been one of his favorite subjects.

"You cannot be serious," his mother said, scowling at him. "Surely you don't approve of this scheme," she cried, turning toward his father.

"No, I do not approve, and I'll be damned if I give you one quid for you to travel abroad," he grumbled.

"You need not give me anything, as the trip is paid for," Alexander announced. "In fact, it's a trip for two."

"Two?" Edwin repeated with a raised brow.

"He's done it," Lydia shouted. "I knew he would do it." She pushed Edwin on the arm. "Didn't I tell you he would propose?"

Suddenly, the table became a yelling match of opinions demanding to be heard. Alexander's father commanded to know what he had done. His mother gasped and covered her mouth. Richard laughed, and Edwin and Lydia had a spat about a bet.

"I have asked Beth Edwards to marry me, and she has accepted my proposal," Alexander announced, sitting up straight like a proud, puffed-up peacock.

His father pushed back his chair, stood to his feet, and threw his napkin down on the table. "You stupid, foolish, irresponsible man," he said. "I swear if you do this, I shall disinherit you." His face turned beet red.

"Then disinherit me," Alexander calmly replied. "Today, I break free of your demands and gain control over my life, Father. And there is nothing you can do about it."

"Oh, Alexander, you cannot be serious," his mother wailed.

"Let him go," Lydia said. "I am happy for him."

"Me too," Richard announced.

Alexander looked at Edwin. "And what of you, brother? What say you?"

"Bastard," he railed. "With you away, Father will hound me even harder to marry for money. Damn you, Alexander!"

Expecting the reaction, Alexander did not take it to

heart as Edwin stormed away from the table. Lydia threw her arms around his neck, and Richard gave him a pat on the back.

"You better write me," he said. "I want to know everything about Egypt."

"I will," Alexander agreed, happy for their congratulations.

He glanced at his mother, who quietly removed herself from the dining room with tears. His father stomped down the hall to his study and slammed the door.

"Give them time," Lydia said. "They will come around."

"I would like to leave on good terms," Alexander remarked. He knew that he could not expect their support, but he did not wish to sever familial ties forever.

"Richard and I will attempt to soften the blow. We have a month to do it," Lydia encouraged.

"Sweet of you, sis, but I fear your efforts will be for naught."

It was almost comical as half of the table departed. Alexander couldn't help but notice Benson's eyes twinkling in approval over what had transpired.

"Well, stay with me, Lydia and Richard, and let us enjoy dessert together. Perhaps they will return."

When the following morning arrived, Alexander only had one thought on his mind—Beth. With the return of her brother, he feared that he would assert his influence to rescind her acceptance of his proposal. Upon Francis hearing that Alexander planned to spirit her away to a foreign land, it undoubtedly would not sit well with him. He wanted to call upon the Wilson household before Francis forced Beth back to Dunwich and away from his grasp.

After bathing and dressing for the day, he joined the family for breakfast. Apprehensive that he would be unwelcomed, he walked into the dining room as if nothing were amiss. His father was absent, but his mother sat at the table, nibbling on a piece of toast, appearing as if she had not slept a wink. Lydia and Richard smiled at him, while Edwin glared at him with an unwelcomed frown.

"Good morning," he said, going to the sideboard and filling a plate with food. After retrieving a hearty portion, he sat down. "Is Father not joining us this morning?" His mother raised her head and looked at him with swollen eyes from weeping the night before.

"He is in his study and does not wish to be disturbed. You can thank yourself since he does not wish to lay eyes upon you this morning."

"Well, that's too bad, because I have another matter to discuss with him before I call on the Wilsons," Alexander announced.

"Are you going there to see that Edwards girl?"

"That Edwards girl is my fiancée, Mother," he reminded her in a stern tone.

"She is very nice, Mama," Lydia added. "You should be happy for Alexander. They make a delightful couple."

"I have no objection," Richard announced. "Not that you care, Mother, what I think."

Alexander smiled, enjoying their support, although it fell upon deaf ears.

"Well, it is abominable that you have defied your father's wishes," his mother said. "It's a terrible thing for a son to do. I'm not surprised he has disowned you." She sniffled again as if she would break out in tears.

Alexander hated that she attempted to manipulate his choices with her motherly wiles of tossing guilt upon him. He ignored the maneuver.

"It is a shame that you think that way, Mother, but I shall not change my mind to please you or Father."

Alexander gulped his breakfast, took a sip of tea, and then rose from the table. "Now, if you will excuse me, I have matters to attend to," he said, leaving and heading to his father's study.

He came to the closed door and halted for a moment. Refusing denial for entrance, he rapped on the door with his knuckles until he heard his father's voice.

"Yes, who is it?"

Rather than answering, Alexander turned the door-knob and entered his office uninvited. He wasn't about to wait for his father's command to go away.

"Good morning, Father. Might I have a word with you?" He closed the door behind him, strode in the room with confidence, taking a seat in front of the desk.

"I don't wish to see you," his father protested.

"Well, I wish to speak with you as I have a question regarding an urgent matter," Alexander announced.

"What question?" His father narrowed his eyes at him in disdain.

"Yesterday, a secret kept for over twenty years came out into the open that I had not been privy to," Alexander said.

"What secret?"

"That Celia Wilson is the daughter of Lord Howard and Catherine Ashby."

"Poppycock," his father sputtered.

He averted direct eye contact, which told Alexander he intended on skirting the matter rather than answering truthfully.

"I doubt it. Francis Edwards discovered letters from the Wilsons to Catherine, detailing Celia's upbringing. From what I've been told, you and Mother helped arrange for Catherine's seclusion before the baby was born, and the Wilsons agreed to take the child to raise as their own. I understand that Lord Howard has no idea that Celia is his daughter."

Finally, his announcement caught his father's attention, and he turned his gaze.

"And what if we did? Celia is no wiser to the situation either," he remarked.

"She knows now or will soon be told. The Wilsons have explained the entire fiasco to Francis and Beth about Celia's parentage. I daresay you and the Wilsons pulled off a rather grand scheme that no one discovered. If it hadn't been for the unearthing of the letters that Catherine hid in her home, the secret would remain buried."

His father stared at him oddly as if he were looking through Alexander and to the wall behind him. If he didn't know any better, he would think his mind whirled around in a circle on a totally different subject.

"Interesting it should come out now," his father pensively remarked. "Are they going to tell Howard?"

"I doubt it, but I'm not sure," Alexander remarked.

"Probably best not to as he will certainly deny culpability as he has done since he impregnated poor Catherine."

Surprised by his father's sympathetic tone, they both fell silent for a few moments. After a continuation of deep thought on his part, he finally spoke.

"Is that all you have to say? No announcement in your change of plans to marry Miss Edwards or traipse off to Egypt?"

"No, I am determined to follow this path," Alexander steadfastly announced. "My hope is that Mother and you will come to accept it, even if you do not agree before I depart. There is no telling when or if we shall see each other again." With those words, Alexander stood to his feet and walked to the door and opened it. "Good day, Father," he coolly remarked. It was time to turn his attentions elsewhere.

CHAPTER THIRTY-FIVE

Accepting the Inevitable

Perhaps Beth should have been nervous about her impending conversation with Francis. Instead, she dealt with the shock of Celia being their half sister, which threw her into a tizzy of emotions. Pondering how her poor mother had been seduced by Lord Howard was enough to make her want to hire a carriage to Rosemont Park and slap the man hard across the face. What irked Beth even further had been the bald-faced lie the earl perpetrated to cast blame upon his dead father. She had lost all trust in the man.

All had emphatically agreed the evening before that Lord Howard would continue to be ignorant of the fact that Celia was his daughter. Celia naturally had mixed emotions over being the illegitimate offspring of an earl. She wanted to confront him, but after receiving advice, she abandoned the idea for fear of rejection.

As Beth pondered her poor mother's circumstances, she did not harshly judge her weakness. They would never really know how the earl convinced her to lay with him. Perhaps the enticement contained false promises of becoming his wife, when all along, he merely wanted another conquest. Since he had convinced everyone that the death of his wife had devastated him, perhaps that was a ruse too. The man was reprehensible, and unfortunately, Annie had no idea about the real character of her uncle. Possibly marrying Percival would be the best thing for her rather than staying at Rosemont Park with a snake in the grass.

When the clock on the mantel struck eight o'clock in the morning, Beth knew that Francis would soon knock upon her bedroom door and wasn't surprised when it arrived.

"Come in," she called, standing to her feet. Francis opened the door and entered, closing it softly behind him.

"Punctual as usual," she remarked.

"Naturally, as I'm eager to start the conversation at hand."

Beth didn't want him to assert his usual control over the situation, so she took no time in expressing her thoughts.

"Before you say anything, I want you to hear me," she announced, sitting on the edge of the bed. Francis took a seat in the empty chair by the window.

"All right," he said, keeping his opinions captive for the time being.

"Alexander has followed his heart, Francis, both in his business and personal life," she solemnly reported. "He is to become an agent for Lord Montrose and will travel to Cairo to set up an office there. They are starting an import business."

"Well, perhaps I should thank this Lord Montrose for taking Alexander out of the country," Francis remarked. "Do you intend to wait for his return from this excursion?"

"No, I intend to marry him and travel with him to Cairo as his wife. We will live there for the unforeseeable future." Beth braced herself, fully expecting Francis to burst into a raging madman at the concept of her departure. Instead, he sat there motionless and scowled, shifting in his chair. He dug his nails into the armrest and puffed a few times from between his lips. If she didn't know any better, she would have thought he was about to have one of her attacks. When the color returned to his face, he spoke.

"And you have no fear following him to the ends of the earth?"

"None whatsoever," Beth replied. "When I am with Alexander, I am at peace. My heart is at rest, and he makes me feel safe. He has promised to take care of me, and I believe him completely."

Francis stared at her. In his eyes, she saw a mixture of emotions flash from concern to resignation.

"You know that I love you, Beth, and want the best for your life," he admitted.

Beth saw the pain in his countenance. "I know Francis, but it is time to let me go. You can see that, don't you?" Beth reasoned with him. "I love Alexander, and now it is time for me to leave your side, and time for you to find a wife and start your family."

"When is this wedding, and when will you leave?" Francis asked. She sensed a slight tremble in his voice.

"We have not set a date, but we will leave in a month for Egypt. The passage has been paid by Lord Montrose," she announced.

"I see." Francis stood to his feet. "Well, I suppose then we should have that wedding before I return to Dunwich, as I must walk you down the aisle." A slight grin curled his mouth. "You do want me to walk you down the aisle?" Francis's eyes glistened as if he were on the verge of tears.

"Oh Francis," Beth said, coming toward him and giving him a hug. "Thank you." After placing a kiss on his cheek, she looked at him with affection. "I shall miss you terribly and promise to write often."

"And I shall endeavor to write you back, assuming that it takes two months for the letter to arrive, it shouldn't be too burdensome of a chore."

After speaking for a few more minutes about arranging a rather quick wedding, Francis asked. "I imagine that the elder Mr. Davenport is not too happy with your intended."

"Furious, no doubt, but I shall not worry about it. I am very proud of Alexander finding the courage to break away and find his way in life on his terms. It is one thing I admire about him."

"Then I must admit, as hard as it is to swallow, that I have unjustly judged his character and motives." He grimaced as if it hurt to confess his wrongdoing.

"My goodness, Francis Edwards," Beth smirked. "You, admitting wrong?"

"Well, with you away, I'll now have Celia's interest at heart. She may be sorry to have me as a brother," he said, grinning.

"Oh dear," Beth said. "I will have to warn her what is to come."

After talking for a few more minutes in private, Beth and Francis made their way downstairs for breakfast. The Wilsons sat at the table with Celia, who smiled when they entered the room. Beth had not yet told anyone her news with all the revelations yesterday about Celia. As they settled into their seats, she glanced at Francis.

"Should I tell them?"

"You might as well," he encouraged her.

"What news now?" Celia asked, scrunching her brows together.

Beth smiled. "Alexander has asked me to marry him, and I have accepted his proposal."

Benjamin nearly choked on his tea, while Prudence's eyes grew wide as saucers.

"And—and his father has approved?" Benjamin stuttered.

"Approved or not," Celia said. "Congratulations, Beth! I'm so happy for you."

"There is much more," Francis remarked.

"What else?" Prudence said. Benjamin stared at Beth with his mouth gaping open.

"Alexander has been offered a position in Egypt as an agent for Lord Montrose. Beth and Alexander will leave England to live in Cairo."

"Good God! When did this come about?" Benjamin bellowed.

"Within the past day," Beth replied. "The duke and his son were visiting Rosemont Park, as Lord Montrose is Annie's intended. He and Alexander spoke about Egypt and a commercial venture that His Lordship had in mind. One thing led to another, and they forged a business arrangement."

"Oh, my dear," Prudence remarked. "His father must be beside himself."

"Good for him," Celia said. "I am happy for Alexander. His father wrongly pressured him to marry for money, just like he did Edwin." She looked at Beth. "And you told me that you were just friends," she scoffed. "I knew you loved him."

"What will he do now?" Prudence said, shaking her head. "Oh, Benjamin, you should go call on James and speak with him this morning. He will need your support." She reached over and touched his hand.

"Why are you not happy for Alexander?" Beth asked. "You seem to think his father has suffered some substantial loss when, in reality, you should be happy for Alexander for building his future."

"The man has given his life to Aycliffe and held great hope in his sons to help turn the town around," Mr. Wilson admitted. "The city is on the verge of bankruptcy. Now all hope is lost." A groan of disappointment left his throat.

"Well, there's always Edwin," Celia snidely reminded them. "I'm sure he can find his way up the skirts of some daughter of another aristocrat or heiress of a rich manufacturer."

"Celia, really," Prudence scolded.

Celia's face brightened. "Well, that means Francis will be alone." She looked at him, flashing an impish smile. "I wouldn't mind coming to Dunwich to keep you company while Beth goes to Egypt. Would you consider such an arrangement?"

Beth could hardly believe Celia's suggestion. It sounded outrageous but also timely.

"Oh, Celia, if you live with Francis, he shall attempt to control you as he did me. Do you actually want to subject yourself to such shenanigans?" Beth laughed.

"Celia, you would leave us?" Prudence asked, looking hurt.

"I think it a fine idea. I know you both very well, having spent the past twenty-four years of my life under this roof. Now, I have a sibling who I scarcely know and would like to get to know him better." She reached out and touched Francis's forearm. "What say you, brother? Shall I keep you company while Beth rides camels in Egypt?"

Francis appeared flustered at the proposition, attempting to swallow a mouthful of food. At first, Beth worried he might choke. Eventually, the lump went down his throat. Thinking some encouragement on her behalf might help, she spoke.

"Oh, Francis, that's a delightful idea. I won't worry

about you being alone. She can keep an eye on you for me, and I'll know you are in good hands."

"Well, I. . ." His words trailed off as if he couldn't finish the thought.

"Perhaps you can find him a wife," Beth added.

"And perhaps he can find me a husband," Celia countered. "Oh, come and agree, Francis. I shan't be a burden to you. I promise."

A slow smile spread across his face, and Beth could see that a different kind of affection had taken hold. Celia was his half sister. Why wouldn't he allow her to live with him in Dunwich?

"I suppose there will be some explaining to do with the townspeople," he said. "They may think it inappropriate, seeing a strange woman residing in the household."

"Yes, I suppose you are right," Beth admitted, not having considered the consequences to her mother's memory. "People will ask. When we tell her about Celia's identity, it will cause a gossip storm indeed." Beth woefully spoke. "How shall we protect Mother?"

"Beth is right. It's a terrible idea. You should protect Catherine at all costs," Prudence interrupted, attempting to dissuade Celia from the idea.

"We could tell them she's my cousin," Francis suggested, "but it would be a falsehood to hide the secret my mother hoped to keep buried."

"You may call me your cousin," Celia agreed. "I do not find it troublesome on my part. We can live as such if it protects Catherine."

Beth thought it a viable solution. "I see no problem in that arrangement. It would have to be on Father's side of the family, of course, as most know Mother had no living relatives to speak of."

"If you are sure you can tolerate me," Francis said,

"then you are welcome at Dunwich."

"Then I will travel there after Alexander and Beth leave for Egypt," Celia said. "Would that be convenient?"

"Yes, and you can have Beth's room that I am redecorating."

"Redecorating?" Beth squeaked. "Then you best tell him your favorite colors, Celia, or he shall wallpaper it with some ugly pattern."

The three of them laughed while Mr. and Mrs. Wilson sat quietly listening to their banter. Beth wanted to encourage and comfort them but struggled to find the right words. Benjamin arose from his seat.

"I supposed I should call upon Mr. Davenport," he said.

Beth watched as he excused himself, while Prudence followed him to the door.

"Alexander will visit soon," Beth mentioned. She looked at Francis. "You will be kind to him, won't you?"

"With great difficulty," Francis replied. "With great difficulty, indeed."

Beth appreciated Francis's honesty, for she knew letting her go would not be an easy task.

CHAPTER THIRTY-SIX

The Nuptials

Francis had faced disappointment in life that often weighed heavily upon his shoulders. With the passing of his father, mother, and now about to give Beth away to marry, he bemoaned a deep-seated sense of abandonment. Perhaps Celia would help to fill the void when she visited Dunwich, but he worried about the future.

Once Francis had made peace with Alexander, the concern for his sister's well-being subsided. The assurance that he had given Francis regarding his love and care for Beth had been genuine. Beth's affection for Alexander had also been abiding. Nevertheless, the thought of her leaving for Egypt broke his heart. It would hurt to say goodbye.

The wedding day arrived, and as promised, he walked Beth down the aisle. The Wilsons helped with the preparations, despite Benjamin being disappointed in Alexander's choices in life. Celia and Prudence found the perfect dress for her wedding day. Francis paid for the gown as well as giving Beth a substantial allowance to buying clothing for her fresh life abroad. He also purchased a trunk for her travels.

Though Beth had no dowry to speak of put aside by their father, Francis had generously gifted a small sum of money to Alexander. He wanted assurance that upon their arrival in Cairo, they could obtain suitable housing. Surprised by the offer, Alexander refused the funds, stating he had saved enough money to start their life without need. Francis insisted that he take it for safekeeping for Beth to use in case of difficulties. Alexander swallowed his pride and reluctantly agreed.

The guests at the wedding were few. Since there were not enough weeks before their departure to read the banns in an Anglican church, Alexander and Beth married in a small nonconformist chapel. Alexander's parents refused to attend, leaving behind a scarred relationship with their son. Instead, Lydia and Richard participated, but Edwin stayed away. Annie and her new fiancé, Lord Montrose, attended the ceremony. Lord Howard had not been invited. Mr. and Mrs. Wilson agreed to witness the marriage.

As Francis stood in the foyer of the small chapel, he glanced at Beth. The bittersweet moment of giving her away had arrived.

"You look beautiful," he said. "I am sure that Mother and Father would be so proud of you right now."

"I miss them enormously," Beth confessed.

"Perhaps they are here in spirit, watching us." Francis wished it were so.

He walked Beth slowly as if to savor each second left with his sister. Alexander waited at the altar, smiling as Beth came near.

"Who gives this woman to be wed?" the minister asked.

"I do," Francis said. He placed her hand in Alexander's and then stepped back to the pew to watch the ceremony unfold. Celia sat next to him and whispered in his ear.

"She will be fine, Francis."

Her assuring words barely eased the gut-wrenching heartache of saying goodbye. For Beth's sake, he would give his blessing and pray for her happiness.

The ceremony did not take long, and quickly they had been pronounced man and wife. Beth's face lit with excitement, and Alexander could not stop grinning from ear to ear.

"Congratulations," he said, approaching them.

"I'll take excellent care of her," Alexander reminded him. "You have my word."

A flurry of good wishes came from the attendees. They retired to the Wilson residence for a wedding breakfast, except for Annie and Lord Percival, who excused themselves to return to Rosemont Park. Before leaving, Beth said her goodbyes to her friend with promises to write. No doubt, since Montrose had employed Alexander, their connection would remain for some years to come.

"How are you?" Celia asked, coming to Francis's side.

"I feel as if the universe is testing my character," he admitted. "Releasing Beth has not been easy, but I have come to terms with it. Her happiness is far more important than my self-centered whining." He looked at Celia and smiled. "Since I have you in my life, I shall have something else to focus upon."

"Yes, but you shall not control me, Francis. Let me make that perfectly clear before I pack my bags and follow you to Dunwich."

Francis's brow rose above his eye, hearing Celia's emphatic declaration. "Well, our cohabitation should be an interesting event then."

"I shall make it my purpose to marry you off," Celia announced. "If I play matchmaker, it will keep me entertained."

Francis laughed aloud and rolled his eyes at the idea

of it. "I'm afraid you may find that task somewhat difficult. However, if that is the pursuit you wish, then I shall return the favor and find you a husband."

"Well then, we have our work cut out for us," Celia agreed, smirking at him.

"You do know that Dunwich is not the sprawling city of London, filled with high society. It's a small village with minimal prospects."

"That may be true," Celia remarked, "but it shall not deter me."

As they retired to the dining room to enjoy their meal, Francis enjoyed Beth's glowing countenance. Seeing her happiness put a salve upon his selfish wound, and he had the profound sense that his parents would have approved.

"So, when do you leave for Egypt?" Benjamin asked as they sat down to eat luncheon.

"Next week."

"It must be an arduous trip," Prudence remarked.

"One that is well traveled," Alexander remarked. "Tourism in Egypt is at its peak."

"Aren't you afraid to go so far away?" Prudence asked Beth, as if she wanted to stir up trouble.

"Not in the least. I am extremely excited to undertake the adventure," Beth admitted.

Francis believed her declaration.

After spending a good deal of time around the table with amicable discussion and good food, Beth and Alexander excused themselves. Alexander had booked a suite at the Aycliffe Hotel to use for the next few days until their departure. Soon Beth would become a woman in every sense of the word, and he wished his mother had been alive to counsel her beforehand.

"I shall take my leave to Dunwich in a day," Francis announced.

"So soon?" Beth inquired with a surprised look on her face.

"Yes, dear sister. We shall say our goodbyes, for if I prolong it, I may embarrass myself by becoming a blubbering fool."

"Very well then," Beth agreed. "And Celia, will you go with him? I do hope."

"Yes, we have discussed the matter. You need not worry about Francis as I plan to keep him out of trouble."

"Trouble?" Francis balked.

"I am sure my brother will be in good hands," Beth acknowledged with a smile.

Alexander, appearing restless to break the bonds, grabbed Beth's hand. "We should go."

With those words, Francis watched his sister climb into the carriage with her husband and waved at them as they pulled away. He heaved a sigh and turned around to see Celia shed a tear.

Beth held Alexander's hand tightly as her stomach churned with butterflies. The ceremony had been beautiful, although it seemed to fly by like a bird—here one second and over the next. Mr. and Mrs. Wilson had kindly put on a lavish wedding luncheon, but Beth found it challenging to eat anything substantial.

"Francis appeared to take everything in stride," Alexander remarked. "It is good that Celia will be going to Dunwich. It should fill the void of your absence."

"Yes, I think it will keep his mind occupied." Beth said. "I have a sense that Celia may be a handful."

Alexander glanced out the window as the carriage

passed his home. The disappointment over his parent's refusal to attend the wedding hurt him deeply.

"I'm so sorry they have not supported you," Beth said, squeezing his hand.

"As am I, but I shall not fret or allow their actions to taint the happiness of this day. We are husband and wife now, and soon we will leave Aycliffe forever." He looked lovingly into Beth's eyes. "I have no regrets and would not change this moment for anything."

The horses trotted toward the hotel, and a few minutes later, they arrived. Alexander helped Beth and escorted her indoors to the lavish lobby. They had already delivered their belongings. He signed the register, obtained the key, and proceeded to the suite.

Beth pushed aside her nervous jitters over the impending private moments they would share. She knew in her heart that Alexander would be loving and gentle, leading her into womanhood. Not long before her mother fell ill, a conversation had occurred between them. Recalling that discussion turned Beth's thoughts to that terrible moment that her mother had relinquished herself to Lord Howard. His persuasiveness must have caught her off guard, or at the very least, his insistence that she comply with his advances were too difficult to fend off. Though no one had suggested that he had forced himself upon her mother, the possibility existed.

Alexander opened the door to the room and, without warning, swooped her up in his arms. Beth let out a yelp of surprise and giggled.

"Alexander, what are you doing?"

"Carrying you over the threshold, my dear," he announced. "Though this is not our home, it will have to do for the moment until we reach Cairo. Then I shall carry you again."

He set her down and grinned. "I do love you, my dearest Beth."

"I love you too." Beth recognized the undeniable look of desire in a man's eyes. Soon he would take her.

"Trust me?" he asked, with a lopsided grin.

"Completely." She embraced him, losing herself in a passionate kiss. When she felt his arousal, Beth knew it wouldn't be long before she would become his wife in the flesh.

CHAPTER THIRTY-SEVEN

The Extortion

James Davenport had no desire to attend his son's wedding. Neither did his wife or Edwin. He didn't quite know how long he would keep the grudge against Alexander as he climbed out of bed that morning. It all depended on how the day turned out. One thing was for sure, he had come into information that he knew he could use to his advantage and had no qualms in doing so.

He dressed for the day, had a leisurely breakfast, and then left shortly after Alexander departed for the church. With a ready carriage and directions to his driver, he sat back and pondered the discussion that would soon occur at Rosemont Park. The day had turned out to be a fine one with blue skies and puffy white clouds. There was nothing like beautiful weather to keep one's spirits afloat and instill confidence to make a rash move.

The carriage slowed and stopped at the entrance, and James gave instructions for his driver to wait. "It shouldn't take more than a half hour at the most," he said. After walking to the door, he rapped it with the tip of his cane, and Clifford greeted him.

"Mr. Davenport to call upon His Lordship," he announced.

Clifford stared at him as if to remind him that he

had arrived uninvited and without an appointment. Regardless, he would not allow the man opportunity to refuse his entrance.

"I come on urgent business, and I need a private word with His Lordship," he reiterated, enunciating the word private. "Now, if you do not mind, please announce my arrival." With that declaration, he boldly pushed past Clifford into the foyer.

"Wait here," he said, tensing his jaw to show his displeasure.

James glanced around the opulent interior that he always found too flashy for his taste. The crystal chandelier hung above his head, the gold gilded staircase with red carpet, and portraits of ancestral family members scowled at him from above. A few minutes later, Clifford returned.

"His Lordship will receive you in the sitting room," he announced. A footman took his hat and cane, and James followed Clifford down the hallway. When he reached the double doors, he glanced about the room to make sure they were alone.

"Thank you for seeing me," he began.

Clifford closed the double doors behind him for privacy.

"I do not make it a habit of receiving uninvited guests without an appointment," Lord Howard remarked in a peeved tone. "You are lucky to find me in a good mood."

The comment made James chuckle inwardly because, in a few minutes, the man would certainly not be in a pleasant mood.

"What urgent matter do you wish to speak about in private?" The earl motioned to an empty chair, and James sat down. "I thought your son was getting married this morning," he remarked. "Do you not approve of his choice?" A smirk curled his lips, and James knew that the comment was intended to ruffle his feathers.

"Not exactly," he truthfully answered. "It seems, though, that your household and its guests have done well in influencing my son's decisions. First, by agreeing that Miss Edwards is a suitable match, and second by enticing him to Egypt with a business scheme."

"You may not realize this, Mr. Davenport, but your son was ripe for the picking. I think he had enough of your demands to marry for money."

"Yes, he has made that point quite clear to me." James inhaled a deep breath before continuing. "Nevertheless, I am not here to discuss my son's marriage or his recent career choice, regardless if I believe both are ill advised."

"Then why are you here? Get on with it, man. I'm busy," Lord Howard complained.

"Well, it appears that there has been a shocking development in the Wilson household," James noted with dark amusement.

"I couldn't care less what happens in the Wilson household," the earl quipped.

"Oh, I think you should care, Your Lordship. A secret has arisen from the mire due to a recent discovery. Apparently, some very illuminating correspondence kept by Catherine Ashby has surfaced."

The earl's eyes tapered, suggesting that James had finally gotten his undivided attention. "And what do these letters say?" he asked in a gruff tone.

"Well, as we both know, Your Lordship, you seduced Catherine Ashby many years ago and impregnated the poor girl. Do you deny it?"

Lord Howard stared at him like a jaguar, ready to pounce at any moment. James kept a steady stare, refusing to back down.

"I seem to remember she claimed to be pregnant by me, but I discarded it as her ill attempt to gain a position as my wife. She was nothing more than another upstart, like your sons, attempting to raise her social status at my expense. I denied culpability and thus thwarted her effort to ensnare me. As you know, she left Aycliffe and disappeared."

The earl rose to his feet and walked over to a decanter, pouring himself a drink of brandy. Without an ounce of civility to offer James one, he brought the glass with him and sat back down again in the chair. He took a gulp and swallowed the liquid.

"Unfortunately, Your Lordship, you are quite mistaken," James continued. He spoke in a slow and determined manner. "Catherine Ashby was indeed pregnant. My wife and I took it upon ourselves to provide a place of seclusion not far from Aycliffe where she could have the baby in private. No one knew about the arrangement except the Wilsons." His Lordship clutched the glass in his hand.

"What of it?" he barked. "The baby must have been stillborn or died not long after."

"No, Catherine entrusted the child to the Wilsons to raise as their own daughter, because Catherine could not care for her." The earl's eyes narrowed as he concluded the astounding revelation. "Celia Wilson is your daughter."

Davenport found great satisfaction in watching the man's reaction. His knuckles turned white, clutching the glass to such an extent he thought it would shatter at any moment. Lord Howard set the glass down with a clank on a side table, and grit his teeth together before articulating his sentiments. With a beet-red face, he growled his answer.

"Like hell she is. What proof do you have?"

"The Wilsons can attest to the matter, as well as my wife and me. Francis and Beth know because of the correspondence they discovered hidden by their mother that testifies to the fact. The Wilsons wrote to her these past twenty years, keeping Catherine informed of the young girl's progress in life." James smirked, enhancing the announcement with an implied threat. "Indeed, Your Lordship, Celia Wilson, is your daughter, and we are all ready to testify to that fact."

What he had just uttered wasn't the truth, but James didn't care. He needed to make a point—many people could affirm the affair. Benjamin had insisted that Lord Howard never find out the truth. As James sat there, revealing the sordid details, the Wilsons were none the wiser that he betrayed their confidence. More was at stake than their reputations.

"I don't believe it," Lord Howard grumbled in return. "It's a pack of lies."

"Whether you do or not, it is the truth."

Lord Howard glowered in return, no doubt considering the consequences.

"Is this Celia girl now going to end up on my doorstep with demands? I shall deny her as I denied her mother," he coldly remarked, showing no empathy for Celia.

"She has no intention of doing so. In fact, she will move to Dunwich to be with Francis as his newfound sister."

Howard fell silent, ruminating inwardly over the exposure. "Is that all you came here to tell me, some sordid story from the past?"

"No," James said, shaking his head. "I thought it was my duty to warn you. You should consider that the gossipmongers of Aycliffe could get word of this scandalous affair. Tongues love to wag, and I would hate to see your reputation sullied in town or throughout the county, for that matter. As you know, many remember Catherine as a fine young lady and are well acquainted with the Wilsons and Celia."

"Catherine Ashby was a slut, like any other who succumbs to a man's advances," the earl said as if to diminish his guilt.

The comment irritated Davenport. Catherine was no slut. He and his wife knew her enough to understand her innocence and naivety that Howard had used to his advantage. They had allowed her too many liberties while living in Aycliffe, which perhaps led to her downfall. At that moment, he regretted once more not having watched over Catherine more carefully. When they discovered her pregnancy, he and his wife did all they could to help her through the wretched affair. He could not help but wonder if she had willingly surrendered to his seduction.

"Did you force yourself upon her?"

"What do you take me for, man?" the earl bellowed. "Some farm boy who ruts in the field?"

"Well, however the affair happened behind closed doors, I would think you would want to bury the secret regarding Celia being your daughter. Especially now that your Annie will marry the son of a duke. I would hate a family scandal swirling around the community right now that could put their relationship in jeopardy."

The earl's hands closed into a fist, and for a split second, James thought he would beat him to death. He had never seen such fire in the man's eyes.

"What is it you want, Davenport? Money? More funds for your damnable town? Will that buy your silence?"

"Well, I am glad that you see the value in investing in Aycliffe so we can shore up the infrastructure and return it to its glory. I'm sure once the town regains its popularity, you will see it as more of an investment rather than a payment."

"If it were not for my current circumstances, I would say the hell with you."

Lord Howard paused, glowering at James as if determining whether he would spread the seed of gossip. James had no qualms about doing so if the man refused him again. Revenge would be sweet, and the knowledge he possessed could be used against the earl for some time to come. Lord Howard finally decided upon the merits of agreeing.

"For Annie's sake, I'll consider it."

"Yes, if it were not for Annie, my son would not have been enticed to traipse off to Egypt at the invitation of Lord Montrose. Since you saw fit to entice him elsewhere, it's only fit that I find another source of income to make up for the loss."

"You are a sly bastard, Davenport," he snarled.

"I could say the same of you when it comes to vulnerable females," he responded. "Bravo, by the way, on your acting abilities in front of Beth and Francis. Very impressive. Not a hint of disdain for the slut you impregnated. Only feigned condolences and accolades, praising their mother's beauty and character. You are a damnable hypocrite."

"I think you have overstayed your welcome," Lord Howard announced, standing to his feet.

"I expect you at my office first thing Monday morning to discuss the needed funds," James firmly instructed. "My attorney will be present to draw up a binding agreement. I am more than willing to engage you in my plans since you will invest a rather sizeable sum of money."

"You will be sorry that you have blackmailed me," he

threatened.

James did not take his parting words to heart, for he knew well that he held the winning card in his hand. Lord Howard would not risk the rumors floating about town about Celia being his daughter. The tittle-tattle would never cease or the judgmental looks of disgust. Of course, most aristocrats had bastard children strewn about here and there. It would not surprise James should there be others the earl had fathered. It was a miracle, frankly, that he had not accosted Beth while she stayed under his roof.

"Until Monday, Your Lordship." He nodded in deference when he could have spit in the man's face.

As the carriage returned to town, James felt little guilt. Perhaps he should have considered Celia and the Wilsons in his little extortion plot. If the truth came out, Celia would be subject to embarrassment and the Wilsons to scorn. He had gambled with their lives, but it was worth it. The town, his livelihood, and his family's fortune would be saved. As a result of his bold move, James Davenport felt reborn. A tremendous burden lifted from his shoulders. It was a glorious day indeed, thanks to the buried letters of Catherine Ashby.

CHAPTER THIRTY-EIGHT

The Farewells

Beth could not believe the time had arrived to say goodbye to Francis. She feared that she would cry for hours, but Alexander's encouragement had given her strength.

"We will come back to England occasionally," he assured them as she stood before Francis with trembling lips.

"I shall miss you. You are a wonderful brother, Francis."

"And I shall miss you, Beth. Do write, and I shall endeavor to answer."

"One of us will answer," Celia said, standing by Francis's side.

Celia had packed a trunk of her clothing, and Francis had loaded his suitcase onto the coach to Dunwich. The Wilsons looked brokenhearted, saying their goodbyes.

"You will write to me, won't you?" Prudence asked.

"Of course, Mother, I shall write."

It was good to hear Celia use the endearing term to the woman who had raised her since a babe, even if they were not her actual parents.

"You are welcome to visit us in Dunwich," Francis announced. "My home is open to you anytime, and I am more than happy to return the hospitality."

"We might take your offer up," Mr. Wilson said.

"Well," Francis announced, inhaling a shaky breath. "I fear it is time for us to leave." He approached Beth and embraced her tightly, giving her a kiss on the cheek. When he let go, he offered his hand to Alexander. "Take good care of her."

"Indeed. I shall guard Beth with my life," he assured him.

Celia hugged Mr. and Mrs. Wilson, equally long, giving them a kiss on the cheek. "Thank you for allowing me to go and enjoy my newfound brother. I have not forgotten your love and your kindness in bringing me up."

Poor Prudence cried large rounded tears down her cheeks. "Come on now," Mr. Wilson said, putting his arm around her shoulder. "Don't make it worse than it already is."

With that, Celia and Francis boarded the coach and waved their goodbyes as it pulled down the street and out of sight.

"A couple of days, and we shall say our farewells to you," Mr. Wilson said, looking at Alexander.

"Yes, indeed. Beth and I are excited to start our journey."

"Will you say goodbye to your father? I do hope you will stop by and give your regards," Benjamin encouraged.

Beth smiled and answered for him. "We are on our way to visit him now. Regardless, Alexander wants to say goodbye to his family."

"Glad to hear of it," he said. "Good luck."

Prudence continued to weep, and Beth gave her a quick hug goodbye. She took Alexander's arm, and they walked to his family residence, hopeful they would be received.

"He won't turn us away at the door, will he?" The thought made her feel dreadful.

"I don't think so. It's still the family home, and I doubt the servants will hinder me from walking in the door." He chuckled, making light of it, but Beth knew the apprehension he held.

"I am not knocking," he said. He took the doorknob and opened the door. A servant caught sight of him and smiled.

"Mr. Davenport, you have come to visit?"

"I have. Are my parents in the sitting room?"

"No, they have just sat down for lunch. You will find them at the dining room table with your siblings."

"Better yet," Alexander said, striding with Beth by his side to interrupt their luncheon. He stopped at the doorway and stood there until they were noticed.

"Alexander!" Lydia jumped to her feet.

"Hello, Lydia."

Richard grinned, and Alexander acknowledged him with a friendly wink.

"Edwin," he said, turning to his brother.

"Alexander." He refused to look him in the eye.

"Mother, Father."

They both glimpsed at him, which Beth thought encouraging if nothing else.

"What are you doing here?" his father asked.

"Beth and I have come to say our goodbyes. We leave in two days."

"Off to Egypt, is it?" he sardonically quipped.

"Yes, off to Egypt."

"How was the wedding?" Mrs. Davenport asked.

Beth couldn't believe his mother cared enough to inquire. "It was wonderful," Beth answered.

"I see." She turned her gaze back to her bowl of soup, acting indifferent.

"I had hoped that you would wish us well before we go," Alexander announced.

His father remained silent for a few minutes and then put his napkin down by his plate. In a surprising move, he stood to his feet and walked over to face Alexander, extending his hand.

"This is the best I can do under the circumstances," he solemnly remarked. "You have chosen your path, now follow it to your best abilities. Have a safe trip, and write when you can."

"Father," Alexander said, flabbergasted at the offering and words. After a hearty handshake, James poked his wife.

"Get up, woman, and give your son a hug goodbye. Lord knows if you will ever see his face again," he barked.

She jumped in her seat and glanced warily at Alexander. With a quivering lip, she did as commanded and came and stood before him. "You have broken my heart," she admitted. "Severely broken my heart."

"I am sorry, Mother. That was not my intention. May we part without a quarrel?"

She gave him a hug. "Take care of yourself," she ordered in a motherly tone. "Don't fall off the back of some damnable camel and break your neck."

"I will make sure he is careful," Beth said.

"I suppose you will."

Mrs. Davenport eyed Beth for a few seconds as if to decide whether she was worth accepting as a daughter-in-law. "I shall not hug you," she defiantly remarked. "But I will wish you well."

"Thank you," Beth replied. "I accepted your kind well-wishes."

Finally, Lydia and Richard came to say their good-byes. Alexander's father scowled at Edwin, who eventually relented and faced his brother. "Have a safe trip, you lucky bastard."

Alexander grinned. "Thank you, Edwin. Take care of Father."

"Oh, I think Father can take care of himself," he said. "It appears he's convinced the earl to invest in the town again."

"You are kidding?" Alexander shot a surprised glance.

"Indeed, I have. Apparently, I still have the power of persuasion."

"Good news, indeed. Write and let me know how the progress goes on the revitalization. I am keen to know."

"If you weren't off to Egypt, you could help me."

"Perhaps, but I'm happy with my choice, regardless."

"Very well," he relented.

Pleased that their visit had gone far beyond their imaginations, Beth took Alexander by the arm, suggesting that they leave. By the painful expression on his face, she understood his reluctance. Farewells to his family members were as difficult as what she experienced with Francis.

"Goodbye then," he said.

"Goodbye, and God bless you all," Beth said, waving as she left the room. Alexander pulled her by his side.

"I am thankful that it went so well," Beth remarked.

"Surprisingly well," Alexander replied, swallowing a lump in his throat.

Beth glimpsed at Alexander, experiencing a swelling pride at how brave he had been to follow his heart. She admired him deeply, for it gave her courage.

"It won't be long now, and we shall travel together to a faraway land." She squeezed his arm. "Your daydreams are turning into reality."

"Who would have thought everything I desired in

life would come to pass. I am so thankful for the blessings and for you by my side."

"It's a beautiful day. Can we take a stroll on the beach together before our scenery turns to a desert?" Beth chuckled.

"Yes, I admit that I will miss the ocean, but our eyes will have new visions of wondrous things."

They slowly strolled to the sandy shore and stood together hand in hand, enjoying the view. Soon they would leave Aycliffe behind, not knowing when or if they would ever return. Beth knew she would miss the ocean, trading it for a mysterious and exotic country at Alexander's side.

As the waves sloshed toward shore, her mind drifted to her mother. She would never know how her choices in life had reached from the grave and set in motion changes for so many people. Though the seduction by Lord Howard had attempted to ruin her life, she overcame it. Out of the bittersweet event came new beginnings. In due course, Catherine married a man who loved her, she bore two children, and enjoyed a contented life. Her death and the invitation from the Wilsons led to the discovery of a secret seaside affair.

"If my mother had never come to Aycliffe, we would have never met," Beth said. "Isn't it strange how her life has set in motion ours? Even Francis and Celia are embarking on a new chapter."

"Indeed, it is," Alexander said, putting his arm around her waist.

They stood watching the waves for another few minutes. Beth's soul stirred with anxiousness. "We should get back to the hotel and finish packing," she reluctantly suggested. "There is still much to do."

Alexander turned and faced her. "Not before we enjoy our last kiss on the sandy shores of Aycliffe," he said, taking her in his arms.

Beth closed her eyes. As their lips met, she listened to the rumble of the breaking waves, the screeching of the seabirds overhead. A steady ocean breeze swirled around their bodies, joining them together. She would remember the moment for years to come.

EPILOGUE

Cairo

Beth stood on the balcony of their lavish apartment that overlooked the bustling cobblestone street below. The warm atmosphere filled her nostrils with a variety of smells, some of which she had never experienced. Her eyes admired the architectural creations, which were far different from anything she had seen in England. Mosques with spires rose to the heavens. Fountains, bazaars, and markets crowded the district. Cairo stimulated her senses in a thousand ways.

If the sights, sounds, and smells were not enough, the people were fascinating. Men dressed in long garments, wearing turbans on their heads. They clad devout Muslim women in black from head to toe, revealing only their eyes. Other women freely let their long flowing hair dangle down their backs while dressed in exotic and colorful robes. Light, loose cotton was the typical clothing for men and women to keep cool in the scorching summer. Compared to the cold and damp climate in England, Beth embraced the warmth.

Cairo bustled from morning until night. Instead of carriages, there were camels and donkeys transporting people and moving goods on carts. Rather than stores, there were bazaars and open markets where merchants sold their wares from expensive silk to jewelry of scarab beetles, which supposedly brought good luck.

Sometimes musicians would parade down the street, leading wedding processions. Belly dancing had been banned in Cairo ten years earlier, but women in upper Egypt still practiced the art. She wondered what it was like to see scantily clad females shimmy and twist their hips, using exotic movements to entertain men. Such a practice would be scandalous in England, but here with the embellishments of fringed garments, jewels, and sequins on their outfits, the eye-catching outfits allured the audiences. Egypt had proven to be as fascinating and mysterious as Alexander promised.

"Enjoying the view?"

Alexander came up behind her and put his arms around her waist. He kissed her on the neck, and she leaned into him. It had been three months since their arrival. They had set the office up, hired buyers, and Alexander had used his skills to start the business for Lord Montrose. Percival and Annie had married and were planning a trip to visit them in the next month. Everything fell into place. Alexander found contentment with Beth by his side.

"I am enjoying the view," she said, turning around to face him. "Thank you."

"For what?"

"For loving me, marrying me, and bringing me with you. I couldn't be happier, Alexander."

"Nor I," he admitted, kissing her softly on the lips.

They found freedom from family restraints and expectations while binding themselves to each other.

"Is that a letter from Francis?" He stepped over to the desk and picked up the correspondence. "Anything of interest?"

Beth giggled. "It is filled with his humor and complaints about how Celia is attempting to control him. Naturally, he misses me but is happy and well."

"I'm glad to hear it." Alexander stood in front of Beth and grinned mischievously. "I have an announcement to make."

"About what?"

"Well, I have been so busy since our coming here, tending to the business, that I have neglected you in some respects," he confessed.

"Perhaps, but I understand." Beth squeezed his hand in reassurance.

"Tomorrow we are going on a trip."

"What kind of trip?"

"To see the great pyramid of Giza, and we are traveling by camel."

"Camel?" Beth squealed. "Oh my. It's really going to happen. We will ride a camel." Beth felt like a little girl on Christmas morning. Excited, she threw her arms around Alexander's neck.

"No more daydreaming, Beth. We are living our dreams," Alexander said, looking at her with loving eyes.

"Yes, we are, my dearest. We found the courage together, didn't we?"

Alexander flashed a roguish smile, and Beth knew what he meant to happen next. Married to a kind and generous lover, she welcomed his advances.

"I better lend you a pair of my trousers," he announced. "You need to mount the camel like a man rides a horse."

"You mean swing one leg over it?" Beth laughed aloud.

"I'm afraid so."

"Then lend me some trousers, for I will let nothing impede camel riding."

Alexander swept her off her feet and walked her over to the bed. "God, I love you," he said, kissing her deeply.

Beth rejoiced in their situation, assured that their adventures together would be glorious.

~The End~

For research and background information about the setting of The Seaside Affair, visit:
https://theseasideaffair.wordpress.com/

The story continues with
"The Village Affair" and "The Resort Affair."

ABOUT THE AUTHOR

With Russian blood on my father's side and English on my mother's, I blame my ancestors for the lethal combination of my DNA that influences my stories. Tragedy and drama might be found between the pages, but I eventually give readers a happy ending.

I live in the beautiful but rainy Pacific Northwest. My hobby (more of an obsession) is researching my English ancestry and expanding my family tree. To keep the memory of my ancestors alive, I often use their names in my novels or dedications.

My usual genre is historical fiction with romantic elements and historical romance set in the Victorian and Edwardian eras. My books include:

- ❖ The Price of Innocence (Book One of the Legacy Series)
- ❖ The Price of Deception (Book Two of the Legacy Series)
- ❖ The Price of Love (Book Three of the Legacy Series)
- ❖ The Price of Passion (Book Four of the Legacy Series)
- ❖ The Phantom of Valletta
- ❖ Dark Persuasion
- ❖ A Christmas Oath (Novelette)
- ❖ A Christmas Mission (Novelette)
- ❖ Lady Isabella (Ladies of Disgrace)
- ❖ Lady Grace (Ladies of Disgrace)

- Lady Charlotte (Ladies of Disgrace)
- Lady Jane (Ladies of Disgrace)
- Toil Under the Sun
- The Seaside Affair (Venturous Hearts Series)
- The Village Affair (Venturous Hearts Series)
- The Resort Affair (Venturous Hearts Series)

Romance with a Kiss of Suspense
- Thorncroft Manor
- Whitefield Hall
- Blythe Court

Gothic Romance
- The Baron's Obsession, by Victoria Raven

Contemporary Romance:
- Conflicting Hearts, by J.D. Burrows -
  Contemporary Romance/Women's Fiction

Sign up for my newsletter and blog by visiting my official website. Vicki Hopkins, Author - http://vickihopkins.com

The best way to thank an author, is to write a review.